THE
AFTERLIFE
OF THE
PARTY

AUTHOR OF THE BESTSELLING **DEAD IS** SERIES
MARLENE PEREZ

THE AFTERLIFE
OF THE
PARTY

AUTHOR OF THE **DEAD IS** SERIES

MARLENE PEREZ

Entangled Publishing, LLC
10940 S Parker Road
Suite 327
Parker, CO 80134
rights@entangledpublishing.com

Entangled Teen is an imprint of Entangled Publishing, LLC.

Visit our website at www.entangledpublishing.com.

Edited by Stacy Abrams and Liz Pelletier
Cover design by Covers By Juan
Cover images by
FlexDreams/shutterstock and
Isabell Schatz/shutterstock and
Irina Ulianova/shutterstock and
NikhomTreeVector/shutterstock
Interior design by Toni Kerr

ISBN 978-1-64063-902-7
Ebook ISBN 978-1-64063-903-4

Manufactured in the United States of America

First Edition February 2021

10 9 8 7 6 5 4 3 2 1

entangled teen
an imprint of Entangled Publishing LLC

ALSO BY MARLENE PEREZ

Dead Is series

Dead Is the New Black
Dead Is a State Of Mind
Dead Is So Last Year
Dead Is Just a Rumor
Dead Is Not an Option
Dead Is a Battlefield
Dead Is a Killer Tune
Dead Is Just a Dream

"One thing about living in Santa Carla I never could stomach: all the damn vampires."

—*The Lost Boys*

"Hell is empty, and the devils are all here."

—*The Tempest*

To the friends who won't leave you behind.

Chapter One

When my best friend, Skyler, told me about this party in the Hollywood Hills, I was less than enthused. The last thing I wanted to do was fight traffic for the privilege of watching her flirt with some guy, but I didn't want to let her go alone, either.

She was determined to go and friends don't let friends go to parties without backup, so Vaughn and I were tagging along. I was riding shotgun and Vaughn was wedged into the tiny back seat of Skyler's convertible. The top was down and a summer breeze ruffled his thick, dark hair.

"Why are we driving all the way to L.A. again?" I asked.

"I've been talking to this guy…" Sky replied, her gaze trained on the car in front of us, but she was biting her lip. That meant a long night ahead.

I didn't even try to suppress my groan. "Skyler."

She'd been my best friend since I first came to live with Granny Mariotti. Granny had been running story time at the library, where Skyler and I had fought over a copy of *Mama, Do You Love Me?* Pretty ironic, since we'd both been ditched by our own moms, but Granny made us sit and read the book together. We met Vaughn at the library story time a few weeks later.

Skyler took a turn too fast and Vaughn made an exasperated sound. My gaze darted to the back seat, but he was looking down at his phone. Probably texting Ashley.

Now it was my turn to let out an exasperated groan, but I was mad at myself. Why couldn't I get over my crush? Luckily, Vaughn had no idea how I felt about him.

I'd been tempted to do something about it so many times, but it was too late now. He had a girlfriend.

"I wanted you to get dressed up and flirt with boys," Skyler added. "You might meet someone, too, you know."

I groaned louder this time.

"Tansy only likes to flirt with me," Vaughn teased, and I tried not to squirm as heat flooded my cheeks. He had no idea how right he was—and if I was lucky, he never would.

"Meet *single* dudes." Skyler clarified with an eyeroll. "You, my friend, are very taken."

"Ashley and I broke up," Vaughn replied. Succinct.

I turned around to study his face. He didn't seem to be suffering, but I had to check. "Are you okay?"

"I'm not eating ice cream and listening to sad boy band music," he said. No trace of emotion in his gray eyes or in his voice, but I knew he often tried to keep his feelings hidden.

"Hey, that happened *once*," Skyler said, bugging out her eyes comically.

Vaughn and I laughed like she wanted us to, but it was nervous laughter. Although Skyler wasn't BFFs with Ben & Jerry any longer, she still hadn't recovered from Connor, and we all knew it.

"It's been a long time coming," Vaughn said. "And I

don't want to analyze it to death."

"When did this happen?" I asked.

Vaughn was silent but then finally supplied details. "Three days ago."

"Three days ago?" she asked. "Wasn't that right after Christian asked you out, Tansy?"

Why was she changing the subject? I wanted to know why Vaughn and Ashley had broken up.

"Christian Choi or Christian Guerra?" Vaughn asked.

I slid her a look. *What are you doing?*

She gave me a look back and shook her head.

Vaughn's lips tightened. "They *both* asked you out?"

"Yes," I said.

"They're both assholes."

"I thought you liked Christian, both of them," I said.

He looked at me like he wanted to say something, but instead, he just shrugged.

"You snooze, you lose, Sheridan," Skyler said to him.

"What are you talking about?" I asked her.

She kept her eyes on the road, but there was an aggravating smile on her face, like she knew something I didn't.

I looked back at Vaughn. He was blushing. For a second, I wished I could read his mind, but it wasn't possible, not even for a Mariotti witch like me.

I could feel warmth on my own face, too. *Vaughn's single for the first time in forever.*

It shouldn't make a difference, but it did. It felt riskier somehow. For the first time, I noticed Vaughn was more dressed up than usual. He wore a gray button-down shirt with the sleeves rolled up and jeans that fit him perfectly.

I leaned back in the passenger seat and closed my eyes. "I'm glad we're hanging out tonight."

"Me too." I heard the smile in Sky's voice, and I felt warm inside knowing I'd put it there. There'd been something off about her the past few weeks. I'd blamed it on her breakup with Connor, but maybe it was more than that.

Skyler put on a song from a band I'd never heard of. "Play The Drainers," she commanded, and the voice-activated playlist started.

We listened in silence for a few songs. "The Drainers?" I asked.

"They're a newer band. Don't you just love them?" she asked. Which meant she wanted me to like their music. I did not like their music.

In the back seat, Vaughn snorted but cut it off when Skyler glared at him in the rearview mirror.

"Vaughn's a music snob, but I thought you'd like it," she told me. Vaughn wasn't a snob, not really, but he was a talented musician and pickier than most.

"Emo's not really my thing right now." I settled for a polite but evasive answer. It wasn't strictly true. Emo *was* my thing if it was done well. Which…this was not. The lead singer hadn't found a note he didn't like—even the off-key ones.

She bounced in her seat, in no way fazed by my lack of enthusiasm. "It will be."

The party was off Mulholland, and Skyler took the turns with reckless abandon, which made talking for the next ten minutes nearly impossible as my stomach was firmly lodged in the back of my throat. When we pulled up, there were cars lining the street.

Skyler circled the block, but there were no parking spots to be found within a mile radius. She stopped at a red light and turned to me.

"We're going to be late," she said. She had tears in her eyes, which seemed extra, but she'd been more emotional lately.

"Do that thing you do," she begged.

"Skyler, you shouldn't ask her that," Vaughn said sharply.

"It's not a big deal," I said.

"Your granny wouldn't want you to use your magic on this," Vaughn pointed out.

He was right. My grandmother would be disappointed in me if I used my powers for something so trivial as a parking spot, but my friendship with Skyler wasn't trivial and she rarely asked me for anything.

"Please, Tansy," she said. She was my best friend, and it wasn't like she was asking me to turn her ex into a toad or anything.

There was magic in the world if you knew where to look. Finding a parking spot in L.A. required luck and, sometimes, a little magic. My two friends were the only ones at school who knew I was a witch, and neither of them had ever needed me to prove it. But *I'd* needed it, so I'd shown them what I could do.

It hadn't been a big deal the first time I'd done magic in front of them, but for some reason, it felt like it was tonight. That if I used my magic right now, it would change the course of the night.

But I decided to do it anyway. "Go around the block again," I said. "Slowly." Skyler squealed, knowing she would be getting her way.

"Thank you, thank you," she said. The fervent note in her voice gave me pause, but I closed my eyes and concentrated on the spell.

We were back to the party location. At first, I thought the spell hadn't worked, that we could turn around, head home, and eat popcorn and watch a horror movie on Netflix instead of going to this party.

Two houses down, a Tesla pulled out of a space, and Skyler crowed triumphantly before nabbing it.

What I hadn't told my friends, because I didn't want them to worry, was that magic always had a price, and I'd have to pay it eventually.

Skyler turned off the convertible, but she didn't get out immediately. "I have a surprise for you."

"Spill it." Her excited smile reminded me of the Skyler she used to be, loud and happy and sharing every secret with me. Until Connor.

"My new guy's band is playing here tonight!" She clapped her hands and bounced in her seat. "Isn't that the best?"

I smiled at her. "It is." I loved music, all kinds of music, but especially live performances. There was something special about seeing a band live for the first time. Maybe this party wouldn't be so terrible after all.

I nearly twisted an ankle on our way to the house, but Vaughn caught me by the elbow to steady me. Sky had no trouble in her impossibly high heels and a dress that masqueraded as a slightly long T-shirt. I was wearing a pink dress Skyler's stepmom had discarded and, in honor of the momentous occasion, a freshly washed scowl.

I'd finally pieced together what was different about Sky tonight. She wasn't wearing her charm necklace, the one that matched mine. The ones that Granny Mariotti added charms to on every special occasion for both of us.

"Where's your necklace?" I instinctively touched mine. It was heavy with memories of our friendship, like a laminated corner of a ticket from our first concert, a tiny silver witch's broom she'd given me for my sixteenth birthday, and a miniature of a photo of Skyler and me that Granny had taken when we were seven. We were covered in stepmother number one's expensive makeup, arms entwined, grinning at the camera.

Those necklaces were the story of us and were imbued with protective magic. It had been the first spell I'd ever cast.

"The clasp broke," she said. She tugged on the diamond stud in her left ear. She only did that when she was lying, which made my stomach hurt.

I stopped walking—which made her stop, too—and narrowed my eyes at her. "The clasp broke and you didn't say anything?"

"Yes," she replied flatly.

"Skyler—" I said, but her phone buzzed with a text.

"C'mon, hurry or we'll miss it," she said. Even though I was taller than she was, she walked so fast that I couldn't keep up. She was used to walking in heels; I was not.

From the outside, the house looked like your average multimillion-dollar home. It was a modern structure of concrete and glass, but it looked like an expensive prison to me.

There was the sound of someone's loud, slightly off-key singing, accompanied by jangled instruments that just managed to stay in time together.

Skyler beamed. "That's The Drainers."

Vaughn winced but then wiped his expression clean when she glared at him.

She said the name of the band the way Granny Mariotti talked about The Grateful Dead. Or Bowie.

The music improved, though, the closer we got. The jarring sounds were slowly replaced by music that wrapped around me like an embrace, pulling me in. The song was full of longing and promise, the singer whispering that he knew all my secrets but they didn't matter. He would love me anyway. Forever.

Now I understood what Skyler was talking about. I only wished I'd discovered the band first. I walked faster, suddenly eager to get closer to the music.

Everyone seemed to be poolside, so we walked through a breathtaking living room and kitchen to the back of the house.

The music was louder here, and a crowd had gathered around a small stage. A tall blond guy wearing leather pants with a leather vest but no shirt sang in a husky, compelling voice that oozed lust and longing.

My jaw dropped. Three other guys, nearly the most attractive I'd ever seen—and I lived in Southern California, the home of models and movie stars—played instruments while the blond sang. Another guy, this one looking like a young Jason Momoa, with long dark hair and electric-green eyes, wore shorts and a black-and-white-checked flannel shirt over his tee as he strummed a guitar. A dark-haired guy was on keyboards, in a sharp suit with cheekbones a model would envy, and a tatted-up, muscular ginger played the drums as sweat poured down his bare chest.

Sky didn't take her eyes from the stage—from the lead singer. A horde of girls pushed and shoved one another to get to the band members, particularly the guy in leather pants and no shirt. A part of me wanted to join the mayhem, but I managed to hang back.

What was happening to me? I felt a little dizzy and had to fight the urge to jump onstage and beg one of them to kiss me.

The lead singer held a ball of flame in his hands while the audience shouted for more, until suddenly the music ended in a loud crescendo. But something must have gone wrong with the special effects because the fire sailed over the audience's heads and landed in the branches of a tree. And as quickly as the feeling of wanting to jump onstage had overtaken me, it vanished.

Everyone else was still entranced with the band, not paying attention to the fire hazard or to me, so I whispered a little spell, and the fire went out.

Most of the girls in the audience wore the same debutante white. "Is this some kind of cult?" I asked.

"It's summer," Sky replied. Summer meant people in Southern California wore lighter colors, but I'd never seen so many white dresses in one place.

"I recognize that look in your eyes," I said to Skyler. "You are in lust."

"Not lust—love," she said. "Aren't you just obsessed with The Drainers? And Travis?"

"Is Travis the lead singer?"

Someone next to me snorted. This guy had obviously been listening in on our conversation. "You think this derivative bunch of posers is good?"

Sky sent him her best death glare, but it didn't stop him.

"That steaming pile up onstage known as The Drainers?" he said. "I just don't get it. Every woman here thinks this band is the next Rolling Stones or something. Is everyone tone-deaf?"

"Hater," Sky whispered.

"It's like everyone is hypnotized," the guy continued. I followed his gaze. The crowd *was* mostly female, but there were a couple of guys who'd had the same heart-eyes expression as they watched the band.

"You have no taste," Skyler huffed. The guy looked at me, and I stared at him.

I wondered why this guy was still smiling if he hated the band so much, and then I saw his earplugs. "My girlfriend gave me the album," he said, noticing my stare.

"What do you think?" I asked Vaughn.

"Some bands are just better live," he said. "Will you be okay for a few minutes? I'm going to find a bathroom."

"We'll be fine," I said.

Skyler edged closer to the stage, and I followed her.

As we walked by the pool, a shoving match started, and two girls fell into the pool. They broke the surface of the water and continued to pull each other's hair. I thought one of the guys in the band might try to help, but instead, they moved to lounge chairs at the other end.

"Look at these people," I said. "Making asses of themselves over a guy."

"I can't believe it, either," Sky replied. "Let's go over there."

I tugged on her hand. "I don't think so."

"Please," she coaxed. "I want you to meet Travis."

"I'm your best friend, so I'm always here for you," I pointed out, "but something about this doesn't feel right."

"Never mind—he's coming this way." She fluffed her hair. "How do I look?"

"Gorgeous as usual," I said.

The tall, blond lead singer was making a beeline for her. I was struck by the fluid way he moved through the crowd. Skyler went to meet him halfway, but I stayed where I was to give them a moment of privacy.

She said something to him, and his smile faded.

I hustled over to join them.

"Travis, I missed you so much," Skyler cooed, ignoring me.

Was she for real? What was happening right now?

He bypassed her and sidled up to me. This was the guy Sky was so into? Was it possible he had a doppelganger—one with better grooming habits and some manners, maybe?

"I'm Travis," he said. He took my hand and drew it close to his heart. "You will join us."

"I'm Tansy," I said. "And I don't think so."

He was good-looking but pasty, which was saying something, coming from me.

He returned his attention to Skyler. "Did you have any punch, baby?"

"Not yet," she replied.

"Get some," he said. "It'll make you taste sweet."

When I shuddered, he leered at me, but when I glared right back at him, he seemed to remember Skyler. "My little beauty Schuler," he said.

"Her name is Skyler," I snapped.

But my best friend didn't seem to care that this creeper didn't remember her name. Instead, she kissed him. "I missed you, baby," she said.

They kissed again, this time with tongue. It was almost unbearable to watch them, like when I'd slept over at Callie Humphrey's and her dad, my high school science teacher, stumbled down to breakfast the next morning sporting only a pair of boxers with hearts all over them—he'd totally forgotten I'd spent the night, obviously—and I'd not been able to raise my hand again in his class all year.

They finally pulled apart, and my mind was racing with how to peel Skyler from this douche and head out.

"I thought I told you to wear white." Travis frowned.

I expected Skyler to tell him to go to hell, or at least roll her eyes at him, but instead, she said, "I'll change."

"You too," Travis said. It took me a minute to realize he was talking to me.

"White's not my color," I said.

I kept my temper with difficulty. This guy was just another short-term solution; we'd laugh about him next week. In the meantime, I needed to stay close to Skyler.

"I will teach you many pleasures," Travis said.

"Hard pass." I glanced over at Sky, but she was still gazing at him dreamily. It was like she hadn't even heard her guy hitting on me.

He whispered something into Skyler's ear, and then he was leading her inside.

For about the tenth time that month, I had visions of braining Connor when I saw him again. Skyler wouldn't be willing to hook up with a guy like Travis if she weren't trying to wipe away the memory of her ex.

I hesitated for a second as they turned to head indoors. I probably should drag her away, but sometimes it takes a loser to get over a loser. I watched the crowd. There were even more girls here, including a few college-aged ones. They weren't much older than me, but their faces were drawn and hungry-looking.

"Want to dance?" The guy was cute, with long, dark hair and full lips, but I wasn't there to hook up.

"No thanks."

"How about a kiss?" He leaned in, and I leaned away.

Vaughn returned as I was dealing with this creep. He frowned when he saw the guy next to me. "Is he bothering you?"

"I'm here with my friend," I said, gesturing toward Vaughn.

"Your friend won't mind," the guy said, leaning in again.

I recoiled. "*I* mind."

Vaughn grabbed the guy by the back of the shirt. "Get lost, dude. She said no."

The asshole finally got the hint and walked away.

"Sorry, the line for the bathroom was really long," he said. "Where's Skyler?"

"Where else?" I said. "With Lover Boy."

"We may as well get comfortable," Vaughn said. "Want anything to drink?"

I shook my head.

We found an unoccupied sofa in the corner of the living room and sat next to each other silently for a few seconds.

His eyes locked on me. "You look beautiful tonight."

"Thank you," I said. The way he looked at me made fireworks light up my insides.

"That's a nice dress. I like the way you look in pink," Vaughn said. "You don't wear that color very often."

I smoothed down the fabric of my soft pink dress. "Clashes with my hair," I said. "And the dress is one of Gertie's hand-me-downs." Gertie was Skyler's stepmother and a former Vegas showgirl. Nothing Skyler owned would ever fit me. Skyler was delicate lines, and I was all curves, but inside, where it counted, we fit.

I changed the subject. "Do you have to work this weekend?"

A guy threw himself on the empty spot next to me and proceeded to pass out.

Vaughn put an arm around my shoulder. "Scoot in closer," he said.

We talked about the latest gossip at his dad's catering company where we both worked, about bands we liked, and about how we didn't want summer to end. We talked about everything under the sun, except for one thing: why he and Ashley had broken up.

As much as I was enjoying Vaughn's undivided attention, I wondered what was keeping Skyler.

"I'm going to send Skyler a text," I finally said. "You have to work tomorrow."

We waited, but she didn't respond. "It's getting late," I told Vaughn. "We should look for her."

"Will you be okay if we split up?" he asked. "We can cover more territory that way." The house was huge with at least ten bedrooms and a casita out by the pool.

"I'll take the upstairs," I said with a nod. It wouldn't surprise me if Travis and Skyler were holed up in one of the bedrooms.

There was still a line for the bathroom, but Skyler wasn't in it, so I moved on. I searched every bedroom until I found a locked door. I knocked. "Sky, are you in there? It's Tansy. We need to go." Nobody answered, but I thought I heard male laughter followed by Skyler's softer voice.

"Let me in!" I pounded on the door.

I was still pounding ferociously when it opened, and I stumbled into the room. Travis stood just inside the doorway. He'd lost the leather vest; now he wore his leather pants and not much else. Skyler was behind him, her dark-brown hair tousled.

As she'd promised Travis, she'd changed into a white sundress. She must have been carrying it in her bag.

One of the straps had fallen. A trail of something dark and sticky-looking ran down her front, and my stomach rolled as I realized what she'd probably been letting him do. There were three other guys in the dank-smelling room with them. Everything about this screamed *get out*.

My heart pounded in my chest.

"C'mon, Skyler, let's go," I begged. But she just stood there.

"I can't find my necklace," she said. She got down on her hands and knees.

"Sky, it's okay," I said. "I'll let you wear mine, all right?"

She stopped crawling around. I helped her stand up before I removed mine and draped it around her neck. "See? All better."

Travis frowned. "I thought I threw that out."

"You threw it out? You had no right," I said.

He ignored my confrontational words and leered at me instead. "Pretty pink pinup," Travis said. "What can I do for you?"

It wasn't the first time someone had compared me to something pink and white. I was as pale as moonlight, and my hair was strawberry blond. And tonight, I wore Gertie's cast-off-but-glorious pink dress. But it still got on my nerves: my best friend's boyfriend should not be handing me a line.

"Not a thing," I said. "Just taking my friend home."

He ignored me and kept talking. "I drank one of those in the fifties. She tasted like a strawberry milkshake. You look like a strawberry milkshake."

"I'm cold like one, too," I said, a note of warning in my voice. Travis was too close to me. He smelled wrong—they all did. I needed to help Skyler get the hell out of here.

"You smell like strawberries, too," he said, inhaling deeply. "And vanilla."

I moved past him, toward Skyler, and noticed her eyes were dilated. She didn't even seem to recognize me.

"What did you give her?" I asked.

Nobody answered, but a couple of the other guys snickered.

"Sit down," Travis said. Immediately, Skyler sat on the white leather sofa.

Even in the dim light, I could see brown stains on the furniture. I grimaced. "I don't think so."

He blinked his red-rimmed eyes, and his brow furrowed like I was the toughest answer to a crossword puzzle. Five-letter word for mouthy girl. Tansy.

"You...don't think so?" he asked.

"Nope. I know what you've been doing," I said. A million alarms went off in my head, all of them screaming at me to run.

"C'mon, Skyler. Let's get out of here."

"I said sit down." Travis was louder this time. Something slithered in his eyes, cold and reptilian. "Sit down and shut up."

I sensed it then—some sort of dark hypnosis, twisting tighter and tighter with every word he spoke. It was easier for me to resist than the music had been, but I'd been taken by surprise then, not expecting compulsion via emo music.

There were four of them and two of us. One and a half, really, since Skyler was barely conscious. I could try carrying her out, but I wasn't sure she'd cooperate in the state she was in. So I sat and hoped she would sober up quickly, because I was starting to realize we were in a room with supernatural predators.

And we were outnumbered.

Chapter Two

The silence was oppressive. I was sitting in a dimly lit room with my out-of-it best friend and her latest bad decision. The other guys in the band didn't say a word; they seemed to be waiting for something. It was clear that Travis was the leader of the group. He sat between Skyler and me, which meant I couldn't see her expression.

Travis had one arm resting on the couch, his long fingers draped over Skyler's shoulder. He tried to drape his other arm over me, but I shifted away.

I leaned around Travis and whispered to Skyler, "It's as funky as the devil's armpit in here." She didn't respond.

I waited for introductions, but the other band members just stared at me. I shifted uncomfortably. "Who are you guys?"

"That's Fang, our drummer," Travis said, pointing to the red-haired guy. There was a towel around his neck, and he used it to wipe the sweat off his chest.

"Ozzie's the bass player, and Armando's our keyboardist. And I'm the lead singer and guitarist."

Ozzie was dressed in eighties grunge, like he thought he was the next Eddie Vedder, and Armando wore a sharp black suit with a white shirt and black tie. Apparently, the wardrobe budget all went to Armando's suits.

"Did you enjoy the concert?" Fang, the drummer, asked me. His words were slow and deliberate, like he didn't talk very often.

"It was…interesting," I said.

"You'll come to our next show," Travis said. "You can be my number-one groupie."

I made a face, and he must have misinterpreted it as confusion.

"A groupie is like a friend of the band who likes to do things for us."

"I know what a groupie is," I said. "And you're sugar-coating it."

I didn't appreciate how he was trying to mansplain.

"Thanks for the invitation, but I don't think so," I said. I tried to pull Skyler to her feet, but it was like trying to teach a wet noodle to walk.

Travis leaned toward me until our faces were only inches apart. "You are beautiful. I will make you very happy."

My gaze narrowed on his high cheekbones. "Are you wearing glitter?"

Skyler reached out slowly and touched his face, but he swatted her hand away.

"It's stage makeup," he replied defensively.

"Skyler, I think it's time to go," I said.

He gave me the creeps. There was a dark splotch of something on the corner of his mouth, and a word tickled my brain. *Vampire.*

I'd heard my granny talk about them before, but she

always mentioned them as evil and soul sucking. I mean, Travis was dirty-hot, but in that I'm-too-cool-to-call-you-later sort of way, not the I-eat-hearts-for-breakfast kind of way.

He locked eyes with me. I didn't look away, even when a headache began to build. A voice that I instinctively knew no one else could hear told me to give in, to yield, to do what I was told. But I refused, jerking my gaze away. Still, even though I fought it, my gaze went back to him.

The smells of graveyard dirt and dried blood hit my nose, and my stomach roiled. Something tugged at my mind, but I resisted it. I wasn't looking at a human. I was looking at a vampire. But as soon as the thought occurred to me, it was gone.

"What were we talking about again?" I asked. My head was spinning. I'd forgotten something. What was it?

Travis gave me a satisfied smile. "Just getting to know each other."

"I'm hungry," the drummer whined like a tired toddler.

"You already ate," Travis snapped.

Fang looked at me and licked his lips. "I want dessert."

Travis glared at him. "No one gets dessert before I do."

"I want my necklace," Skyler slurred suddenly. "Need it."

"You don't need that thing, baby," Travis said, but Skyler continued to mumble.

"You're wearing it already, Sky," I said, lifting it up to show her where my charm necklace was draped around her neck. "Here you go." She was too out of it to be able to tell the difference. I'd help her find hers in the morning.

Downstairs, someone put on a playlist.

"Baby, they're playing your song," Skyler cooed.

"That doesn't sound like the same band," I said.

"We're better live," Armando said.

I thought auto-tuning made everyone sound better, but apparently not. It was hard to believe it was the same band. I'd never heard anything more ear-numbingly awful than The Drainers album playing on the sound system. I was relieved until I realized the music was so loud that nobody would hear our screams.

"I'll be right back, Sky." I made for the door alone this time. I'd go get help, find Vaughn.

But Travis was in front of it, blocking the way. He was fast, so fast, even though he was drunk. Or high. Or something. Something that made his face flushed, his eyes red and beady like a rat's.

"What's your hurry?" Travis said. "You're having fun. You want to stay."

"No, I do not."

Again with the surprised face. I had a hard time believing that a guy like Travis hadn't heard the word "no" before, but he acted like it was a unique experience.

Then there was this squeezing sensation, like someone had put my brain in a vise and was twisting it tighter and tighter.

A tiny part of my mind tried to tell me this wasn't just a headache. But suddenly, the room was spinning, and a queasy feeling reminded me of the one time I'd been seasick, spinning and sloshing. I hadn't had anything to drink, had I? It felt like he was there, in my head, telling me to go with him. Something inside me knew to resist. I wasn't the kind of girl who let some asshole boss her around, so I gathered all my strength and silently yelled, *"Get out of my head."*

When I looked up, Travis seemed shaken.

He leaned in and sniffed me, then tried to nuzzle my neck. "You smell good," he said. "I've never smelled anyone like you before."

"No means no, asshole," I said. I shoved him away, but not before he leaned in close and sniffed my neck, grazing it with his teeth.

"You're resisting me?" Travis asked. "But girls can't resist me."

I rolled my eyes at his monumental ego. "This one can."

He made a move toward me again, and I brought my leg up and kneed him in the groin. He crumpled to the ground.

The room tilted, my vision blurred, and a burning sensation went down my neck to my chest, but I managed to stay upright.

I was so out of there.

I grabbed Skyler, who thankfully seemed to be coming out of it, whatever *it was.*

The other two guys snarled, but I put up a hand. "You two stay back. We are leaving, and you're not going to stop us." I'd scream the house down if I had to, but I was hoping I could bluff my way out of it.

Travis still writhed on the floor. He started to get up, but I raised my leg like I was going to kick him again, and he decided to stay put.

The drummer, who had muscular arms as big as my thighs, blocked the door.

"Hi, Fang," Skyler said. She gave him a dazed smile.

"Skyler, Travis doesn't want you to leave," he replied.

"Too bad," I said. "We're gone." I briefly wondered if I should bust out a spell of some kind, but then I realized I had no idea what might work on vampires—probably best to just hightail it out of there.

"What are you?" the guy asked. There was a strange note of curiosity in his voice.

"I'm going to be your worst nightmare if you don't open that door," I said.

I was seconds from screaming, but I tried not to let my fear show. "Let us go." I stood my ground but avoided staring into his reddened eyes, until he unlocked the door and stepped aside.

I half dragged, half carried Sky. I nearly turned my ankle again in my heels, but our pace didn't slow until I knew we were out of their sight.

I helped her downstairs to find Vaughn waiting for us. *Thank god.* The tension in my body relaxed a fraction, but we needed to get out of here. *Now.*

"We're leaving," I said shortly.

"Is she okay?"

"She will be. We just need to get her out of here."

"Okay." Vaughn was usually unbelievably chill. Everyone at his dad's catering company liked working with him. Always calm in a crisis.

That's when I noticed the red stain on Skyler's dress. "That's blood," I said.

Vaughn knew what that meant—the sight of blood made me pass out. "Breathe, Tansy," he said as he checked Sky for wounds.

Even a little cut could cause me to get light-headed and weak, and I was realizing there was way more than a little blood all over Skyler's white dress. I took shallow breaths, one after the other.

I couldn't faint when Skyler needed me.

"We have to keep her away from The Drainers," I said. "Especially Travis."

Skyler stirred when she heard his name. "Travis loves me."

"She seems okay except for these two marks on her

shoulder," he said as he took Skyler from me and hoisted her into his arms. He grunted. "She's heavier than she looks."

"She's all muscle and unrequited love," I said. "Which weighs more than you'd think."

Skyler had been reckless, going out and looking for love in all the wrong places, ever since Con broke her heart and headed off for a study-abroad program in Europe. But tonight was the first time I'd been truly scared for her.

I looked more closely at her shoulder, and sure enough, there were two bite marks. Damn vampires. "We need to get her to the hospital."

She smiled up at me. "I'm in love with Travis."

"You barely know the guy." I rolled my eyes, teasing her even though my heart was pounding in my chest. "Wipe that smile off your face."

"I can't help it." She continued to rhapsodize about Travis, but I tuned her out.

I was gasping when we got to the car, but despite his initial complaint, Vaughn carried Skyler with no problem and didn't even look winded.

"Where are her keys?" he asked.

I fished them out of Skyler's tiny cross-body purse, which fortunately, she still had with her.

Vaughn placed Skyler gently in the back seat, and I got in beside her. He put the roof up on the convertible and took off.

"How're you doing back there?" he said as we started down the narrow, twisting road that led to the freeway.

We'd barely made it onto the main road when Skyler started screaming.

I tried to soothe her, but she snapped her teeth at me when I tried to hug her. I'd never seen Skyler like this, not even at her worst.

"What's wrong with her?" Vaughn asked. She hissed when he flicked on the overhead light with one hand while keeping his other firmly on the wheel.

She panted like a dog, her tongue hanging out. She opened her mouth to scream again, and I froze. Fuck my life. She had long, pointed fangs.

It was hard to believe what I was seeing, but I'd grown up on Granny Mariotti's stories of the hidden world.

"Vampire," I whispered. "The Drainers turned you into a vampire."

She heard me and laughed. "He's coming for me. Our love is eternal."

Her whole body contorted, her limbs moving impossibly fast. She nearly ripped the car door off its hinges trying to escape.

"Skyler, close the door," I said. "Stay calm. We can help you."

To my relief, she obeyed me, but she started saying Travis's name, over and over, like a chant.

"Ignore it," Vaughn said. Clearly he hadn't heard my earlier revelation. "She'll be fine once we get her home."

Skyler snaked an arm around his neck and tried to pull him into the back seat, nearly causing Vaughn to lose control. He was forced to let go of the steering wheel, and the car swerved wildly as he tried to pry her hands from his neck. I tugged at her hands, too, but she had a death grip on him.

Before we ended up wrapped around a tree, Vaughn grabbed the wheel again and managed to maneuver the car to the side of the road.

"Stop it right now!" I shouted. Skyler released him but began to claw at her own skin. There was the bite mark on her neck and another lower down, near her collarbone. Would this happen to me? I rubbed my neck, at what I hoped was just a scratch and not a bite, then drew my hand away quickly. I'd think about my own *scraping* from Travis after we helped my best friend.

"What's the matter with her?" Vaughn asked. "Did she take something at the party?" Drugs might explain some of Skyler's bizarre behavior, but she never touched anything stronger than booze. This was something *much* worse.

"Do you have any rope in the trunk?" I asked Vaughn.

His eyebrows shot up, but he got out and popped the trunk open, then returned with the rope he used for rock climbing and handed it to me. "I thought we were taking her home."

"Nope," I said. "We need to crash Granny's book club."

Skyler's eyes went bloodred, and she lunged for Vaughn's throat before I could stop her. He jumped back. "Jesus, what the hell is wrong with her?"

Maybe most people would think they were hallucinating or being pranked if their best friend suddenly sprouted fangs and a bad attitude, but I was a Mariotti.

"Fucking vampires," I muttered under my breath again, but Vaughn heard me.

"Vampires? Sky is dating a vampire? Are *you* high?"

"I know it sounds preposterous, but it adds up," I explained. "The Drainers had fangs. Fangs mean vampires. And I got a look at them—they weren't fake. Plus, Sky has bite marks."

I was sure it sounded far-fetched to Vaughn, but I knew what I saw.

"I think you're right," Vaughn said after a very long pause. "Skyler doesn't do drugs, and you saw something. Sometimes the most obvious answer is the right one."

Vaughn had never doubted my family history, but I was grateful that he also believed me about the vampires.

Our popular culture was inundated with stories of vampires. There was even a non-scary vampire on a beloved kids' show. Maybe there was more to it than just stories to make you shiver.

Skyler thrashed wildly as we wound the rope around her. "Not too tight," I said. "But make sure she can't get loose."

Her dress rode up, and I noticed a bite on her thigh. It was an old mark, faded, but the skin looked ripped and swollen.

I sucked in my breath. "Those jerks."

"What are we going to do at the book club?"

"Find out how to kill a bunch of asshole vampires." I stared at the night sky. The moon was full and bright, a typical romantic setting, but there was a dark blot in the sky, and it was coming toward us. I stood frozen, my heartbeat loud and fast.

Vaughn came up next to me. "Get in the car, Tansy," he said. He repeated it a couple of times before my brain, which had been locked down in terror, finally started working again.

"Help me with Sky," I said.

He bent and, in one swift motion, picked up Skyler and carried her in a bridal hold to the car. She tried to bite his ear.

"Sky, stop it," he said. "Or I swear I'm going to drop you on your ass."

She growled at him like a feral cat, her teeth snapping, but he managed to dodge her.

I opened the door, and he shoved her into the back seat. I jumped in after her, and then Vaughn got in the driver's seat and we sped home.

"I can hear you being all judgy over there," I said. "Cut it out."

"I'm not being judgy," Vaughn said. "It's just that—"

I cut him off. "Your best friend broke her."

"Con didn't break her," Vaughn said. "He broke *up* with her."

"Same difference," I said, a hot feeling in my stomach all over again at the way Connor had dropped Sky so suddenly.

"Not always," he replied carefully. "Sometimes, a breakup is a good thing—especially if one of the people is in love with someone else."

My mouth fell open. "Connor's in love with someone else?"

"No, I'm not talking about Connor," he said.

"Who, then?"

He took his eyes off the road for a brief second, and something in his gaze made my heart pound in my ears. "Can we talk later?" he asked.

I nodded, barely restraining myself from asking more questions. From hoping.

He returned his attention to driving. "Good," he murmured.

We'd reached PCH when a heavy fog rolled in, obscuring the road. Vaughn slowed down but kept a steady pace as the fog grew thicker.

"I've never seen a marine layer like this," he muttered.

There was a sound like hail falling on the roof. Then something hit the windshield and clung there—a skeletal creature with wings like a bat but the face of a man. Its cheek pressed to the driver's side, its mouth in a silent scream. Vaughn and I were both screaming now.

"What is that thing?" I yelled. The creature raised its

bony hand and tried to punch through the glass to get to Vaughn.

"What the hell?" Vaughn swore but kept driving.

This night had been a freak show from beginning to end, and I'd had enough of things that go bump in the night.

"Leave him alone!" I screamed. The car swerved...

And then the creature was gone.

Chapter Three

It was a miracle, but Vaughn managed to turn onto PCH without crashing the car. In the back seat, I was shaking. "What was that thing?"

My question made Skyler laugh, but the wild and screechy sound wasn't like anything I'd heard from her before. Her warm brown eyes had turned a violent red. "He's coming for me." She cackled again.

I flinched, which made her cackle louder. I started to tremble, which made her dissolve into another bout of malicious mirth.

When we reached Granny's, Vaughn scooped Skyler up, and we dashed from the driveway into the house.

Our bungalow had been in our family for generations. Granny said all the houses in the neighborhood used to look like ours, but now it was the house the neighbors called a "tear-down."

It was a block from the beach with a killer view, but it *had* seen better days. Still, I loved the small Craftsman with its wide front porch, dark wood bookcases and floors,

and the backyard with Granny's herb garden, avocado
trees ripe with fruit, and the eucalyptus tree that Skyler
said smelled like pee.

"Mariotti witches have always lived by the sea," Granny
had often said. *"That's why I'll never sell this place."*

After the night we'd had, it felt like a refuge.

"Granny, I need you!" I shouted the second the door
swung open.

"You're home early," Granny Mariotti said placidly
as she blinked at me from the couch. Granny was nearly
as fair-skinned as I was, although her hair had once been
black. She had brown eyes, not green like mine, and she
was thin and wiry. Sometimes, it seemed impossible that
we could be related, but Granny assured me that we were.

She wasn't alone. Her friends Edna and Evelyn were
still there.

"Can I fix you a snack?" Edna asked. "You look tired,
Tansy. Doesn't she look tired, Evelyn?" I'd been the
ringbearer at their wedding when I was five, and sometimes
they still treated me like I was that age.

They studied me, and I realized that I was standing
in the doorway, blocking their view of my friends, and
stepped to the side.

"I have a little bit of a problem." I undersold it, then
motioned to Skyler, who snarled.

"My, you must have had an interesting evening," Evelyn
said.

"There's something wrong with Sky," I said, stating the
obvious. Vaughn placed Skyler on the blue velvet chaise.
"I think she's in thrall to a vampire."

She just lay there panting until Granny crossed the
room to examine her. Granny didn't even flinch when
Skyler, who'd somehow managed to work an arm free,

tried to claw her face.

"Tell me what happened tonight," Granny said. "Quickly, now."

The story came out in a rush. When I was done, Granny didn't say anything, just went into the kitchen. The bungalow was small, with no walls between the kitchen and living room, so I watched her as she got out a copper pot and began throwing herbs and other ingredients into it. She turned the stove burner on high and then occasionally stirred it, muttering under her breath as she did.

"Can you help her?" I asked.

Skyler was quiet, busy trying to use her sharp incisors to gnaw through the rope.

"I'll try," Granny said. She sniffed the concoction. "This will ease the symptoms. Think you can get her to drink it?"

"Maybe." I tried to coax Skyler into trying some of the frothy purple liquid, but in the end, Vaughn had to hold her while I pinched her nostrils closed and forced it down. She spit the first bit out, right into my face, but I managed to get the rest into her.

"I will tear out your heart and have it for breakfast," she said in a low voice I almost didn't recognize.

"No, you won't," I said. "You never eat breakfast."

Vaughn choked back a laugh while Skyler snarled at me.

I did my best to ignore her, but it didn't exactly feel great when she started muttering about how she wanted to bathe in my blood.

"That's probably really unsanitary," I said calmly.

It took a few minutes, but Skyler eventually fell into an uneasy sleep.

Evelyn studied Skyler critically. "Fascinating," she said. "I've read about it, of course, but I don't think there's been this kind of hidden world sighting since the eighties."

I almost expected her to whip out her lab coat and microscope, but instead, she reached into her purse and took out a spiral notebook and pencil and started scribbling something down.

"Hidden world?" Vaughn asked.

"The first rule of the hidden world is you don't talk about the hidden world," I said, knowing he'd get the movie reference.

Vaughn gave a little snort in acknowledgment, which was adorable.

"Vampires, werewolves, ghosts," Edna said. Her long black hair was tied up in braids, which highlighted the perfect skin of someone twenty years younger. She was a dermatologist, after all.

"Vampires, werewolves, ghosts?" he repeated. "That all?"

"Not even close," I said. "Maybe if I'd been paying attention, this wouldn't have happened to Skyler. I'm a witch, and it took me way too long to recognize a vampire when he was standing right in front of me."

Granny frowned. "How do you think vampires have managed to remain hidden? They're sneaky and secretive, and they manipulate their victims to help themselves stay undetected. Skyler was probably deliberately concealing things from you. Unless this was the first time they'd met?"

I shook my head. "I don't think so," I said. "She mentioned they'd been talking for a few weeks."

"So the hidden world means vampires and witches?" Vaughn asked.

"The hidden world includes any of the supernatural, really," Edna said.

"I thought vampires were just legends," Vaughn said. "Myths. Made up."

I nudged him. "You believe I'm a witch but don't

believe in vampires?"

The older women were all shaking their heads. "Not made-up. Real. Rare, usually hidden—hence the name— but real enough," Edna said.

He sighed and ran a hand through his hair. "It's just a lot to take in."

"After I get Skyler settled, I want to read up on vampires. Do you have suggestions?" Books were librarian catnip. Granny would have a stack of reading material for me before the end of the night.

I turned to Vaughn. "Can you carry Sky to my room?" Then I turned back to Granny. "We'll be back. We need to talk."

Vaughn carried Skyler to my bedroom, and I pulled down the RBG quilt Granny had made for my seventeenth birthday.

"Still a fan, I see?" Vaughn nodded at the quilt. My love for Ruth Bader Ginsburg was well-known. When I was younger, I'd dressed like her for Halloween.

"Always and forever," I replied. I was nothing if not loyal.

Vaughn set Skyler down gently. I noticed my floor was covered in dirty clothes. Vaughn grinned at me when he caught me kicking my sturdiest bra under the bed.

"Sky's been acting secretive for weeks," I said softly.

"She'll be okay," he said.

"I need to get her out of those bloody clothes," I said.

He nodded and then left the room.

I clicked on the bedside lamp. Its soft glow made Skyler look younger somehow. I eased the stained dress over her head and replaced it with a long T-shirt, then tucked her in and tiptoed out of the room.

Vaughn was sitting on the sofa across from Granny, so

I plopped down next to him.

"What a night," he said.

He smelled so good. He must be using a new cologne now that he was single because I could barely restrain myself from snuggling into him. I fanned my face, ignoring the twinkle in Granny's eyes. She'd caught me checking out Vaughn and his hotness, but I played it off like it was the heat making my cheeks flushed. We didn't have AC. That was my story. Sticking to it.

"What do you think is wrong with Skyler?" I asked.

I wound my hair up into a bun and secured it with one of the hair ties I always kept on hand. My hair was thick and unruly.

"Where's your necklace?" Evelyn asked. She and Granny exchanged a look.

"Sky's wearing it," I explained. "She was upset she didn't have hers."

To be honest, my neck felt bare without it, but Skyler had needed it more than I did.

"What's that on your neck?" my grandmother said. There was a strange note in her voice.

"That asshole Travis sniffed me, and then he bit me," I said indignantly, not wanting to think about what that might mean. "Without my permission."

Vaughn glared at the mark on my neck. "I wanted to kill him for what he did to Skyler, but I really want to watch him bleed for what he did to you."

Granny put her hands on my shoulders. "Sit here, in the light, so we can get a better look." She guided me to a barstool in front of the kitchen counter.

Evelyn and Edna put down their drinks and joined us. Granny put on her glasses and examined the small wound.

"I've never heard of a golden vampire bite. I'll research

it," Edna said. "I like the weird stuff."

I shivered. Golden vampire *bite*? I wasn't ready to ask more questions about that yet.

"You *are* the weird stuff," Evelyn replied. "And I love it."

Edna became absorbed in Granny's bookshelves while I made myself a glass of iced tea. I was so thirsty.

"Is Sky a vampire?" I asked.

Edna shook her head.

"Why not?"

"Think of vampirism as a transformation," Edna explained. "There are steps to it. Sometimes, vampires only compel their victims and drink their blood until the victim either gets away or dies. Usually the latter. Those victims will never become a vampire."

"Then what's the first step?" Vaughn asked.

"The first step is when the vampire creates a psychic bond as he drinks his victim's blood," Edna continued.

"The more he drinks, the stronger the connection," Granny added. "And the harder that connection is to break."

"So what's the big deal about my bite, then?" I asked. "He only did it once, and it happened so fast, there was definitely not a connection, psychic or otherwise."

"There's good news," Evelyn chimed in. "You have not yet received the kiss that kills."

I stared at Granny, but she wouldn't meet my eyes. Evelyn said I wasn't a vampire *yet*.

The kiss that kills?

"Although vampirism is transmitted through the blood, it requires the maker to completely drain the victim dry to the point of death," Edna said. "And then the vampire feeds the baby vamp their vampire blood. It becomes irreversible when the baby vamp finds and kills a human by drinking *their* blood."

"Gross," I said. "That's never going to happen."

"Witches are special cases," Granny said. "That's why vampires go out of their way to avoid biting a witch. The smart ones, anyway."

"Then what *exactly is* going to happen to Tansy?" Vaughn growled.

Evelyn turned to Edna. "You know what a vampire bite does to a witch."

"Striga vie," Edna crowed triumphantly. "There hasn't been one in hundreds of years."

"What does that mean?" Vaughn asked. He stood a few feet away, watching us with storm-gray eyes.

"Vampire witch," Granny translated, and I flinched. "A hybrid. It can only happen when a vampire bites a witch, which rarely happens, resulting in someone who has the strength of a vampire and the magic of a witch. When those two powers are combined…"

She didn't finish her sentence. I wasn't ready to think about what that meant.

"Do you know how she got mixed up with this Travis fellow?" Granny asked.

"Before tonight, she hadn't even mentioned him," I admitted.

I would have to be a sucker not to consider that we were dealing with some serious supernatural stuff, but I was relieved to hear Granny say it, like saying the word would lessen its power somehow.

"What else can you tell us about vampires?" Vaughn asked. His expression was deadpan, but his knee jiggled nervously.

"Vampirism is transmitted through bodily fluids," Granny said.

"Like an STD," Edna supplied oh so helpfully.

Evelyn paced. "It might still be possible to save Skyler."

"We'll save her," I said. "Tell me how."

"Tansy, have something to eat," Granny said. She nudged a bowl of dip in front of me and then handed me the tray of crackers.

I scooped up a big bite of the delicious-smelling dip and shoved it in my mouth. I realized I hadn't had dinner and shoveled in another helping but stopped mid-chew. "Why are you all looking at me like that?"

"Like what?" Evelyn said, but she wouldn't meet my eyes.

"Like you know something I don't?"

"There's a ton of garlic in the dip," Granny replied calmly. "Evelyn was worried that you would spontaneously combust once it hit your bloodstream."

"And you let her eat it?" Vaughn asked. He reached over and snatched the cracker out of my hand. He glared at the older women, but they ignored him.

I took the cracker back and swallowed it, practically without chewing, before I said, "Stop worrying, Vaughn. I'm fine."

"You're not *fine*," Granny corrected. "But you were able to resist a vampire. He was probably one of the younger ones."

"He almost did get me," I admitted. I told them about how the closer I got to the music, the more I was drawn to it. I shook my head, suddenly not hungry any longer. "What can we do about Skyler?"

"You and Vaughn should get some sleep," Granny said.

I hesitated. "Will she be okay?"

"I've given her something to counteract the effects," Granny said.

She hadn't answered my question. My stomach

clenched, roiling from tension and fear. I couldn't lose my best friend. "We have to fix this, Granny."

"We'll do our best," she said as she folded me into her arms. This was as close to a promise as I'd get from her, but it was enough.

Suddenly, I was exhausted.

Granny took one of the vintage charms off her bracelet and handed it to Vaughn. "Keep this on you at all times."

I tried to see which charm she'd given him, but he put it in his pocket before I had the chance. "Thank you," he replied. "I will."

Granny said, "Tansy, help Vaughn get settled in the library." Vaughn was tall and muscular. One night on the library's small daybed might kill him, but walking home after midnight definitely could.

I narrowed my eyes at her. She just smiled.

I showed Vaughn where we kept the extra toothbrushes and helped him put clean sheets on the bed.

He hesitated. "We'll figure everything out."

I bit my lip, still worried about Skyler.

"We'll help her, Tansy," he said. "I promise. Tomorrow we'll research The Drainers. Get some sleep, and things will look better in the morning."

"That's a good idea," I said. "Good night."

The night had been one of the weirdest of my existence, but I brushed my teeth and put on my pajamas like always.

I headed to the kitchen for a glass of water. Granny and her friends were talking in the living room, and I was in the hallway, out of sight, when I heard a name that made me stop in my tracks: *Vanessa.*

My mother.

Granny rarely talked about my mother. She'd dumped me with Granny and never looked back. And then she'd died. Or at least that's what I'd been told.

"I think you should tell Tansy the truth," Evelyn said.

"She's better off not knowing," Granny replied. I recognized that stubborn tone. She wasn't going to tell me anything, which made me feel a little better about eavesdropping.

"She's already met a vampire," Edna said. "That's a lot for one night. Maybe we should save emotional revelations for another day."

Evelyn cleared her throat. "What about Vanessa? Tansy should know her mother is still alive."

"You want me to tell Tansy that Vanessa is *alive*?" Granny's voice was tight.

My mother is still alive? I blinked away tears. What else had she lied to me about?

When I was in fourth grade, Granny had told me that my mother had died. Skyler had helped me through that terrible year. I hadn't known my mother, but that didn't mean I hadn't missed her. You *can* miss what you've never had.

I returned my attention to eavesdropping, where they were still handing out truth bombs.

"You know it, and I know it," Granny said. "Skyler will run back to that creature."

There was a long silence, and I could feel my granny's displeasure, even though I couldn't see it.

"You haven't shown her enough to deal with this." Usually when they tried to convince Granny of something, Evelyn was the more diplomatic of the two, but tonight there was no good cop/bad cop. It was bad cop/bad cop all the way.

I almost felt sorry for Granny until I remembered that she'd been keeping secrets from me.

"Vanessa had read all the books and was nearly finished with her training when she was Tansy's age," Edna said.

"And look how that turned out." The grief in Granny's voice cut right through me. "I can't lose Tansy, too."

I tiptoed away, hydration needs forgotten as I analyzed the conversation I'd just heard.

When I went back to my room, Skyler was sleeping like the dead, barely moving, the quilt over her despite the warm night, one arm dangling off the bed. I touched her skin. It was so cold.

Nobody had called asking where she was. Mr. Avrett was away on business (he was always away on business), so I'd texted stepmother number three to let her know Sky was sleeping at my house. Gertie texted a short *ok* back. Skyler slept over at my house a lot, so Gertie didn't ask any questions.

I grabbed some blankets from the linen chest and made a pallet on the floor. I wanted to be nearby in case Skyler needed anything.

It had been a long, stressful evening. I'd learned my dead mother was alive and my best friend had hooked up with a vampire.

And that wasn't even my biggest problem. You know how sometimes you crave chocolate? Like when you're PMSing, or feel bloated, or just epically failed your bio exam, or broke up with your boyfriend, or all of the above in the same day? Since the party, I'd been getting that feeling a lot.

But it wasn't chocolate I craved. It was blood.

Worst. Party. Ever.

Chapter Four

I t was barely six a.m. when I stumbled into the kitchen, and Granny was already drinking coffee at the counter. A new wreath of garlic hung in the kitchen window.

"How's Skyler?" Granny asked.

"Still sleeping," I said. "Vaughn up yet?"

"Already left," Granny said. "Something about summer conditioning. He said he'd text you later."

Vaughn didn't get all those muscles by sleeping in. He was either practicing with the baseball team or running a mile or ten.

Granny hesitated like she knew I wouldn't like what she had to tell me. "This musician most likely has created a physical and psychic connection. Abruptly breaking it could do more harm than good."

"Is that why Sky freaked out last night?"

"Most likely," Granny said.

"I have to help her," I said. "Is there a spell that could work?"

"Not one that I know of," Granny said. "I'll ask the

book club for help. I have to go to pick up an author at LAX. Will you be okay?"

"Sure," I said.

Granny had a long day ahead at work. She had the closing shift at the library because they had some famous nonfiction writer presenting a talk on the science of folk medicine.

She was dressed for work, except for the rubber ducky slippers on her feet. "There's some elixir in the fridge," she said. "Make sure Skyler drinks it."

"I will. Granny—" I hesitated again. I wanted to ask her more about being a striga vie—and about my mother, but she needed to get to work.

She slipped her heels on and grabbed her car keys but waited for me to finish my sentence.

"Have a good day," I finally said.

After she left, I sat at the kitchen counter, thinking.

I didn't know any spell to get me out of an AP Calc test or a magical way to erase the tiny freckles on my nose. I'd always thought spells were more about "the peaceful way," which was the main thing Granny emphasized when she was raising me.

I had a temper, and when one of the kids in my class had made a smart-ass remark about my mom abandoning me (the truth, it does hurt), I punched her in her smarmy little face.

Granny had sat me down and talked to me about why striking someone else was not the right way. Not the peaceful way. I knew people called her a witch, but to me, it seemed like it was kind of a new-age philosophy that had been handed down for generations, like the old books in the spare bedroom, which we jokingly called the library.

I headed there and grabbed as many books as I could

find with any mention of bloodsuckers or vampires or compulsion.

I settled on the daybed by the window and hit the books. At first, my reading didn't come up with anything I couldn't have discovered from a quick read of Bram Stoker's *Dracula*. I kept looking, and finally, in a book called *The Twenty-First Century Bloodsucker*, I found a paragraph about vampire talents, which seemed like a good lead.

According to the research, all vampires had a special talent, along with the ones that had made it into popular culture, such as turning into a bat, not having a reflection, and drinking blood. One of the rarer talents she listed was the ability to "day walk," which was a fairly obvious term for a vampire who could walk in the sun.

There wasn't any mention of compulsion through song, but maybe that was another rare talent. Assuming all vampires were the same was like saying all people were the same.

The words were starting to blur, so I closed the book and put it in my bag.

It didn't take a genius to figure out I'd been bitten by a vampire, even if he masqueraded as a wannabe emo-boy musician with an oral fixation.

I spent the next few minutes following The Drainers on social media and reading articles and reviews. Several mentioned the amazing pyrotechnics at their shows, but I wondered if it had more to do with vampire talent than special effects. I made a note to research vampire fire and see what I could find.

They'd posted their tour schedule on their website, and there were upcoming gigs listed in and around Diablo, a beach town north of L.A. My phone lit up with a notification. Vaughn had texted that he was coming over to check on Sky.

It was getting late, and she still wasn't awake. I took the drink Granny had left for Skyler to my room, but it was empty.

Oh no. No, no, no. What would I do if Skyler had gone back to Travis?

My necklace lay discarded on the neatly made bed. I scooped it up and put it around my neck. I lifted my hair and studied the two puncture marks carefully. Travis hadn't had time to get more than a sip, but the wound ached.

The protective magic hadn't done its job, and I needed to cast a stronger spell. It wasn't my imagination that Travis had wanted to get rid of it, though.

I mean, I did have an overactive imagination. Like the time I thought there was something hinky going on with Vaughn's baseball coach, so I accused him of drinking between innings. He *was* drinking, but it was just Gatorade. My granny made me send him a written apology. I felt somewhat vindicated when, a year later, the coach ran off with fifty thousand dollars of the league's money.

I had the same strange feeling in the pit of my stomach now. I needed to get Skyler away from The Drainers for good, but I wasn't sure how. I had to figure out what to do.

Granny had said that it was hard to break vampire hypnosis, but I had to try. Maybe there was something she didn't know or had overlooked. I took another quick look at her hidden-world research books. I spotted a neglected looking volume on the bottom shelf. Judging by the layer of dust, Granny hadn't opened it in decades. Probably because it was written in German: *Des Nachzehers.*

A quick visit to a translation app confirmed it was a book about German vampire mythology, and I honed in on something that looked like it could be a recipe and typed it in.

Not a recipe—a spell. I'd found a separation spell to break a vampire's hold. I felt my body sag with relief. And it didn't seem too complicated, either. I needed a freshly shorn lock of Skyler's hair. That meant I couldn't just sneak a strand or two from her hairbrush, but it should be easy enough to get once I found her.

But then I read on. I also needed a lock of hair or a fingernail from the vampire controlling her and a "filet of fenny snake," whatever that was. Not as easy, but I'd find a way. I jumped to my feet and got into the shower.

Vaughn wasn't going to like it, but I had a plan.

I threw on a pair of shorts and a T-shirt. I could practically see Skyler rolling her eyes at my choice of outfit, and the idea choked me up. What kind of friend was I? I hadn't even noticed she hadn't been herself for a long time. Probably since Connor had ghosted her and left the country without a word to anybody.

The epic disaster that was Skyler and Connor's love story made me hesitate about Vaughn. Our friendship was solid, but Skyler and Connor had been friends first, too, and look how that had turned out.

I threw some clothes in a duffel bag and then added the reference books. While I was at it, I applied a little mascara and lipstick.

While I was waiting for Vaughn, I opened Instagram and noticed a new post from Skyler. It wasn't much—just a picture of an all-access pass to a Drainers concert.

I was pacing on the front porch when I saw Vaughn pull up.

I'd already written a note for Granny, which I hoped she wouldn't find until she came home late tonight.

I practically dragged him inside. "Sky's gone."

"What?" Vaughn said. We almost collided going through the kitchen door at the same time, so he put his hands on my hips to steady me. We both froze and stared at each other, his gray eyes turning the color of pewter.

Neither of us moved, but one more step and we'd be in each other's arms. Our eyes remained locked until I finally took a step back.

Vaughn followed me when I went to get my luggage, so I filled him in on the morning's events. He insisted on carrying my duffel bag for me. "What's all this?" he asked as he put the bag in the trunk of the Deathtrap, which was my loving nickname for my beater car, a pink Lincoln.

"I'm going after Skyler," I admitted. I explained to him about what I'd learned and where I thought Skyler had gone.

"I'm coming with you," Vaughn said. "Follow me to my house. I'll grab a few things, and we'll hit the road."

It didn't look like anybody was home when we got to Vaughn's.

"I'll wait here," I said.

It didn't take long before Vaughn came out of the house, a gym bag slung over his shoulder and two travel mugs in his hands.

I jumped out and opened his car door for him. He handed me one of the mugs, and I inhaled the scent of the delicious elixir known as coffee.

"Dark and bitter as my soul," I joked.

"As warm as your heart," he countered. "But only half as sweet." In other words, he remembered I liked my coffee with one sugar and a splash of cream. Granny was an espresso-or-die kind of woman, but I liked my beans a little watered down.

We were already in the Deathtrap when my phone started to chime with notifications. I'd set up alerts, and The Drainers were trending.

I ignored the phone for now and headed to Skyler's. Maybe we could catch her before she left.

Gertie answered the door and greeted us with a smile. "Why, hello, you two."

"Is Sky here?"

"She left a few hours ago," she said. "Grabbed some stuff and headed out."

"She left my house without saying goodbye," I said.

I wanted to kick myself for blurting out the information, but Gertie just shrugged. "Some girl came, and they took off."

"A girl? What did she look like?"

"Dark-haired and pretty," Gertie said. "Her name was Natalie, I think. She said they were going to see a band."

I didn't know who the girl was, but I was certain the band was The Drainers. "I'm sure she'll text me later."

"I'm sure," Gertie replied.

"If you hear from her, tell her to call me?" I asked.

Gertie nodded. "Everything all right, Tansy?"

"It will be," I said.

I dialed Skyler's number as Vaughn and I walked back to the car, but it went straight to voicemail. After I read my notifications, I knew where Skyler had gone — and I didn't like it one bit. Skyler was headed to a show in Diablo.

Granny's words echoed in my brain. *Never date a musician. Or a bartender. Or a Raiders quarterback who blew out his knee in '03.* That last part was awfully specific. Perhaps a hint to who my dad was?

I had to ignore my emotional upheaval for now and concentrate on helping Skyler. Learning that my mom was alive—that my granny had been lying to me for almost my whole life—those things had to wait.

Skyler had always been there for me, and I was going to be there for her.

"We have to find her, Vaughn," I said.

His warm gray eyes crinkled at the corners as he glanced at me. "We will."

"What if we don't?" I tried to keep my voice steady. I needed to find my friend before Travis hurt her more than he already had.

"Hey," he said, "we're in this together."

I quickly swiped at the tears welling in my eyes and changed the subject. "I get to pick the music."

"I never expected anything else," he assured me. "Maybe we'll get lucky. We should check the house in the Hollywood Hills where they had the party. Maybe she went back there."

I tapped the address into the app on my phone. Apps like this were invented for the directionally challenged like me. "Hollywood, here we come."

Chapter Five

The Deathtrap had a full tank of gas, and there wasn't much traffic. Bonus: I only got lost once, when my GPS signal dropped up in the hills.

There were a few cars parked near the house where we'd met Travis, but none of them was Skyler's little red convertible. Everything was quiet and still, except for the far-off sound of sirens, which wasn't unusual in the city.

"No sign of life," Vaughn said.

"We *are* dealing with vampires," I said. The more times I said it aloud, the more I believed it. "They're probably still sleeping."

Musicians and vampires had a similar schedule—sleep all day, up all night—which was convenient if, like The Drainers, you were vampires in a band.

I told myself that maybe Skyler was already safe back in Huntington Beach. I told myself that, but I already knew it wasn't the truth. Skyler had gone to find Travis.

But I needed to check anyway.

Vaughn and I got out of the car. I knocked on the door,

but no one answered. I knocked again, harder this time, and the door creaked open on its own.

Which wasn't creepy at all.

Vaughn's phone rang, and I jumped. "It's my dad," he said. "I've got to take this. Wait for me. I'll be a few minutes."

I'd forgotten I was supposed to work this week. "I have a shift scheduled on Thursday."

"I'll take care of it," he said. "I'll ask Dad for a few days off for both of us."

I hoped it wouldn't take that long to find Skyler, but it might take me a while to get the ingredients for the spell I needed to cast.

I fumbled for a light switch and was relieved by the sudden brightness. The house looked empty, but all the curtains had been closed to shut out the sun. A bra hung from the chandelier, and an overflowing bag of trash stunk up the kitchen, but there was no sign of life, human or otherwise.

There was a lot of conflicting information about vampires, but I was pretty sure they were creatures of the night, which again made The Drainers' musical profession convenient.

A weird scraping sound, like someone was dragging something along the marble floor, startled me. A tall blond girl appeared, pulling a ladder behind her. She wore a halter top, denim cutoffs, and cowboy boots.

"Have you seen Travis?" I asked.

Her blue eyes narrowed. "Who are you? And why do you want to know?"

"He's a…" I hesitated and then forced the words out. "Friend of mine."

She snorted. "You need to get better friends."

"More like a friend of a friend. My best friend is dating

him." I shuddered as the ladder screeched its way across the room.

"You should probably pick that up or you'll scratch the floor," I offered.

"I know," she said with twangy satisfaction. Her Southern accent was slight but noticeable. "It'd serve him right. I hope he loses his deposit."

"This is Travis's house?"

"The band probably rented it while they were in L.A.," the blonde said.

"When did they leave?"

She shook her head. "Bus pulled out at around three a.m."

I wondered if she knew what the guys really were. "They travel during the day?"

"They sleep on the bus," she replied. "Gary drives."

"Who's Gary?" I didn't recall any of them having that name.

She stared at me. "He's The Drainers' roadie. Their human servant. He guards their coffins. They usually just call him Renfield—get it?"

"Renfield? Like in *Dracula*? So you know?"

"That they're vampires? Sure do," she said. "I also know they're assholes."

I couldn't argue with that. I wondered how she knew so much about The Drainers. She didn't have that vacant stare that some of their superfans had.

She stopped below the chandelier and propped up the ladder, then climbed it and snagged the bra hanging off a crystal teardrop.

"I wondered where this thing went," she said with a cheerful smile, then climbed back down and took a seat on the bottom rung of the ladder. She stared off into space and twirled the bra idly. Not only was she built, she had a heart-shaped face and big blue eyes. She was definitely beautiful.

"I'm Tansy," I offered.

Her hair was the shade of blond that let people underestimate her, but underneath all that gorgeousness, I saw fierce intelligence.

"Bobbie Jean," she said. "I suppose you're one of the rat bastard's groupies?"

"Rat bastard?"

"That jerk Travis," she said. "I wish I had my daddy's hunting rifle about now, but they wouldn't let me take it on the plane. Not that it would do any good to shoot him, but it would sure make me feel a little better."

I inched away from her, but she didn't notice.

"I tracked him from Texas," she said. "Finally cornered him last night. He pretended to be glad to see me, but, afterward, when I fell asleep, he skedaddled."

"Afterward?"

"After...you know," she said. "Oh, honey, don't tell me you fell for that soul mates stuff? Me too, at first."

I felt like throwing up. Travis had had a busy night. Skyler was out there somewhere with a lying, cheating douchebag who used girls like they were his own personal blood bank.

"I didn't fall for anything," I said. At least I hadn't fallen for *Travis's* BS. The bite on my neck throbbed. "My best friend did."

"I *thought* you looked too smart to be one of Travis's Bleeders." She studied me. "Or a Sundowner, either."

"What are those?"

"His followers," she said. At my blank look, she clarified. "The Bleeders are groupies. The Drainers have thousands of them. They follow the band, do anything they ask." That explained some of the hashtags I'd seen.

"Why is their live music so amazing and the recorded stuff so terrible?" I asked.

She giggled but sobered quickly. "Don't say that in front of Natasha," she cautioned.

"Who's that?"

"The president of The Drainers' fan club. The number-one Bleeder," she said.

Natasha? Could that be the "Natalie" who Skyler had taken off with? Maybe Gertie had her name wrong.

"I thought you said they were called Sundowners."

"Sundowners are waiting for the final kiss," she said. "The Bleeders are just…wannabe Sundowners." She said it like it clarified everything.

"There's a hierarchy for their band groupies?"

"Bleeders are more like…the band's food source," she said. "They follow them everywhere."

"Gross." But despite how disgusting all of this was, it started to make sense. It was like a fog was slowly lifting from my brain. "He's using my best friend as an appetizer," I said. "She keeps going back to him."

"There's not a snowball's chance in hell she'll leave him," Bobbie Jean replied. "Once she's under his spell, there's not a lot you can do."

"I have to try. She's my best friend," I said. "Did you happen to see her last night? Petite brunette with brown eyes."

She shrugged. "Maybe. What's her name?"

"Skyler," I said.

She shook her head. "Doesn't sound familiar, but there were *a lot* of girls here last night. I mean, I knew The Drainers were a gluttonous bunch, but hoo-wee."

"Do you have one of these?" I craned my neck so she could see the bite mark.

She nodded. "But I can't show you mine."

Relief swept through me. "You mean it faded?"

She blushed. "It's somewhere…private," she said.

"Oh."

Silence. We both stared at the floor.

"Some of The Drainers' superfans seem into the whole vampire thing," I said.

She nodded. "They *want* The Drainers to bite them. But it takes more than one bite to make a vampire, or you and I would be screwed."

"Do you know what it does take to make a vampire?" I asked, trying to keep the trembling from my voice, hoping to confirm what Granny had told me.

"Travis would have to drink you dry and then give you some of his blood," she replied. I made a face. So Granny was right.

"Why are you looking for him?" I asked her.

"Revenge," Bobbie Jean said.

"Because he bit you without permission?" I asked. "I can relate to that one."

She shook her head. "He took something of mine," she said. "And I want it back."

"I…get that one, too," I said, thinking of Sky.

"What are you going to do now?" Bobbie Jean asked.

I shrugged. "I have no idea. I'm assuming you have the other symptoms, too?"

She nodded. "Daddy slaughtered a cow last week, and I knocked him over trying to get the blood."

I thought about what she'd told me so far. "What will happen to you?"

"Travis left that part out when he was whispering sweet

nothings in my ear. Like how I smelled so good and he was sure I was the one."

"And how your love would be eternal?" I said with a shudder.

"Hello?" a girl said from the doorway, and I turned. She had pink hair and was dressed in a vintage floral dress and white gloves, which made her look like she was ready for a garden tea party. "I am Rose. Is this the residence of Travis, lead singer of The Drainers?"

She was asking about a vampire, but she looked human and didn't have that weird decaying smell that Travis and the guys had. She must be human. Or at least not a vampire.

"Travis seems to be pretty popular today," I replied. "But you just missed him."

"A tragic loss," another girl said, stepping in from behind her. Instead of pink hair, she had jet-black hair in a braid and wore a belted oversize white T-shirt over unicorn-print leggings. Some sort of weapon was strapped to one thigh in a Lara Croft–like holder. Her big blue eyes matched the other girl's. Despite their different hair colors and clothing styles, it was clear they were twins. Probably a few years older than me.

Rose frowned at her. "What Thorn meant to say is that we have a message for him from the pack." She may have looked eighteen, but she sounded eighty.

"The pack?" I asked.

Rose shook her head. "Not the pack, the PAC. The Paranormal Activities Committee. The people we work for."

The girl beside her snorted. "Or Pain-in-the-Ass Creeps." She definitely didn't like her bosses.

There was a committee to govern paranormal activity? Of course there was. And I'd bet she was using the word "people" loosely.

"Let me guess," I said. "A bunch of old white dudes making decisions for everyone."

"They *are* very old," Thorn said solemnly. "And very white. But that is because most of them are dead. No blood flow, you understand."

"What does the PAC do?" I asked.

"Each kingdom has a representative on the committee. They agree on policies," she said. "Or, more often, disagree. Sometimes, they have to make executive decisions."

"What kind of executive decisions?"

"Deadly ones," she replied. "That's where we come in. If the PAC feels threatened, we *manage* that threat."

Politics, sheesh.

I wasn't very impressed with the way regular old politicians treated women. Vampire politicians were probably a hundred times worse.

Thorn snorted again, louder this time.

"Thorn, please refrain from making that ungodly sound," Rose said.

I gaped at her. "Your names are Rose and Thorn?" Though now that I thought about it, the names seemed to suit their personalities. Rose was soft-spoken and formal, and Thorn seemed outspoken and sharp as the dagger she had strapped to her thigh.

Suddenly, I was incredibly tired. I wanted to go home to the boring life I'd left behind in Orange County in all its beige glory.

"What do you want with Travis?" I asked.

"That's classified," Thorn said. Then Ms. Bossy Pants added, "You know, it is very likely you both were infected."

"We know," Bobbie Jean and I said in unison.

"It is more than likely that Travis has already fled the city," she added.

"We know," we chorused again.

"But do you know that there's still a chance to save all those girls?" she asked. "And yourselves, too, of course."

"Tell us how," I said. I'd overheard Granny say we shouldn't try to save Skyler, but I had to. Giving up on my best friend wasn't an option. And there were other girls, too?

"If he has ingested their blood but they have not ingested his, there is still a chance to save them," Rose said.

"And if they've had some of his blood?"

"It's hopeless," Bobbie Jean said.

Thorn made a scoffing noise. Rose frowned at her, but Thorn said, "It's not hopeless, just *almost* hopeless."

"What?" I asked her. "Tell me what can be done if Skyler's already drunk Travis's blood."

"You can kill him," she said. "If you kill the sire, all his progeny will return to human."

I nodded. "Then that's what I'll do," I said.

Skyler might not make it through the summer. I had to find her and save her from Travis *now*.

That seemed to deflate Rose a tiny bit, but she soldiered on. "What else have you determined?"

"We both hooked up with Travis," Bobbie Jean said.

I shuddered. Oh hell no. "I didn't hook up with Travis." I shook my head for added emphasis. "He just bit me without permission."

"Then what happened?" Rose asked.

"Then I kneed him in the balls," I replied with satisfaction. "But my best friend was bitten, too. The Drainers didn't want to let us leave, but we did."

"I got bit at his gig in Austin and then again last night," Bobbie Jean said.

"My friend had fangs," I said.

"What color were her eyes?" Thorn blurted out. "All red and squinty like a rat's?"

"Her eyes?" I asked. "Normal color. Brown." I wasn't ready to tell them my secrets.

"That is good news," she said.

Rose fished a thick file out of her purse and scribbled madly. The pen had silver ink. I tried to read over her shoulder, but she blocked my view. "So what else?"

"Skyler was bit when we were at the party here last night," I said. But then I thought of the weird way Skyler had been acting. "It's possible it was more than one time.

"She's my best friend," I continued stubbornly. "I'm not going back home without her."

"Perhaps there's hope for her," Rose said. "As long as she doesn't drink any of the prince's blood."

"Gross," I said, making a face. "Who's the prince?"

I'd just started to get my head around the idea of vampires, and now Rose was telling me there was a hierarchy?

"He goes by the name Travis," she said. "His father is the king of the vampires. California realm."

"His *royal* blood is probably swimming with communicable disease," I replied. "But my friend Skyler thinks she's in love with him. And that he loves her."

Thorn studied my face. "The prince thinks of women only two ways," she said. "For feeding and for f—"

I interrupted her before she could finish that sentence. "I've no intention of staying here and waiting," I said.

"You are a Mariotti witch." Rose narrowed her eyes. "But you still do not know what you are getting yourself into."

How did she know I was a Mariotti? Who *were* these girls?

Things were getting less clear the more I learned—but saving Skyler was more important than anything right now. "It doesn't matter," I said. "Skyler is my best friend."

"Then be prepared to face the consequences," she said.

I tried to ignore the dread pooling in my stomach at what I'd find when we finally caught up with Skyler. If that jerk had hurt her, I was going to find a spell that would make his fangs as useful as flip-flops in Siberia and see how long he survived.

Chapter Six

"Tansy, where are you?" I heard Vaughn's voice calling me.

"Who is that?" Thorn asked.

Good question. Who *was* Vaughn, exactly? Friend? Potential boyfriend?

While I was dithering about labels, Thorn whipped out a wicked-looking dagger.

"He's a friend," I answered hastily as Vaughn walked into the room.

Bobbie Jean looked him up and down. "He's bitable."

I glared at her. "Don't even think about it."

Vaughn ignored everyone but me. "Sorry that took so long," he said. "Everything okay here?"

I lifted an eyebrow. "What did your dad say about you leaving?"

Vaughn lifted an eyebrow back. "He was pissed at first, but everything's okay now. He got Angela and Rohan to cover our shifts."

The other girls watched us like our conversation was a

yellow tennis ball we were batting back and forth.

"Hi, I'm Vaughn," he said and gave them all a wave. They didn't wave back or even introduce themselves. Thorn was still holding the dagger like she *wanted* him to make a wrong move. "Ohh...kay..."

"Is he your boyfriend?" Bobbie Jean asked, stepping over to him.

I said no quickly and maybe a little too loudly. Vaughn raised an eyebrow at me again but didn't say anything.

"You should give him a chance." Bobbie Jean winked. "If you don't, I will." Her top lip curled up just enough to reveal a fang, her eyes intent on him, hungry.

Not happening.

The sisters seemed to lose interest in Vaughn and me and returned to arguing about who would get to make Travis pay.

"I have ways of making him talk," Thorn said. "The prince won't get away with this."

"I'm going, too," Bobbie Jean said stubbornly.

"We can travel much faster without you," Thorn said.

"What my sister means to say—" Rose started to add, but Thorn interrupted her.

"*Your sister* can speak for herself. And I said what I meant. The prince's castoff will slow us down."

I sat on the floor and listened to the argument going on all around me.

Vaughn sat beside me and held my hand. "Tansy, I'm sorry it took so long. My dad was going on and on about his new girlfriend." He rolled his eyes.

I squeezed his back. "It's okay." I hoped my hands weren't sweaty, but holding his hand was a lot. I'd probably faint if he ever kissed me.

My phone buzzed with a text from Sky, and my pulse

thudded in my ears as I scrambled to open the message. Maybe she'd sent me her location? But all it said was: **Don't try to find me**.

That was never going to happen. Vaughn and I would find her, whether she liked it or not. My best friend was in trouble, and no text message would stop me from doing whatever it took to help her.

"Skyler's trying to get us to leave her alone," I told Vaughn. I showed him the text, and he swore under his breath.

"What's she up to?" he asked.

I pulled up The Drainers' Instagram. There was a picture of Skyler and another girl snuggled up to Travis and Ozzie. They were somewhere gloomy and sitting on what looked like coffins.

Rose peered over my shoulder. "Is that your friend?" I nodded.

I put a hand up to my neck, everything I'd learned— especially those words, *striga vie*—swirling around in my head.

Rose came over to me. "Let me see your bites," she said. I shook my head. "Bite. Singular."

Vaughn nudged me. "Tansy, you should show them. Maybe they can help."

"Fine." I craned my neck and pointed to the mark. "Is that what yours looks like?"

Everyone in the room but me gasped.

"What? What is it?" They were all staring at my neck.

"I don't have a bite like *that*," Bobbie Jean said.

"Like what?" I asked, truly alarmed now. I mean, how much worse could it be?

She wordlessly handed me the compact from her purse.

My bite marks were now perfect circles and glowing gold.

Even Thorn looked shocked. She stared at the mark and then woke her cell phone. "I need to make some calls," she said before walking out of the room.

"Do you know where The Drainers are staying?" I asked Bobbie Jean.

"There's only one way to find out," Bobbie Jean replied. She whipped out her phone and started typing madly.

"When were you born?" Rose asked out of the blue. Thorn had finished her call already and returned.

Nosy much?

"Her birthday is April first," Vaughn said. He shot me a look and winked. That was not my birthday. I glared at him, but then realized he was just messing with them. He wasn't going to give a stranger my birthday. Next they'd be asking for my social and the pin number to my checking account.

"Was there anything unusual about your birth?"

"Nothing I can think of," I said.

For the first time, I wondered if there was something more to my birth that Granny had concealed from me. "Why do you want to know, anyway?"

"It is better that you do not know more until I can verify a few facts," Rose replied.

That didn't sound ominous at all.

"What if I kill Travis?" I asked. "That's how they do it in the movies, and you said it would make Skyler human again. Kill the head vampire, reverse the transformation."

"You can't just kill Travis," Bobbie Jean said, her eyes as wide as saucers.

"Why not?" Why did she care if I killed him?

"It's not exactly easy, for starters."

"He compels people to give him blood." If my rage alone were enough to kill him, he'd be pushing up daisies. "He did that to you, didn't he? And probably a bunch of other people, too," I said to Bobbie Jean. "Why *shouldn't* I kill him?" I looked at Thorn for confirmation.

She shrugged. "You could try. But it's true: vampires aren't that easy to kill."

"And you should worry about yourself," Rose said.

"I'm not going to turn into a vampire," I said, horrified by the idea. "But he fed on Bobbie Jean," I said. I turned to her and started to ask, *"How are you feeling?"* but she was already gone.

"Anything else you want to tell us?" I asked Thorn, who seemed to be more forthcoming.

Vaughn stopped his pacing long enough to ask, "What if we just find Sky, grab her, and go?"

I arched an eyebrow. "Because that worked so well last night?"

"You may have a point," he conceded.

"That's a terrible plan," Thorn said. "Bleeders often bond with their makers emotionally."

"Do not use that degrading term," Rose snapped at her sister. "They are human beings."

"They *were* human beings," Thorn said. "Now they are mindless food sources."

"Harsh," I said. "Anything else we should know?"

"Vampires cannot go into the sunlight or they die," Rose said, speaking to me as if I were a toddler.

"That's true?" It might help explain why the fan club president had picked up Skyler instead of Travis.

"Popular culture gets a few things right," Rose said.

"Most vamps can't enjoy the sunshine," Thorn said. "But there have been a few daywalker reports."

Her sister frowned at her. "Unsubstantiated rumors." She sniffed.

So some of the things in Granny Mariotti's books *had*

been true. I was glad I'd thrown them into my bag before leaving.

"Please do not tell anyone I gave this to you—the committee would not be pleased." Rose rummaged in a tote and then handed me a manila file.

"Then why are you giving it to me?" I asked, but it was her sister, Thorn, who replied.

"Because you're going to need all the help you can get."

Chapter Seven

We said goodbye to our new friends, but they followed us outside.

The twins crossed the street and stood by a nondescript sedan, and it was clear they were arguing, even though I couldn't hear what they were saying. The unflappable Rose threw her hands up in the air, and Thorn responded with a rude gesture before storming to the driver's side and getting in. It looked like Thorn made her sister stand there waiting for Thorn to unlock the door, which she took her sweet time about. Baller move.

I gave Rose a little wave as we got into the Deathtrap.

Vaughn started up the car. "Ready to go? Or should we wait for them to leave?"

"Let's go," I answered, still stunned.

My phone rang. Not a text—it was my grandmother calling. How did she find out I was gone already?

"I can't believe you left without telling me," she said.

I can't believe you lied to me about my own mother. "Hi to you, too," I said. "And I left a note."

"I found it," she said. "That's why I'm calling. What were you thinking, Tansy Morgan Mariotti?"

Granny was middle-naming me. She must be really pissed.

I ignored the question and replied with one of my own. "Why are you home so early?"

"Author missed her plane," she replied. "We're rescheduling. Now, explain to me what you were thinking by taking off after a bunch of vampires."

"I was thinking that my best friend in the entire world needs my help," I said. "And Vaughn's with me."

"Of course he is." She laughed.

"What's that mean?"

"That boy ever miss a chance to get up close and personal with you?" Her tone was teasing.

"Granny!" I moaned. "Quit trying to embarrass me."

She snorted again. Granny's snorts all sounded different and conveyed a variety of emotions. This one made me blush.

I glanced at Vaughn and then looked away.

Granny didn't say anything for a long time. "You promise to call me every night?"

"I promise," I replied.

"And you'll keep your necklace on you at all times," she said. "You can't give it to Skyler or anyone else."

Why was Granny so insistent? I knew those charms protected me, but I was a Mariotti witch, more powerful than Skyler, who was only human.

"Those are my conditions," she said. "Take it or leave it. And be safe when you're sharing a bed with Vaughn tonight. Ta-ta!" She hung up.

She was so embarrassing...but the thought of Vaughn and me alone did make me shiver.

We had agreed Vaughn would drive the first shift. I liked the idea because that way I got to pick the music. I scrolled through the track list on my phone until I found the perfect road trip playlist, which included my favorite Billie Eilish song.

We were only on the freeway for twenty minutes before we had to slow down. "Traffic." I groaned the word out.

"It's L.A. There's always traffic." Vaughn adjusted the air vents and the temperature controls, making sure cool air was hitting us both. I didn't have the heart to remind him the Deathtrap didn't do well in bumper-to-bumper traffic *and* with the air full blast. Not yet, at least.

But even the carpool lane was stopped. I sighed. We were likely going to be here a while.

My only comfort was knowing that The Drainers would stop to perform. We'd catch up to them, and I'd somehow snip some hair, cast a separation spell, and break the hold he had on my best friend. I'd do whatever it took. Even if it meant killing Travis.

I had to.

While Vaughn inched us forward, I got out my phone and did some research on The Drainers. They were popular, but there were a lot of comments about how they were best live.

I downloaded a couple of songs, and Vaughn and I listened. I wanted to see if he had the same reaction as I did. Before the first song was over, we agreed with the reviews. Travis singing on a recording was an experience I did not want to repeat.

Why did I have such different reactions to The Drainers' music? Vampires had a variety of powers, including the ability to mesmerize and compel people. Being a descended witch must offer *some* protection. And clearly a recording didn't have the same compulsion, since Vaughn seemed to be unaffected as well.

"That's why everyone thinks they sound great live, but their recorded music sucks. Because they have to be near their victims for it to work."

Vaughn shot me a quizzical look. "What do you mean?"

"When they play live, their music is haunting," I said. "Beautiful. Compelling."

"In other words, not this," Vaughn deadpanned.

I burst out laughing. "Definitely not this."

I noticed my nails were overgrown and got out a nail file from my bag. I filed them down to a reasonable length and then hit up social media streams again.

Their Instagram feed was obnoxious. A girl named Natasha oversaw it, and she featured herself in a lot of the posts. In one photo, she was hanging on Travis's arm; the next, it was the drummer she was all over. There were a lot of #Bleeders references, too.

I wrinkled my nose. "I need brain bleach." I tossed my phone on the console.

"Any pics of Skyler?" Vaughn asked.

"Only a few," I admitted. "There's nothing that stands out, except that I'm pretty sure she's with Natasha, the president of The Drainers' fan club."

"Look further back," he suggested. "Maybe about six weeks earlier."

"But Sky only started talking about Travis a few weeks ago," I argued.

"I think she met him a while back," he said. He kept his eyes on the road, but there was something in his tone that worried me.

"Skyler tells me everything."

He hesitated, then said, "She doesn't tell you everything. In fact, I don't think she's been telling either of us half of what's been going on with her."

"What do you mean?"

"She's been acting funny for weeks," he finally said.

I'd clearly missed the signs that my best friend was in trouble. I wondered what Vaughn's impressions were. "Funny how?"

"Secretive," he said. "Always taking off without either of us."

"She had been partying without us more," I said. "I thought she was getting sick of how much we had to work. I can't believe I didn't notice. I suck as a friend."

"No, you don't," he said sharply. "You can't blame yourself. Skyler lied to you. She lied to us all."

"That makes it worse," I said. "Skyler never lies to me."

"Everyone lies," he said. "Some of us just lie to ourselves most."

"Maybe that's what Skyler was doing, too," I said. "She was scared and didn't know what to do, so she kept it all to herself."

I'd do better in the future, be a better friend, as soon as I found her.

Two hours later, we passed by the accident that had turned the freeway into a parking lot. After that, traffic improved, thank god.

"What's the plan?" Vaughn asked, easing the Deathtrap up to the speed limit.

I shrugged. "We're winging it."

I thought he'd ask me more questions, but instead, he glanced around the interior and said, "This car is so badass."

I nodded. "I just need to remember to fill it up every chance I get."

"I'll pay for the gas," Vaughn said quickly.

I stiffened. "No, you won't." It wasn't easy, but I made sure I always paid my share, despite Sky and Vaughn both coming from wealthy families.

"She's my friend, too," he said softly.

He had a point. "We'll split all expenses," I said. "Fifty-fifty."

"Sixty-forty," he countered. "You're providing the sweet ride."

I crossed my arms in mock anger but couldn't hold it long and ended up in a wide grin. "Fine."

We drove in silence for a mile or two before I remembered the file Rose had given me. Why? What did she have to gain by sharing it?

I hated the way my brain fired off suspicions immediately. Maybe it was why I didn't have many friends. Maybe people could sense my deep distrust and skepticism and stayed away. Or maybe I pushed them away.

It probably didn't help that the one person I trusted the most, my grandmother, had told me my mother was dead when she clearly wasn't.

I flipped the file open. The first page listed the dates and places of The Drainers' concerts for the past two years.

At first, I thought Rose might be a weird superfan, but then I turned to the next page, and there was a list of names, which I soon discovered was a list of murder victims and the locations their bodies had been found.

Many of the dates had been highlighted, and when I compared the two, I noticed in a lot of cases, The Drainers had been in the immediate vicinity near the time of the murder.

My heart had relocated to my throat. I wiped my sweaty hands on my shorts. The Drainers weren't just bloodsuckers; they were murderers.

Chapter Eight

The file was thick with documents, but I wasn't sure I wanted to read the rest, even though I knew I should. My stomach was burning with acid at the thought of Skyler with those monsters.

I turned to tell Vaughn what I learned, but he started talking first.

"Ashley thinks the breakup is temporary," Vaughn said. He kept his eyes on the road.

Okay, so he wants to clear the air about his love life first. Cool.

I swallowed. "Is it?"

"It's not," he said. His jaw clenched so tight, I thought he might crack a molar. "I can't believe you asked me that."

"Jeesh, since when did you get so sensitive?" I asked.

"I'm not. It's just… I'm not interested in Ashley anymore. Okay?"

"Okay," I said, ready to be done with the conversation. I was kind of embarrassed about how jealous I was that he'd dated her for so long anyway.

I changed the subject. "Where was your dad this morning?" I asked. "Just out of curiosity." Vaughn's dad was not the kind of guy who stayed out all night. He was a lot of fun, but the catering company kept him busy.

He'd cater anything. Like the time we worked a Chihuahua's birthday party. Or a Ren Faire–themed wedding. Lots of turkey legs and steins of beer at that one.

"Didn't I tell you?" Vaughn tossed me a quick look. "He's dating someone."

My mouth fell open. "Holy crap, that's right." I'd been so preoccupied with Rose and Thorn's info dump that his mention of his dad's girlfriend hadn't fully registered until right now.

Mr. Sheridan hadn't been on a date the entire time I'd known the family. Or at least not any that Vaughn had told me about.

"Who?" I asked. "When? I need details."

"I don't know," he admitted. "He says it's too early to introduce us."

"A *mystery* woman." I smiled. "Good for him."

"Yeah, good for him," he said, but a shadow crossed his face.

I changed the music, not sure what else to say. When I was around eleven, I'd gone through a classical music phase after Granny had taken me to the Pacific Symphony. I'd eased up a bit, but it was why Skyler still teased me sometimes about being a music snob. She teased Vaughn about it, too, at least.

I turned the volume up a touch and leaned back in the seat for a nap when a flash of red in the side mirror caught my attention. A white pickup swerved in and out of lanes, coming up on us fast. The driver had to be doing at least eighty. People drove like assholes every day in SoCal, but there was something familiar about the blond driver.

Bobbie Jean?

"I think someone's following us," I told Vaughn.

"Friend or foe?" he asked.

I lifted my shoulders. "She seemed friendly enough earlier." I turned around and waved at Bobbie Jean. Her mouth opened, and then she smiled as she jammed a cowboy hat on her head.

"She sure hates Travis, though," I continued. "But I don't understand why she's tailing us."

"Maybe she thinks we can lead her to him?" Vaughn suggested.

Bobbie Jean pulled up alongside us in the right lane. She rolled down her window and shouted something, but I couldn't hear her through my window and over the freeway noise.

She made a rolling motion with her hand, so I opened the window.

"Pull over!" she shouted. "I need to talk to you."

Then why had she been acting so shady about following us? I mean, obviously she'd been following us for a while on the down low before she floored it and snuck in our rearview. Something was definitely up.

"Next exit," I shouted in reply, and she dropped back.

Vaughn eased over into the right lane and then took the next exit. Bobbie Jean followed closely behind as we pulled into a gas station.

Bobbie Jean got out of her truck, but instead of coming over to us, she jogged inside.

"What is she doing?" I asked.

Vaughn shrugged. "Maybe she had to pee."

We waited for almost ten minutes. I scanned the parking lot and then groaned.

"The twins are here, too," I said. At the gas pump, Rose filled up their nondescript sedan.

"What do you think they want?" Vaughn asked.

I reached over and honked the horn, and when Rose looked up, I waved. She waved back a little sheepishly, but Thorn just stared at me from the driver's seat.

I shifted in my seat. "Maybe I should go find her."

"She's probably buying snacks or something."

"Maybe *I* should go buy some snacks," I said. "I know you love those giant slushies."

"I do love a good slushie…" he said. But then someone knocked on the glass, and I jumped.

Bobbie Jean stood there beaming. She handed us a flyer. The ink it was printed with was so cheap that it turned my hands black. "This one has the location."

"What took you so long?" I asked sourly.

"The guy who works there has a sister who follows The Drainers," she said. "It took a little convincing for him to give up the information."

"Convincing?"

She smiled a bright pageant-worthy smile and waggled her eyebrows. "Convincing," she said. "But he was real cute, so it wasn't exactly a hardship."

She'd managed to shut me up.

"See y'all there," she said.

I looked down at the flyer in my hands. "The 'Bat Cave'?" I said. "The concert tonight is at a place called the Bat Cave. Someone thinks he's a superhero."

"Where could it be?" Vaughn asked.

"No idea," I said. "Obviously their fans know, though."

After we got back on the road, I opened the file again. What I didn't know about vampires could fill the Pacific Ocean.

"Rose was telling the truth. Vampires can't go out in sunlight," I said. The file included a page on daylight spontaneous combustion, and she'd helpfully put a neat little V after most of the names. *V is for Vampire.*

There wasn't much to let me know what else could kill a vampire, which made sense. The Paranormal Activity Committee sounded benign, but I bet they wouldn't be happy if she spilled all their secrets.

I read aloud to Vaughn as he drove, but my voice trailed off when I saw there was a thick photocopied stack of information about the Mariotti family. My family.

Someone had made a notation about my possible powers, including that there were signs I was immune to compulsion but was capable of magic mesmerizing.

Vaughn took his eyes from the road for a second. "What did you read that made you go so quiet?"

"Nothing," I lied. "Just getting a headache."

"What time's the show?" Vaughn asked.

I read the flyer Bobbie Jean had given me. "Not until midnight."

We were only ten miles from Diablo. Vaughn took the off-ramp leading to the sleepy beach town—sleepy in the off-season, at least. As soon as we hit the main road, the Deathtrap was caught in a snarl of traffic, so I had time to stare. There were people everywhere: sitting on the outside patios of the restaurants, shopping in the cute little clothing boutiques, and clogging the crosswalks, some of them taking their lives in their hands by jaywalking across busy intersections.

"It wasn't like this the last time I was here," I said. Diablo was a Central Coast popular location for summer vacations. Lots of tourists...with lots of blood.

"You've been to Diablo before?" Vaughn asked.

"Granny Mariotti and I came here right before Thanksgiving for one of her meetings," I said.

"Coven meeting?"

I shook my head. "Library conference," I said, then thought about it for a minute. "But there was some overlap. Granny says all librarians are magic."

"Your granny is usually right," he replied.

"I won't tell her you said *usually*," I added. "You know Granny thinks she's *always* right." I smiled at him, and the grin he gave me back made my heart thump. "So what's the plan?"

He turned back to the road as the car in front of us started moving again.

"We can eat first," he said. "There's a great seafood place nearby."

"You've been here before, too?" Something I didn't know about Vaughn.

He nodded. "Dad used to take Kenzie and me when I was little." Kenzie was his older sister, who was at college on the other side of the country.

"I'd rather keep going," I said. "Maybe if we walk around town, we'll spot Skyler."

"You have to eat something." Then he saw the reluctance on my face and added, "Please. She's probably keeping night hours anyway."

I frowned at that. I wished I knew what was fact and what was myth about vampires.

My stomach growled.

"I'm starving," Vaughn said.

"Me too," I replied. "Obviously."

"Let's see if I can find that seafood place." He used his phone to search for local restaurants and then grinned. "It's two blocks away."

It had a blue roof with two giant surfboards on it, *Splash Pad* spelled out in neon letters on the sign. We parked around back.

The front and rear doors were open, letting in the ocean breeze.

"What's good?" I asked as we strolled up to the end of the order line.

"Everything," he assured me. "They have the best clam chowder I've ever had."

The aroma of fried food made my stomach growl again. I put my hand on my stomach, hopefully forcing it to shut up. I ordered clam chowder, scallops, and fries.

Vaughn grinned. "Same for me." There were a couple of tourist brochures by the register, and he took one and slid it into the pocket of his jeans.

He paid for our food, even though I tried to hand him some cash, and took the little black-and-white ticket number from the cashier. We found a table in the back before continuing our earlier conversation about the concert location.

"Obviously, it's in a cave," he said, then grinned. "An ancient cave with ancient monsters."

"What gave you that idea?"

"My encyclopedic knowledge of horror movies," he said. "And this brochure." He took it out and showed me the photo on the front. It was a picture of about a thousand bats streaming out of the mouth of a cave at sunset.

"You are a genius." I laughed.

A server put our order on the table. "Thank you," I said, but she was busy flipping her hair at Vaughn.

I swallowed back my irritation. *Hello. Right here.*

Besides, I was anxious to get to the show, but we had a few hours. The thought of Travis and the rest of The

Drainers d-bags letting loose among a bunch of college girls made me sick.

"What if we're wrong? What if she's not there?" I asked.

"It's the best lead we've got, unless they post something else on social." He studied my face. "It's only a little after six—you'll feel better after you get some food in you."

The food was delicious. I returned my attention to eating, and before I knew it, my plate was empty.

"Let's walk down to the beach," he suggested. "It'll keep our minds off things for a while."

"Too bad you didn't pack your surfboard," I teased. ·

We tossed our trash and then joined the tourists strolling along the boardwalk. Some guy jostled me when he walked by, and I lost my balance, but Vaughn caught me. "Watch it," Vaughn growled at the guy.

He kept his arm around my shoulder as we walked, and I tried not to read too much into it. Just a friendly arm across the shoulder. Nothing to see here.

I took off my flip-flops when we reached the water. My nails were already growing again. I calmed myself by promising to freak out about this new development later. I needed to focus on saving Skyler from bloodsuckers.

Diablo's shoreline was flat as a pancake and easy to walk along, without many rocks or driftwood marring the white sand.

The sky was a dark violet. I turned to splash Vaughn— and that's when I spotted Fang. The sun had barely gone down and The Drainers' drummer was already thirsty, out looking for "food."

He leaned up against one of the touristy shops, the kind that held tees and picture frames made of shells and kites. He was talking to a petite dark-haired girl taking photos with an honest-to-god camera around her neck instead of the more typical phone. She looked like she was asking him a question. Directions, maybe?

I stiffened when he took her by the hand and tried to lead her away. The girl resisted, and Fang dropped her hand and stomped off. He looked like he'd given up in search of easier prey.

"Vaughn, let's go," I said. "We need to follow that drummer."

Fang didn't look at us as he walked away from the busy pier and the beach. We'd gone about three blocks when I saw The Drainers' tour bus in a three-hour lot.

"How far are we from the car?" I asked.

He winced. "At least another four blocks."

"We've got to hurry before they move the bus. We can't lose them." I told myself not to panic because losing it right now wouldn't help, but I could feel my breathing speed up.

"I don't want to take any chances," he said. "We should stay together."

He was right. We took off running back to our car, but it was summer at the beach, which meant it took us way too long to get back to the public parking lot. I resolved to renew my acquaintance with the gym.

By the time we got back to the three-hour lot, the tour bus was gone. "Hurry," Vaughn said. "Maybe they just left. We could catch up to them."

We scanned the area, but after several minutes of futile searching, I choked back a sob. "It's no use. They're gone."

I was cursing under my breath when Vaughn said, "I see them. Look, heading to the northbound lane."

I bounced in my seat. "Don't lose them. Please don't lose them!"

We caught up and followed the bus. Then we lucked out

when they got off the freeway to gas up the monstrosity that was The Drainers' tour bus.

"I really have to pee," I said. I didn't recognize the guy pumping gas, but my bladder encouraged me to take the chance he wouldn't recognize me.

I asked the clerk to point me in the direction of the bathrooms, which were located at the back of the store, next to the refrigerated beverages. I sprinted there and locked the door. It was cleaner than I had expected. Not clean, exactly, but not a toxic-waste situation.

There was someone waiting when I got out. She stood in the little alcove outside the bathrooms—the petite camera girl Fang had tried to talk into something earlier. He must have persuaded her after all, and my stomach sank. At least she looked unharmed. There weren't any bite marks on her...none that I could see, at least. She grinned as she texted someone and then stepped into the bathroom and closed the door.

As long as we were making a pit stop, I could use some snacks. I was headed for the slushies when I heard a male voice that sounded familiar. *Travis.*

I stayed where I was and scanned the store until I found him. He stood in the middle of the candy aisle with his arms full of three kinds of chips, bags of red licorice, and a six-pack of beer. But Skyler wasn't with him.

My phone pinged, and I looked down. It was a text from a number I didn't recognize. **Not just a Drainers gig. Sundowner initiation tonight after the bat cave concert.**

A midnight initiation. That sounded ominous.

Chapter Nine

I stood frozen until Travis got in line to pay. There wasn't much in the way of healthy food in the store, but I found some decent-looking trail mix and bottles of iced tea. I hung back, not wanting Travis to spot me.

"Renfield, where are you?" Travis bellowed.

"I'm right here," the guy said. "And I told you, my name is Gary."

"What'd I tell you about talking back, *Rennie*?" Travis's voice was hard.

"Not to do it," the man replied, his voice quaking. "Could you at least call me Roadie instead?"

"Your name isn't important, is it, Renfield?" Travis said, his eyes glowing red.

The guy slowly shook his head.

"Good," he said. "Now pay for this stuff."

Travis gave the worker behind the counter a dimpled grin. "It's hard to find good help these days, am I right?"

The worker nodded in the same slow, slightly out-of-it way that poor Gary had.

I didn't breathe until he lost interest in small talk and returned to the bus, leaving Gary/Renfield there to pay for his junk food.

I spotted some cheap earplugs in a bowl by the register and added some to my pile.

After I paid for my goodies, I ran to the car.

Vaughn was still behind the wheel, so I got in the passenger side. "Did you see?"

"The tour bus? Already on it," he replied, then pulled onto the freeway. He stayed far enough behind the bus that I didn't think the driver would notice the pink more-boat-than-car trailing them. "They make it look easy in the movies," he joked. "But following someone is harder than it looks."

"Good thing we stopped for gas," I said. I hadn't seen Skyler, but I knew she had to be with Travis. He had her under his control and probably wouldn't let go until he'd sucked the life from her.

We continued tailing them until they pulled into a state park. It wasn't even midnight yet, and I was already struggling not to fall asleep. The plan was to get a lock of hair from Travis and Skyler, but first, I needed to find her. If she wasn't on the tour bus, she'd turn up at one of the shows, but I was impatient. The longer this took, the worse things he could be doing to my best friend.

This part of the state park wasn't open for overnight camping, but The Drainers' tour bus was too big to miss, and no irate park ranger appeared. There were already several cars in the parking lot near the cave's entrance. We found a spot for the Deathtrap in the back, where hopefully Travis and the guys wouldn't notice us.

A small crowd had gathered, and I recognized a few faces from the band's website photos.

We were far away from the lights of the city, and the stars looked brighter here, brilliant against a dark sky. I could hear the rush of the waves, though Vaughn was holding my hand again, so it could have just been the rushing of blood in my ears I heard. Either way, it was a perfectly romantic night.

Except we were watching a nest of vampires.

"You know, I've been thinking," Vaughn said. "When we're around The Drainers and their followers, we should pose as a couple."

"Really? Why?" I glanced out the window. He'd said *pose*. Had he figured out that I had a crush on him? Sweat broke out as I contemplated the potential humiliation. I might not survive being officially friend-zoned.

"To protect me from The Drainers' groupies and to protect you from The Drainers," he said.

"I...I don't know," I replied.

"Let's just try it out," he said. "See how it feels."

I was sure it would *feel* amazing—so amazing that I would want it to be real. More than I already did. But he did have a point. Travis and the other band members had already met me. We needed to go undercover.

Finally, I nodded. "Okay." I tried to stifle a yawn.

"I can think of something to keep us awake," he suggested.

"Like what?"

Before Vaughn could answer, though, The Drainers' tour bus doors opened, and I sat up straight. "They're on the move."

We watched the band members and various girls in their entourage file out, but there was still no sign of Skyler.

The crowd grew to the point I felt sure Travis wouldn't spot me. A couple of guys were setting up a makeshift stage about a hundred yards from the entrance to the cave.

"Let's see if we can find Skyler," I suggested.

We got out, and Vaughn came around to my side and grabbed my hand. At my startled look, he said, "Just trying out the couple thing to see how it feels."

It felt amazing to have his fingers interwoven with mine, but I knew it wasn't real.

The roadie set up the instruments while the band schmoozed the girls. I tried to see if I could hear anything about the Sundowner initiation mentioned in the text I'd received, but it was mostly giggling and gasping.

"Renfield!" Travis shouted. "Get your ass moving. Our fans want a show."

"My name's Gary," the guy said again.

"We don't care," Ozzie added. Armando and Travis laughed.

Finally, the instruments and mics were ready and the band went on. Their music wrapped around an unwary listener like tentacles, pulling them in, its grip tightening until they were in the arms of a monster.

I didn't want Vaughn to be compelled by the music, so I handed him one of the pairs of earplugs I'd picked up at the gas station, then I plugged my own ears. I wasn't confident that I was strong enough to resist the enchantment coming from The Drainers' music.

Most of the crowd swayed along to the music, so Vaughn put his arm around me and pulled me to his side as he rocked us gently back and forth.

It was a short performance, but the audience seemed pleased. Probably because they'd been forced to be. After the song ended, Travis said, "The rest of the event is invite only, so if you weren't invited, get the fuck out."

Vaughn and I tried to look inconspicuous as we loitered,

and we weren't the only ones.

Travis seemed to grow impatient waiting for the crowd to disperse. "Initiation time. Who wants to be a Sundowner?" Travis said. A few girls in the audience squealed. "Renfield, take the girls to the cave."

Were they going to turn them? I tried to remember what I'd learned about how a vampire was made, but my heart was beating like a kick drum so loudly, I couldn't think.

"But you ordered me to guard the…" Gary hesitated and then spit out, "The coffins, my prince."

Rose and Thorn had been right. The Drainers' human servant, Gary, guarded the coffins.

Travis waved his hand. "They'll be fine. We'll need your help with dinner."

The other guys in the band laughed, and then they all trailed after Renfield and the girls.

"Let's follow them," I said.

"We should search the tour bus first," Vaughn suggested, "while we have the chance and they're occupied."

"Good idea," I agreed. "Maybe they left Skyler alone in there while they're going off to do whatever it is that vampires do to 'initiate' people."

I thought we'd need a bit of luck to even get close to the bus unnoticed, but apparently everyone was busy watching The Drainers and their "guests" disappear into the cave.

After the last Drainer entered the mouth of the cave, Vaughn and I hustled right up to the bus without a care. The tour bus was a luxury model, but it was filthy. As soon as we opened the door, an odor hit us like a slap in the face.

I coughed. "Don't they ever disinfect this place? It has a funk you can almost see."

It was like someone had used Axe body spray to try to

cover up the smell of a blooming corpse flower. Granny and I had waited in line once for the dubious privilege of getting our nose hairs burned. The world should be grateful that plant only bloomed once in a decade or so.

"She's not here," I said.

"Look at this." He motioned to something suspended from the wall like Murphy beds.

"What are they?"

"Lead coffins," he replied. They were all open, except for one.

"You don't think…" I trailed off, too freaked out to say the words.

The lid creaked as he flipped it open. It was empty. He slammed it shut again.

"We can catch up to them," Vaughn suggested. "Maybe Travis is meeting her somewhere."

It was a good suggestion, except for the whole *following vampires into a pitch-black cave* thing.

"Do you have the charm Granny gave you?" I asked Vaughn. I touched my necklace out of habit.

"Granny said to never take it off," he said, as though I'd just suggested he didn't know the sky was blue. Duh.

I nodded. "Let's go, then."

We headed in the direction the vampires had gone, down a steep path leading away from the sand and toward the caves.

I wasn't fond of enclosed spaces, and these caves weren't open to the public, as evidenced by all the Do NOT ENTER signs we saw. My breathing sped up, the ragged sound filling my ears.

"Tansy, maybe I should go by myself," he said.

"No," I said. "I can do it. I promise."

We made our way to the cave's entrance. It was like

walking into a grave, cold and dark, smelling like dirt and decay. The deeper we went, the more the temperature dropped, until I shivered in my thin summer clothing.

"You're freezing. Here," Vaughn said. He shrugged off his hoodie and held it out for me. I put my arms in the sleeves, and then he zipped it closed. We stood in the darkness, so close that I could feel his warm breath as he exhaled.

I started to move closer, but then I picked up a strange odor coming from somewhere in front of us.

"Do you smell that?" I asked him.

"All I smell is dirt and damp," he said.

"I smell something metallic, coppery." I sniffed again. "Blood."

The empty feeling started in my spine. It hollowed out my bones, then left me with an unquenchable hunger. It spread to my stomach and then to my brain, until my entire body thrummed with it. My incisors descended and almost cut my tongue. The strange power that came with the hunger made me feel both more than and less than human.

There was fresh blood in the air, and I wanted some. The realization sickened me, and I stepped closer to Vaughn, unable to stop the shiver that overtook my whole body at the understanding that a vampire's bite was changing me.

In the darkness, something slithered over my foot, and it snapped me out of my spiraling thoughts. I leaped into Vaughn's arms, clinging to him like a baby koala on its mother. "What was that?"

He squeezed me tight and then rubbed my back, his hands making small, comforting circles. "As much as I'm enjoying this," he whispered, his breath tickling my ear, "I probably should let you go."

"You probably should," I whispered. After I was back

on my feet, we kept walking deeper into the cave. "I wish we knew more about vampires."

"We know some things," he said. "They need blood and they can be killed by sunlight."

"I don't think any of The Drainers would just take a stroll in the sunshine."

As we moved deeper, we heard the sound of water dripping. Or at least I hoped it was water. "Maybe we shouldn't continue," Vaughn said. "We don't know what's waiting for us in this cave. I'm distracted…" He trailed off as I pressed my body closer to his.

I took his hand. "C'mon, let's find Skyler and get the hell out of here." There was something wet and sticky on the path, and I hoped it wasn't blood. Or worse.

We walked along hand in hand, moving deeper and deeper into the cave. Eventually Vaughn had to stoop down to duck under the cave roof. This part was almost entirely without light, and I shuddered to think what we were walking into.

"What *is* that stench?" I groaned. The odor was like old gym socks, spoiled milk, and a wet dog had a baby.

Someone screamed, loud and full of pain. Another voice chimed in, the screaming echoing off the cave walls. Then, without warning, it stopped.

I swallowed back my own scream. The quiet was worse than the screaming, but I thought I heard a muffled sound coming from the cave's interior. Then I smelled the blood, fresh and rich. My stomach growled, which was just horrifying.

"Something's wrong," I said and rushed toward the odor, but Vaughn grabbed my arm.

"Hold on," he said as he took out his phone and turned on the flashlight, aiming it at my face for a second before he lit up the path before us. Not blood. Thank God. "Slow down, Tansy. I hear something."

Suddenly, a great whooshing noise descended on us. Vaughn aimed his phone's flashlight at the ceiling just as hundreds of bats streamed from the cavern. I put up my hands as one—a bigger bat with a white streak in its ruff—went for my eyes.

I shrieked. "No!"

It fell back, stunned by the light, but the rest of the bats escaped. There was no sign of the band, but the tang of blood was still in the air, and I knew what we'd find even before Vaughn's flashlight shone on three dead bodies.

One of them was slender with dark hair. Sky?

The brunette was lying facedown, and my hand shook as I reached out, turned her over, and screamed again—her face had been almost completely chewed off. There was a lanyard hanging around her neck. A backstage pass for The Drainers.

My stomach clenched, but I managed to make it a few feet away before I threw up. Vaughn rubbed my back, murmuring quietly, "It's not her, Tansy. It's not Sky."

I sobbed more. He was wrong. The girl looked so much like my best friend.

"It's not her," Vaughn repeated. "That's not her."

His words finally sank in, and I dragged the sleeve of his hoodie across my mouth before I took a deep breath and turned around.

I didn't want to look, but I had to. He was right. On second glance, the dead girl was more muscular than Skyler and several inches shorter.

I didn't know how long I stood there, but Vaughn finally grabbed my hand. "Let's get out of here."

"We can't just leave those people," I said.

"It's a crime scene," Vaughn replied. "We can't move the bodies."

He was right, but it just felt so wrong. I sobbed as we stumbled all the way back to the car. He fumbled with the keys, then finally opened the doors.

We jumped in, and Vaughn called 9-1-1. His voice quavered, hoarse and uncertain. The Drainers and their tour bus were gone.

We stayed in the car, waiting for the police to arrive, and I couldn't stop my hands from trembling on the steering wheel. Hell, my whole body was shaking.

"We need to go," Vaughn said.

"We can't just leave them," I gasped.

"The cops are going to ask what we were doing here," he pointed out.

"Tell them we were…" My brain couldn't come up with a solution.

"We can tell them we were looking for somewhere private," he said.

I stared at him, my mouth open.

He shrugged. "Isn't that what they'd expect from us? Since we're a *couple*, right?"

"O-oh. Right," I blurted out.

Headlights appeared in the darkness, and then a squad car pulled up a few feet from us.

An officer rapped on the windows, shining a flashlight in our eyes. "Are you the kids who called it in?"

Vaughn nodded. She lowered the flashlight before it permanently blinded us and then took our IDs and asked us a few questions.

The smell of decay clung to her skin. *Oh, crap. Vampire.*

"Stay here," she ordered before returning to her squad car.

I couldn't shake the uneasy feeling that had come over me. "What's she doing?"

"Probably running our licenses, just to make sure we're not wanted or something," Vaughn assured me.

Then she and her partner took flashlights into the cave.

It was almost two a.m., and I was freezing. An uneasy feeling swept through me. "We need to leave." I turned the key in the ignition, but the Deathtrap sputtered and died.

"What's wrong?" I wasn't sure if he was talking about the car or why I was freaking out.

"They're vampires," I said. But it was too late.

The officers emerged from the entrance to the cave. One of them stalked over. "There's nothing there, except a mannequin someone obviously left as a prank," he said sternly.

"But we saw…" I started to argue, but Vaughn put his hand on my knee.

"Thank you, Officer," he said. "Sorry to have bothered you."

His partner motioned him over and said something too low for us to hear.

He walked back to us, gun drawn. "Get out of the vehicle."

When he said that, though, I spotted the gleam of his fangs.

Vaughn and I exchanged glances but did as he asked.

"We didn't do anything wrong," Vaughn said.

The cop ignored him. "You're coming with us."

We couldn't get in that car. No matter what.

I twirled my hair around a finger and pouted, trying to channel my inner Skyler. I'd seen her talk her way out of a speeding ticket a couple of weeks ago. I'd been miffed that day that an officer of the law would be so easily convinced a girl was clueless, but today—today, I was praying this particular guy was just a creeper.

"Can't you let us go, Officer? We were just trying to find a place to be alone, if you know what I mean." Eww, I was grossing myself out. I needed a shower. Now.

I glanced at Vaughn under my lashes, but he was staring at me like I'd grown two heads.

And unfortunately, the cop wasn't buying it, either. "No, you need to come with us."

I suddenly remembered my file. It had said I could use something called "magic mesmerizing." I clearly wasn't doing it right, but then I realized I'd asked him a question instead of giving a command.

"Let us go," I said and held his gaze without blinking, my heart racing in my chest. "You're going to get into that squad car with your partner and leave. You're not going to follow us."

I held my breath. At first, the officer just blinked at me, but after a minute, he nodded, returned to his squad car, and drove away.

I was still shaking with nerves and wanted to throw up again. The damp coldness of the cave clung to my skin, and I couldn't blot out the image of a cold, white body, the life bled from her too soon.

"Do you think they work for The Drainers?" I asked. A headache was starting to pound at my skull.

"It was a little weird that a vampire cop would show up," he said. As if he could hear the fear in my voice, he wrapped my hand in his, his fingers curling around mine and squeezing.

I pulled my hand from his. I'd just done something scary and I didn't deserve his warmth. Vaughn looked at me in astonishment. "You totally Jedi Mind Tricked him."

"I think it was magical mesmerizing," I corrected him. "I'm a witch, remember?"

It was true. I was a Mariotti witch, and for the first time, I understood what that really meant. It wasn't just primo parking spots and minor magic. The thought was actually a little comforting until I admitted I was becoming a vampire, too. And I was a striga vie.

I was so, so screwed.

Chapter Ten

After I calmed down enough to drive, I grabbed the key and turned the ignition, and this time, the Deathtrap roared to life. "*Now* you decide to work," I muttered, but I was relieved.

"We should find somewhere safe to park the car and get a few hours of sleep."

"I'm not sure I can," I said. "Not after seeing that dead girl."

"I think they did something with the body," Vaughn said. "And obviously, there are more vampires than we thought."

I nodded. The understatement of the century. "Since most of the world thinks that vampires exist only in the pages of their favorite paranormal romance, I think you're right," I replied. How many vampires were there, exactly? I didn't want to think about it.

We drove around until Vaughn spotted somewhere that looked safe: a big-box store that opened early. I pulled the Deathtrap into the farthest corner of the lot, then we kicked off our shoes and crawled into the back.

We lay facing each other in the small space, eyes locked, almost close enough for our bodies to touch. It was like there was no one else left in the world.

"I can't sleep," he whispered in the silence.

"Me either," I whispered back. "Today has been tough." Our bodies drifted closer, and our hands tangled.

"Not just today," he said softly, reaching up to push a strand of hair behind my ear. "The whole week. But there's been one bright spot in this whole mess."

"What's that?" I swallowed.

"You," he said. "You're the best thing about my day, Tansy."

I gave up on trying to sleep after that. I was learning new things about Vaughn. Was he just flirting with me? Did he have romantic feelings for me? Flirting was fun, but it didn't mean you wanted to get serious about the other person. We were friends, but were we more than friends? I had no idea. Either way, though, I liked it. I liked it a lot.

I had expected a weird sort of awkwardness the next morning, but there wasn't any, even though we'd woken curled up together. Vaughn was spooning me, his arm tightly around my waist.

I'd stretched like a cat as I yawned—and then realized my butt was now right up against his junk. "Oh god, sorry," I whispered and bolted upright.

"It's okay," he said. "You smell like strawberries." His delivery was deadpan, but his eyes were twinkling.

Before we'd fallen asleep, I'd told him about Travis's weird obsession with the way I smelled. I gave him a little shove. "Shut up. *You* smell like strawberries."

He lifted his arms over his head, and his T-shirt rode up, giving me a glimpse of his stomach. "I smell like something, but it isn't strawberries."

We looked at each other and burst out laughing.

"Let's get breakfast and then find Skyler," he said.

Ten minutes later, we pulled into the parking lot of a McDonald's.

"I need to brush my teeth," Vaughn said. I definitely did, too, but I wasn't going to advertise it.

We split up to brush our teeth in the restaurant bathrooms before we ordered breakfast sandwiches and smoothies. It was nearly empty, but I still showed the girl behind the counter Sky's photo and asked if she'd seen her. She hadn't.

Vaughn and I spent the day showing strangers a picture of Skyler, but nobody seemed to recognize her. I had the urge to call the police and report her as missing now, real fear beating against my chest, but we couldn't be certain the cop who took our statements wouldn't just be another vampire.

Throughout the day, I caught myself turning to tell Skyler something, to text her a silly GIF or ask her where she wanted to go for lunch, but she was never there. "I miss her so much."

"We'll find her," Vaughn said with so much conviction that I believed him, especially when he pulled up The Drainers' Instagram page and showed me a post from today that said something about "Dead in Diablo."

"They're still in town."

But by the end of the day, my faith was wearing thin.

"What's next?" I asked. It was late, and I wasn't looking forward to sleeping in the Deathtrap again. "Do you think we can find a campground with a shower?"

"I think we should get a hotel room," he said.

There weren't butterflies taking up residence in my stomach—they were big black bats. Especially when I remembered the quip Granny Mariotti had made about us sharing a bed...

"Vaughn..." I started to say, but he put up a hand.

"To sleep, Tansy," he said. "I know you're worried about Sky, but you need some rest. We'll find her at their next gig. We need information if we're going to break whatever hold he has on her."

"You know hotels are practically impossible to find this time of year." It was tourist season, which meant rentals were at a premium. I didn't want to tap into my college fund for one night, but Skyler was worth it. I'd spend every penny I had to make her safe again. "Maybe we should just crash in the car."

"It's okay," he said, seeming to read my mind. "Dad gave me permission to use my emergency credit card."

"Of course he did," I said. "Your dad is so nice." Mr. Sheridan was almost too nice, but I was relieved.

"He likes you," Vaughn said softly. "And Sky. He'd want to help."

"Did you tell him what happened to her?" I asked. Vaughn's dad was so practical. I couldn't picture him swallowing the idea that vampires really existed.

"Not exactly," he admitted. "I just told him that Skyler got mixed up with a bad guy and she took off. If I told him about the vampires, he'd think I was hallucinating or something."

"Not a lie," I said.

He gave me that rare, crooked smile of his. "I never lie to my dad."

"I never lie to Granny, either," I admitted. "She'd put a hex on me."

"I think I should call Connor," he said.

My eyebrows shot up. "What?" I asked. "No way. Sky

would kill us. Besides, he's in Europe."

Vaughn's expression changed.

"He *is* in Europe, right?"

"Not exactly," he admitted.

"So on top of everything, Connor is a liar, too?" I blinked back tears. Did everyone lie to me?

"He *was* in Europe," Vaughn defended. "He's back."

"For how long?" I asked. "How long has he been back without texting or calling Skyler?"

"Not that long," he said. "A month. Maybe two."

"Two. Months," I repeated, my fury quickly replacing the hurt. Connor had broken up with her via text and then left. Didn't even tell her where he was going. He'd been back for two months, and the guy couldn't be bothered to pick up a phone to let Skyler know he was home. Or even that he was okay. Or why he'd suddenly decided to study abroad.

I narrowed my eyes at Vaughn. "I didn't see him at school before classes ended."

"He's doing independent study," Vaughn replied.

"He is, is he? You seem to know a lot about it," I said.

"Tansy," he said. "He asked me not to say anything to Skyler."

"And now I'm telling you not to call him about this," I said.

"He'd want to know."

"No, I mean it, Vaughn. Telling Connor Mahoney one single thing about Skyler will only make it worse," I said. "She's wrecked. She doesn't need her ex-boyfriend waltzing in and breaking her heart all over again."

I didn't remind him that it was Connor's fault. If he hadn't broken her heart, Skyler would never have gotten mixed up with an asshole like Travis.

"But—" Vaughn started.

"I don't want to talk about Connor," I said. "He chose to walk away from her. He doesn't get to walk back into her life now."

I didn't know why I was pinning this all on Connor, except that he and Skyler had seemed like the perfect couple, happy and in love, until suddenly, they were over. No explanation, no closure—he was just gone.

My phone pinged with another anonymous text, giving us more details on The Drainers' next gig.

"Did you give Rose or Thorn your phone number just in case?" he asked. "Maybe this is them."

"No, but they probably already had it, judging by the thick file they gave me," I said. "I would have given it to Bobbie Jean, but she took off."

"They'll turn up," Vaughn said. "They're looking for Travis, too."

"I hope the twins don't find him before we find Skyler," I said.

"We'll find her, however long it takes. Let's look for a place to stay," he said. He made a couple of calls and finally found a place that wasn't completely booked up. "We can still make late check-in," he said.

By the time we pulled into the hotel parking lot, I was exhausted. Still, I hesitated near the purple jacaranda framing the front door. "This place looks expensive."

"It was either deluxe or dump," he explained a little sheepishly. "It's tourist season. Tansy, don't worry about it," he said. "I mean it."

I studied his face and then nodded.

He checked us in while I looked around the lobby. The place was swanky, all marble floors and quiet voices.

Our room was on the fifth floor. It was enormous with

plush carpets, a little eat-in area, and a comfortable-looking oversize sofa. I walked around, marveling at the amenities.

The bedroom was separate from the main area. And it had a king-size bed. The drapes were open, which revealed French doors that led to a balcony with an ocean view.

"This room must have been expensive."

He blushed but didn't elaborate.

I swallowed nervously. "This makes the Deathtrap look like a dumpster fire."

"Hey, don't knock your car. It's nice and roomy." He cleared his throat. "So…where should I sleep?" His voice sounded hoarse.

Vaughn had crashed in my bedroom lots of times, but it felt different now, and not just because Skyler wasn't here.

"I'm sure we can sort it out. This bed is massive," I replied, looking anywhere but at Vaughn. Or the bed.

"Okay," he said. "We can order room service later. I need a shower and some sleep before we go out again."

I nodded. "Me too. You go first while I check in with Granny."

"You should give her the address of the hotel," he added. "I reserved the room for the week."

"Do you think it'll take that long?" I asked.

"It might be a while. We don't know where Skyler is, and you'd mentioned their concert site said they were playing here all week," he pointed out.

He went to take a shower while I sat and fretted. The worry about whether or not I was doing the right thing didn't leave me, even when I sent Granny a text to check in and she replied with a thumbs-up emoji. I felt a glow of pride that she trusted my witchy abilities enough to let me take on a band of vampires in order to save Skyler.

Vaughn came out of the bathroom. He'd put on joggers,

but his shirt was still in his hands. "Your turn."

I was too stunned by all the muscular sun-kissed skin he'd revealed. "Tansy?"

"I—I." I was stuttering

"I've rendered you speechless." He gave me a cocky grin like he knew the effect he was having on me. I didn't know why I was reacting like this. I'd seen his bare chest a million times at the beach. It felt different somehow.

"Not at all," I finally managed. "I just remembered I forgot to pack body wash."

I made a dash for the shower before he could say anything else.

After my shower, I dressed in a comfy tee and shorts and headed into the main area. "Anything new on Skyler?"

"Nothing," Vaughn replied. He saw my expression and added, "We're tracking the band through their social media. It's a start."

"Speaking of which," I started as I pulled up the band's website. "There's a new video." The camera jumped around a bit, but it looked like they were in a hotel room with the drapes pulled closed. The only light was from one small lamp.

Armando sprawled on the bed, still in a dark suit but with no tie and his dress shirt unbuttoned. Three girls stood in the background behind him. Travis stepped into view, followed by Skyler, who was holding a small cage, and my heart leaped into my throat.

I gripped Vaughn's arm. "I see her! She's on camera." Skyler handed Travis the cage and then stood next to him, clapping eagerly.

I held out my phone so we both could see, and Vaughn scooted closer to me.

Travis took something out of the cage.

"What's he going to do with that bat?" Vaughn asked.

"An Ozzy Osborne," I guessed, and boy did I hate it when I was right. Travis's fangs sank into the defenseless creature, and he bit off its head. I clicked off the feed, too sickened to watch any longer.

"That dude has been kissing Skyler with that mouth," Vaughn groaned. "I need brain bleach."

"And Skyler just stood there," I said. "She loves animals. All animals. She'd never cheer that on."

But she had.

My stomach twisted as I considered a terrible new thought. What if Skyler truly didn't want to be saved?

Chapter Eleven

Our second day in Diablo had been a bust, and I knew I needed to get some sleep, but I couldn't shake the thought that Skyler wanted us to leave her alone. She'd even told me so in a text.

I opened the heavy drapes and then the balcony door and stepped out to enjoy the sun and, perhaps, to get away from the intimacy of being alone with Vaughn.

But he followed me out. He stepped toward me when a knock at the door made him pause.

I raced back inside and threw open the door before Vaughn could stop me. "Skyler?" But it was Bobbie Jean.

"Did you get my text?" she asked before walking into the room. Without an invitation. Guess she wasn't a full-fledged vampire yet. Or the whole *vampires must be invited in* thing was a myth.

Vaughn sighed. "Bobbie Jean, what are you doing here?"

"How did you find us?" I asked her.

She shrugged. "I saw Rose and Thorn about an hour ago. Rose told me to look for you. And that they'll meet us later."

"What are they doing right now?" I wondered if Bobbie Jean and the twins had started working together. When we'd originally met, I hadn't gotten a sense that they were particularly friendly.

"They're scoping things out. Getting intel," Bobbie Jean explained. "The Drainers always stay together with their roadie; he guards them all day while they sleep. They're too worried one of their pissed-off donors will stake them all."

"Donors?" I snarled the word. "Is that what they call them? Those girls aren't *donating* anything. They're compelling them."

I wanted to tear the vampires apart with my bare hands, but I'd settle for finding Skyler and making sure nothing bad ever happened to her again.

"Why are you here, Bobbie Jean?"

"Same as you," she said. "Looking for Travis. What's your problem?"

I didn't know what my problem was, but she made me nervous. I felt like she was keeping something from me, even though, on the surface, she was sharing information freely.

"Just watch TV or something," I snapped, then sighed. Maybe I was being paranoid. None of this was her fault.

Her blue eyes filled with tears, but she didn't answer me, just sat down on the couch.

She turned to vacantly watch the TV Vaughn had turned on.

"We'll find her, I promise," Vaughn said before he walked over and put his arms around me. "Why don't you get some sleep? I'll keep an eye on Bobbie Jean."

"Maybe I'll just watch a little television, too," I said. I went into the bedroom and stretched out on the bed. Vaughn stood in the doorway, so I patted the spot beside me and then found something to watch. "C'mon, how about some *Friends*?" It was the only show we watched without Skyler. She hated it, lately anyway, because of the whole "on a break" thing. *At least Ross and Rachel* talked *about breaking up*, she'd said. Right before bursting into tears.

Effing Connor. I missed my best friend something fierce. At the thought, tears welled in my eyes.

Vaughn put some water and a couple of sodas on the bedside table. He kicked off his shoes and then climbed in next to me before flinging an arm around me.

"For when we wake up," he said. "I don't know about you, but I'll need something to get me moving."

We watched television until my eyelids drifted shut in the middle of the episode. I felt Vaughn put a blanket over me.

When I woke up, I was draped all over him. The room was dark, except for the glow of the television. Someone had closed the curtains, but I could hear people on the beach.

Vaughn was still asleep, his feet dangling over the edge of the bed. They were bare, but his body was covered by a thin blanket. He smelled so good, like sun and sweat. And blood. My mouth was dry. I tried to slide off the bed, but the movement woke him.

"Feel better?" Vaughn asked huskily.

His body was warm, and he smelled so good. I couldn't help it. I nuzzled into him a little. He bolted up.

"I'd sleep on the couch," he said, "but Bobbie Jean's on it."

"Just stay here," I said sleepily.

"Only if you promise to keep your hands to yourself," he said. I looked up to see what he meant.

He was blushing. Vaughn was actually blushing.

And now I was blushing. I tossed him a pillow and a blanket, and he stretched out next to me. "Let's get some sleep."

"I didn't make you feel uncomfortable, did I? I…I was just joking around," Vaughn added.

"No," I said. "It's fine. I trust you, Vaughn."

He leaned back, but his eyes remained on me.

"Just don't hog the bed," I said. "And try not to snore."

He finally gave me a tiny smile and closed his eyes. "Get some sleep, Tansy. We have to be up in a few hours."

At first, it was awkward to sleep in the same bed. I couldn't get comfortable until finally, Vaughn reached over and tugged me close.

"That's better," he said and closed his eyes. He was right, but I had a hard time dozing off again. Tonight, the walls were closing in.

There was a dark voice in my head. I was half awake, half dreaming, so I couldn't quite catch what it was saying. Something like *I command you*, or maybe it was *I compel you*. I sat up in the bed. I was sticky with sweat.

I got up and crossed to the French doors. *Closer*, the voice whispered.

"No more," I said.

The voice stopped. My tongue felt stuck to the roof of my mouth.

The command, when it came, was stronger this time. *Open the door. Invite me in.* I opened the balcony door. It made a slight creak and I stopped, but Vaughn was still breathing evenly.

I stepped out, even though part of me resisted, tried to stop myself. A man hovered in the air in front of me. Travis. I told myself it was just a dream. We were on the fifth floor. It couldn't be real. But I knew it was.

Something compelled me forward. *Come to me,* his voice commanded. I climbed the railing and stood mere feet from him. His eyes gleamed red in the dark.

"Tansy, what are you doing out here?" Vaughn stood in the doorway. He had something in his hand. "Jesus, get down from there." Then he saw Travis. "Get away from him, Tansy. Now."

I wanted to listen, but I couldn't. Vaughn's voice was drowned out by Travis's. One foot slipped off the railing.

Vaughn grabbed me and yanked me back just as Travis lunged for me. There was a brief tug-of-war, and then Vaughn threw a soda can at him.

Travis swore when the soda hit him. It fell into the darkness without doing any real damage, but the blow must have spooked him. One minute he was there and the next, he was gone.

I stood trembling in Vaughn's arms. He rubbed my back comfortingly. "It's okay," he murmured. "You're okay. I've got you."

There was no way I'd be able to go back to sleep after that.

Back inside, I grabbed a bottle of water.

"Want a snack?" Vaughn asked. He stood there in all his shirtless glory, clad only in a pair of soft-looking gray lounge pants.

I shook my head. "I guess Travis knows we're looking for him."

I was so thirsty. I guzzled my cold beverage, keeping my eyes on Vaughn's bare chest.

"I...like the way you're looking at me," Vaughn said huskily.

Surely Vaughn wasn't flirting with me. I blushed and looked away, but not before noticing he was biting his lip, which made *me* want to bite his lip.

I stepped closer to him, but then fear got the best of me. "We should get some sleep."

"What if I don't want to sleep?" he asked.

I sucked in a breath. The smile on his face now was dangerous.

"It's safer if we go back to bed," I said.

His grin widened.

"Separately," I clarified. I didn't know if I would be able to resist Vaughn's dimples the entire trip. But I was going to try.

Because of course the one guy I wanted to notice me seemed to finally be sending the right signals—just as I was turning into a creature of the night. Who might try to kill him.

The alarm rang at midnight, and when it beeped, Vaughn rolled over and smacked it. "I hate mornings," he said. "Er, I mean, evenings. Damn vampires, my sleep patterns are getting screwed up."

I liked the grumpy, sleep-rumpled Vaughn, but I didn't have time to admire him.

We dressed quickly and headed out to where The Drainers were supposed to be playing, a restaurant that, from my research, was known more for fights than food.

There was no sign of their tour bus, and when we approached the restaurant, there were no lights on. There was a security guard standing nearby, who looked up from his phone when we approached.

"Restaurant's closed," he said. "Rat problem."

I had a rat problem, too, and his name was Travis.

We drove around until two a.m., but we didn't spot the tour bus. We headed back to our hotel and slid back into bed, but I couldn't sleep.

"I wonder how The Drainers can afford to tour," I said. "It's not like they're a big name nationally or anything."

Vaughn was already starting to doze off, but he replied, "Maybe The Drainers make their money off merchandise, or maybe Travis is independently wealthy." He was asleep before I could reply, and a few minutes later, my eyes closed, too.

I didn't wake up until almost noon, but Vaughn was still asleep next to me. I snuck out to grab some food that was cheaper than room service. It was already oppressively hot, and the Deathtrap's AC couldn't keep up, but I didn't mind. I drove around a few minutes, looking for any sign of The Drainers' tour bus, but I didn't see anything.

I bought three large meatball subs, French fries, and three extra-large slushies. Vaughn could drink them all day, and with this heat, a slushie sounded extra good.

When I got back, he was outside waiting for me. "Where'd you go?"

I held up our lunch. "I thought I'd provide sustenance."

"You're the best," he said. "And you remembered my slushie. Here, let me carry some of that." He took the bag of food from me. We went inside and took the elevator up to our room. As it rose, I watched Vaughn. Either he was cuter than yesterday or I was more infatuated.

A drop of sweat slid down Vaughn's neck. The salty scent of his skin mesmerized me. I wanted to lean over and lick his neck, but I forced myself to lean against the elevator wall and keep my tongue to myself.

"Tansy? You okay?"

"Just hungry." I looked away.

We went to the hotel room and set the food and drinks on the table. "Bobbie Jean, breakfast is here," I said, but she didn't answer me.

Bobbie Jean sat on the couch, entranced by the glow of the television. "She's been like that for hours," he said. "She's barely even blinked. Ever since you told her to just watch TV."

"I don't remember doing that," I said and swallowed. My stomach twisted, and suddenly I wasn't hungry at all.

Had I forced her to sit here all night like this?

"You were tired," he said.

What should I say to release her? Maybe simplest was best. "Bobbie Jean, you should do whatever you want now."

She blinked and then stood. "I'm going to take a shower."

I was worried I'd said something else I shouldn't have. I talked in my sleep sometimes, but normally, Granny was the only one who ever heard me. Or Skyler when she stayed over.

"Did I say anything else?"

"Nothing important," he replied. But he was grinning like a fiend. I gave him a suspicious look, but his smile grew even bigger. "Let's eat."

He put a plate in front of me with my meatball sub. Bobbie Jean was still in the shower and my appetite was returning, so I tucked in. It might be the last time real food tasted good if we didn't track down Travis and get some answers.

Vaughn's knee touched mine when he sat down next to me, and a zing went through my body. I scooted closer to him, and when he gave me a cocky smile, I reached for an orange slushie.

"I'm really thirsty," I said.

His eyes gleamed. "Of course," he replied. "I'm thirsty, too."

We weren't any closer to finding Travis or his band of merry murderers.

Plus, I was still trying to wrap my brain around the fact that I had some kind of hold over vampires. I needed more information.

When Bobbie Jean came out of the bathroom, she was wearing the same clothes as before, but her face was scrubbed clean.

"Bobbie Jean, please talk to me. Tell me everything you know about Travis," I said. "But only what you want to talk about," I added hastily.

The thought of taking away someone's free will made me sick, and I resolved to be even more careful about my words in the future.

"I do want to tell you," Bobbie Jean said. Words poured from her. "When The Drainers were in Austin, five girls went missing," she said. "And three of them were found dead with bite marks on their bodies."

Horrific stories of The Drainers and how they treated the girls who followed them came from Bobbie Jean.

"There was this one girl," she said. "The sweetest little thing. She ended up there after following her sister. They never found her."

When Bobbie Jean started to cry, I felt terrible for her. And my anxiety for Skyler was now tripled.

Finally, she finished and wiped her eyes. "And that's all I know."

"Next time I start to get bossy, do me a favor and put your hand over my mouth," I told Vaughn.

Bobbie Jean stood. "I'll see you guys at the gig," she

said. "I'm going to hit a few clubs first. See if I can figure out where The Drainers are staying."

"We'll go with you," I offered.

"You should stay here," she said. "Lay low. "

"Why?"

She shrugged. "I think he's infatuated with you."

With that, she left.

After she was gone, I turned to Vaughn. "Why would a vampire prince be infatuated with me?"

"Why wouldn't he be?" Vaughn replied. "You're pretty amazing."

"You're pretty amazing, too."

He took a step toward me but then seemed to reconsider. "I've been doing some research of my own," Vaughn said.

"What kind of research?" I asked.

"The kind that might help Skyler," he said. "We need to figure out how to kill a vampire, just in case the separation spell doesn't work."

We spent the next hour on the internet, looking up ways to kill a mythical creature who wasn't so mythical after all.

Chapter Twelve

The bedside telephone rang, and I shot Vaughn a look. Nobody but Granny knew we were here.

Vaughn answered it and had a short conversation. "There's a package for you downstairs. Someone's bringing it up."

I jumped when the knock came, then handed the woman a small tip. "Thanks."

After I closed the door, I looked at the return address. "It's from Granny."

I ripped open the box and found a neon-green gift bag.

He glanced over. "More protection?"

"I haven't opened it yet." I pushed the tissue paper aside and stared down at a box of condoms. My face flamed. "You could say that," I wheezed out. I hastily stowed it by my luggage.

"Let's see what's making you blush," he said. I made a mad scramble for the bag, but his arms were longer than mine.

He tore the tissue out of the bag and then stilled. "Open

in case of emergency," he read in a choked voice and then shook his head. "Only Granny Mariotti."

We couldn't look at each other.

After a long, embarrassed silence, I sat back and sighed. "I need to call her and check in."

"While you do that, I'll see if I can scrounge up some candy," he said. "I think I saw some interesting choices in the gift shop."

Vaughn and his sweet tooth. After he kissed my cheek and left the room, I FaceTimed my grandmother.

"Tansy, how is everything going?" she asked.

"Not good enough that I needed a box of condoms," I said. "I'm looking for Skyler, not a hookup, Granny."

"I know that," she said gently. "But I also know that you and Vaughn have a lot of unresolved feelings. I want you to be protected in case you two decide to act on those feelings."

It was embarrassing *and* touching. "Thanks," I said. "I appreciate it. Now, quickly changing the subject—we still haven't found Skyler. But we're pretty sure she's in Diablo."

"With the vampires?"

I flinched at the word. "Yes."

"Then we need to work on a few spells," she said.

"I seem to be able to resist vampire compulsion," I told her. "Not always, but I'm getting better at it."

"Of course you are," she replied. "You're a Mariotti witch. But I've neglected your education."

"Are the charms the reason?" I asked. "Skyler lost her necklace, and since then, she can't seem to resist Travis."

"That's part of it," she said. "It wouldn't work with a really old vampire."

"That's why Travis threw it away."

"Probably."

Part of me wanted to tell her about the file with all our secrets in it, but the other part wanted to keep my mouth shut. I didn't want her to tell me it was too dangerous and that I had to come home. Besides, she wasn't the only one who could keep a secret.

"Okay, Granny," I said. "Let's do this."

"The first thing you need to practice is visualization," she said. Her face looked tiny on my screen, and I suddenly missed her fiercely. Her brown eyes seemed flat and tired, and she was paler than normal. I was still mad at her, but I loved her anyway.

"Close your eyes," she continued. "And think about your intention. What you want to have happen. Now intent into action."

"What should I think about?" I asked.

"That's up to you," she said.

"I want to see if I can move something with my mind."

Granny laughed. "That's not a power most witches can do."

"Okay. Then what *can* they do?" I groaned. When I found Skyler and we were back home, Granny and I were going to have a long talk.

She sighed. "Tansy…that kind of magic is tricky."

"Let me try," I said. "I'll be right back." There were a few apples on the small table, and I went to get one. "Okay, let's do this," I said when I returned.

Granny's lips were in a flat line. "Maybe we shouldn't…" she said.

Maybe you shouldn't lie to me, I thought.

And the apple exploded.

I sucked in a breath. Well, fang my life.

I had more power than I'd ever dreamed.

"Well, that was interesting." Granny must have decided

I'd had enough practice. "Oops, my break's over," she said. "I'm closing at the library tonight. Don't try that again. Love you."

"Love you, too," I said.

Vaughn came back with a bag of chocolate-covered peanuts and a couple of candy bars.

"I can't stand to sit in this room one second longer," I said.

Vaughn glanced around at the exploded apple bits. "Then let's get out of here."

I hesitated. "We can't let their human roadie or any of their human superfans see us. We no longer have the element of surprise to rescue Skyler. I have a feeling he won't let her go without a fight."

"Why don't we take a walk on the beach? Get some air?" Vaughn suggested.

I grabbed a couple of elastic ties and braided my hair into two tight plaits, then piled them on top of my head. I'd brought a hat because, hello, summer in California meant I didn't go anywhere without one.

I put the hat on my head. "See, I'm almost unrecognizable."

"Almost," he said. He grabbed his lightweight hoodie and said, "Wear this. It'll help."

"It'll be huge on me," I said.

"Exactly."

Vaughn helped me into it, zipped it up, and then stared into my eyes for a long minute. I wondered if he was going to kiss me, but instead he asked, "Do I need a disguise, too?"

I studied him. "Sunglasses and a hat will probably be enough."

We grabbed our hotel key cards and left. In the elevator, Vaughn stood close to me.

We took a set of wooden stairs to the beach. When we reached the sand, I kicked off my flip-flops, and Vaughn took my hand. The water shimmered on the horizon, and the rush of the ocean calmed me. We walked along the shoreline, not speaking, our toes burrowing in the sand as we went.

Vaughn bought us ice-cream cones from the snack stand, and we sat on the sand and ate.

"I already feel better," I admitted. He smiled at me, his dimples showing briefly.

He said, "Should we head back?"

I started to answer him when the hairs on my arms stood up. "Someone is watching us."

Out of the corner of my eye, I spotted Rose and Thorn.

They approached us, but Thorn was scowling.

"Why are you following us?" I asked.

"It's our job," Thorn said.

I put my hands on my hips and glared at them. "Why is it your job?"

"We're after Travis Grando, too."

"Why?"

"We're currently assigned to the vampire observation and extermination team," Rose said.

I gaped at them. "You're vampire hunters?"

Rose wrinkled her nose. "That implies we do it for sport. We don't hunt vampires in general, just the rogue ones. The ones who do not follow PAC rules."

"Is Travis not following the rules?"

They didn't answer me at first.

"That has not yet been determined," Rose said, but Thorn's hand went to her side, where her dagger was currently hidden, probably so she didn't scare the tourists.

"You are looking for your friend, yes? We know where

she is," Rose said.

My heart started beating so fast, I couldn't talk, so I just nodded.

"Would you like for us to bring you to her?" she asked. I wished they'd stop following us around, but I'd let them if they helped me find Skyler.

"Yes please," I said.

She nodded. "It's not too far. We can walk."

I started to follow her, but Vaughn caught me by the arm. "Tansy, what if it's a trap?"

I gave him a hard look. "What if it's not?"

Chapter Thirteen

Although the sun had already set, it felt like a hundred degrees outside. The ocean breeze kicked up, which cooled my sweaty face.

We took a shortcut through a park. I spotted universally accessible play areas and an actual zip line. Even though it was past dark, there were kids running around while their parents chased after them. Palm trees lined the path, but something in the air made me uneasy. It smelled rotten.

I wasn't the only one who noticed. Thorn stopped and sniffed the air like a dog. She looked at her sister, and a silent conversation seemed to go on between them. Then out of nowhere, they both took off running into the shadows.

I turned to Vaughn. "Where did they go?"

"I have no idea." His gaze narrowed as he strained to see in the dark.

We walked along, moving into a deserted area of the park, near the empty basketball court. Something rustled in the bushes. I jumped and then laughed when a rabbit ran across the grass.

"What is that?" Vaughn asked. He pointed above our heads, toward a row of palm trees. Red eyes glinted in the darkness.

"Probably a rat," I said. "Granny calls palm trees 'rat condos.'"

"That's the biggest rat I've ever seen," Vaughn replied. "Rose and Thorn looked like they smelled something bad."

I took a closer look. "I don't think it's a rat; I think it's a vamp—"

Something grabbed me. I heard Vaughn shout my name before everything went dark.

I woke to the sound of water dripping. My first fuzzy thought was that Skyler had spent the night and had forgotten to give the bathroom faucet that extra wiggle, like she did every time she stayed over.

Then I realized that I wasn't in my bed. I was hanging upside down, and all the blood had rushed to my head. Some rough material bound my wrists and ankles, and I couldn't seem to open my eyes, no matter how many times I told them to obey me.

My mouth tasted like graveyard dirt, and my head pounded. The tang of blood filled the room. The dripping sound was louder, closer now.

Sleep. The word whispered through my mind, but I fought the command and shook off my grogginess. I needed to open my eyes, but I wanted to listen to the voice in my head.

Instead, I pried my eyes open. My vision was hazy. Two

guys—no, only one guy.

He was on the phone—talking, not texting. "I got her. Yeah, easy as pie," he said.

The bragging voice sounded familiar. Not a guy—a vampire. I was getting better at sensing them.

My vision cleared, and I could finally focus on my surroundings. I was in a warehouse somewhere. Either that or someone had a big online shopping problem, because there were boxes and cases everywhere.

Musical instruments, I realized.

My hands and ankles were bound, and I was sitting on a chair in the middle of the room.

"But I want a bite," the guy whined. "I'm hungry, and she smells like strawberry pie and whipped cream." He sounded like a five-year-old child instead of one of the undead. I almost laughed but then realized he probably wanted a bite of *me*.

He sat in front of a set of drums, holding his phone in one hand and twirling a drumstick with the other.

I looked around and then wished I hadn't, because it wasn't water dripping from a faucet that I'd heard—it was blood draining from the veins of a terrified girl. There was a basin positioned to catch it.

Her eyes blinked rapidly, like she was trying to tell me something. I turned my head and nearly puked at the pain inside my skull.

I didn't recognize the guy at first. Until I focused one blurry eye on him and realized I'd met him before. He had gym-rat arms and pasty skin, and he smelled terrible. The Drainers' drummer. The guy with the poser vampire name, Fang. He clicked his phone off and leered at me.

"Where's Skyler?" I asked. "What have you done with her?"

He snorted. "I'd worry more about what I'm going to do to you."

"What makes you think you'll get the chance?" I said. I tried to keep any trace of nerves from my voice, but I was worried. What had happened to Vaughn? Had Rose and Thorn lured me outside so Fang could kidnap me?

"They told me you're a witch," Fang said.

"I *am* a witch," I said. He hadn't bothered with a gag on either me or the girl slowly bleeding out next to me. Her eyes were now closed—she was probably passing out from loss of blood.

Exactly how many of these assholes were running around killing girls? Entirely too many.

"Your powers are a joke," he sneered.

"*You're* a joke." My fingers started to throb, and I curled them into fists, which made the rope chafe my skin.

My nails bit into the fleshy part of my hand, but I ignored the pain. A couple of drops of blood ran down my wrist, catching the vampire's attention.

"Look, Fred," I said. "Untie me. Please. You don't want to do this. You'll get into trouble."

One of the tasty little tidbits in the report about the Mariotti witches was that they had found a way to resist vampires, but vampires couldn't resist them. Centuries before, my ancestors had been able to control vampires.

Maybe it would have worked if his entire body wasn't focused on the blood welling from my hand.

"Fred," I said sharply but already knew I'd blown it. Reasoning wasn't going to work with him.

"My name's not Fred," he said. "You know it's Fang. I'm the drummer of The Drainers, the best band in California."

I snorted at that.

"You don't think we're the best band?" Aw, Fangy's

feelings were hurt. "But you have to." His voice deepened as he stared into my eyes. "I command you."

"It doesn't work with me," I said. At least I hoped it didn't.

"It works with every girl," he said. He waved his drumstick at me and then let it drop to the floor, where it rolled until it was only inches from me.

"Not me. Which one of you can compel through music?" I asked. "It's how you make your audience think your music is amazing. I bet it's Travis, isn't it?" I'd been guessing, but I knew I was right when I saw his face. "After all, he is the prince. It makes sense that he'd be the powerful one."

"It's not just him. It's all of us together. I can do stuff, too," Fang said.

"The drummer never gets the girl, so you have to kidnap one?" I made my voice sound as insulting as I could.

"I don't have to," he replied. "I wanted to. The blood tastes better with a little terror in it." There was a whole tsunami of terror in my veins. I hoped he choked on it.

But still, it made it hard for me to formulate a plan.

Maybe I could stall long enough for me to get my hands free.

"Really?" I replied. "You sure you're not Fred? You look like a Fred." Fred was the least cool name I could think of.

"What's that supposed to mean?" He took a step toward me.

I smirked at him. "You know. Fred."

"I don't," he said, still watching my bloody hand. "But I've heard from a friend that your blood is delicious."

Travis had a frickin' big mouth. "Too bad you'll never get the chance to find out," I replied.

I wasn't sure what I was doing. Granny had taught me

spells of peace, of protection, of harmony. But I wasn't feeling harmonious.

And I could tell from the look in Fang's eyes that kind of magic wouldn't work anyway.

Nothing I'd been taught had prepared me for this, but I had to work with the tools I had.

"Come closer," I commanded.

While his feet propelled him forward, my teeth grew long and sharp, so I used one to slash at the rope binding my hands together, and then at least my arms were free.

Something strange was happening to me. My body felt cold to its marrow. My lungs breathed in ice. When I looked at him, I could feel his victim's terror, her pain, as he'd taken her blood and nearly her life. White-hot fury pulsed through me. I snatched his discarded drumstick and, with every bit of my strength, stabbed Fang in the heart.

Then there was the sound of crunching bones, and the man who'd been standing next to me was a pile of goo and bone on the floor.

I tried not to look at the dark splotches on the wall, but I couldn't help it. It was like a giant had popped Fang like a pimple.

The only thing left of the guy was staining the hardwood floor. I had killed him.

I picked up the drumstick and wiped the blood off it before sticking it in the back pocket of my jean shorts.

What was Granny going to say? But reasoning with Fang hadn't worked, saying no hadn't worked, and the girl beside me was slowly bleeding to death. I'd had to kill him. I knew it was true, but that didn't stop me from bending over and heaving out the contents of my stomach.

I was starting to understand why Granny had never trained me in magic.

"How'd you do that?" the other girl breathed, fully conscious now.

"I have no idea," I said. "Do you know if there are more of them?"

"More of who?"

"More vampires," I replied.

"Aren't *you* a vampire?" she asked, motioning toward my mouth.

I put my tongue to my teeth. The fangs were still out.

"I'm not a vampire," I said, but she didn't look convinced.

I cut the rope around my ankles and then went to help the other girl. She was losing a lot of blood. I made quick work of the ropes holding her suspended and gently eased her into the chair I'd been sitting in. As the blood rushed into the rest of her body, she seemed to come out of her fog.

I was still wearing Vaughn's hoodie, which meant there was plenty of extra fabric. I tore a strip from the bottom and used it to stop the bleeding at her wrists. She was shaking and pale, but the bleeding was starting to slow already.

She flinched when I touched her. "I won't hurt you. I'm not a vampire," I insisted. "I'm a striga vie."

"What's that?" she asked.

"A vampire-witch hybrid."

"So you *are* a vampire."

"I'm a witch," I said. "Who has a few vampire abilities."

"Sounds like a vampire to me."

I rolled my eyes. "Whatever. We need to get you to an emergency room," I said. "And then call the police."

"No hospital." Her wide gaze held mine. "No police, either."

"But you're hurt."

"I'm okay," she said. "It looked worse than it is. I've

always bled a lot. And what are the police going to do? That guy won't be abducting anybody else." I started to say something, but she interrupted me. "Please."

I wanted to argue, but she looked like she'd bolt if I insisted. The only thing worse than not getting her to a hospital would be to let her wander around alone again.

"Won't your parents be worried about you?" I asked. "They've probably already filed a missing person report."

She snorted. "They probably didn't even notice I was gone."

It felt weird that we didn't know each other's names. "I'm Tansy."

"Misty," she replied.

There was an unfamiliar ringtone, and I eventually identified it as coming from Fang's phone: "I'm Too Sexy" by Right Said Fred. I rolled my eyes. Fang was Right Dead Fred now. I held a finger up to the girl to ask for her silence and then answered.

"Yes?"

"Tiffany?" Travis sounded perplexed. "Why are you answering Fang's phone?"

"Fang can't come to the phone right now." Or ever.

Then I realized what he'd called me.

"Tiffany?" *What's with this guy?* "That's not my name."

I waited, and after a long pause, he said, "Strawberry milkshake. Shay's friend. Whatever."

"My name's Tansy. And you mean Skyler. My best friend," I replied through gritted teeth.

"You mean the girl who is so head over heels for me that she used Daddy's credit card to buy me a new Les Paul guitar? I like her. She tastes good, too. Not as good as you, though."

If I found him, I was going to smash that guitar right

over his head.

"You need to let her go," I said, using my best compelling voice.

He snickered. "It doesn't work over the phone, genius."

"Travis, just let her go," I said. "Please."

"No, I think I'll keep her. Just because you want her back."

I'd made a mistake with him. My hands were gripping the phone so tight that it was in danger of being crushed. I eased up.

"Remember this conversation when I come after you," I said.

He heaved a beleaguered sigh. "Just put Fang on the phone."

"He can't come to the phone right now. Or ever. You're going to have to find a new drummer," I said. Then I hung up on him.

I searched for my phone. I didn't have any numbers memorized, and I needed to let Vaughn know what had happened.

But the phone wasn't in my pocket. I found it on the floor near the door. There were several missed calls from Vaughn.

"It wouldn't stop ringing when he brought you in," the girl said.

As I bent down to grab it, it started ringing again. It was Vaughn.

"I'm all right," I said instead of hello, knowing he was probably freaking out. "You?"

"I'm good," he said, but he didn't sound good. He sounded the opposite of good. "One minute, we were talking about rats in palm trees, and the next, you were gone."

"That particular rat won't be a problem any longer," I said. "And by rat, I mean vampire." My words were blasé, but my voice was shaking.

"Tansy, are you okay?" Vaughn asked. "I can come get you."

"No, don't," I said. I needed time to pull myself together. "I'll text you where to meet me. It'll take a few minutes because first I have to figure out where we are."

"We?" Vaughn asked.

"Another girl. I'll explain later," I said. "We'll be there soon."

It was after midnight. I turned on my maps app, crossing my fingers that the vampire hadn't flown us somewhere a thousand miles away or something, and was relieved to see that we were only about five miles from the hotel.

As much as I hated to, since half the town seemed to be vampires, I ordered a ride from one of those ride-share apps. If the driver tried anything weird with us, he'd regret it—especially after the day I'd had.

While we waited, Misty told me how she'd been walking home around sunset, and then the next thing she knew, she'd been tied up in some creepy warehouse.

"I know this might be hard to talk about," I said. "But why did Fang tie you up instead of compelling you?"

"He did compel me at first," she said. "Or I think that's what happened. He came up and asked me a question—I don't remember what—and then his eyes went all weird and squinty."

She paused to gather her thoughts, and I let out a breath. "Go on."

"He told me to come with him," she said. "And I did, even though I didn't want to, even though every muscle in my body was trying to resist. I couldn't."

"Did he take you to the warehouse right away?"

"I don't remember," she said. "I think I was there at least two days. And it was nothing like those books. I read 'em when I was in middle school, and the creep who grabbed me was not a gorgeous, swoony vampire.

"And," she added indignantly, "he wasn't a vegetarian."

"None of them are," I said.

"To tell you the truth," she added, "I think he tied me up just because he could. He liked hurting me. He liked me helpless."

The thought of it made me clench my fists with rage.

Our rideshare came then—a Mazda with a college-aged guy at the wheel. We were silent the entire drive. I was surprised he was willing to take our fare, but it was nighttime, and I guessed he'd seen pretty much everything as a ride-share driver.

The car pulled up at the hotel where Vaughn and I were staying, and she said, "Now that's more like it."

I glanced out the car window and saw Vaughn standing out front waiting. "He's not a vampire."

"Even better," was all she said in reply. We got out, and Vaughn walked over to us.

"This is Misty," I told him.

He put out a hand to shake, but instead, she took a step closer and grabbed his hand with both of hers. "And you are?"

He lifted his eyebrow. "Vaughn Sheridan," he replied. "Tansy's boyfriend."

Misty dropped his hand like she was afraid I was going to go full vamp on her, and though freshman me wanted to jump up and down and squeal—even though I knew he was practicing for our cover story for The Drainers—instead, I gave him a small smile. "Yup, that's my boyfriend, all right."

Then we went to the room so I could rinse the vampire guts off me. Misty was a bloody mess, too.

I'd offered Misty the first shower, but she declined until Vaughn said he'd wait for us downstairs.

I had the feeling that even though I'd rescued her, she was wary, and I didn't blame her. We were strangers.

I found some clean clothes for Misty. She came out wearing a hotel robe, and then I took my turn at cleanup.

I scrubbed away the vampire blood and gore, and when I was done, my skin was tinged celery green—also known as puke green, but celery green sounded better. To most people, anyway. To me, celery tasted a little bit pukey, so it was a tomato/tomahto situation.

In any case, vampire gunk left a mark.

When I got out of the shower and dressed in fresh clothes that were blissfully guts-free, I joined Vaughn and Misty in the hotel restaurant.

It looked like the place was getting ready to close, and the only server shot me an irritated look when I slid into the booth. Vaughn was telling Misty why we agreed that she shouldn't call the cops.

I gave Vaughn a grateful look. He'd ordered an iced tea for me and a soda and a sandwich for Misty. She must have been starving after being held captive for two days.

"We ran into some vampire cops when we reported something before," Vaughn explained. "And the vampire who took you knew Travis."

"Who's Travis?" Misty asked.

"He's the lead singer of The Drainers," I said.

"Their music sucks," she said.

"I know, right? And his dad is the number-one big bad vampire daddy," I added. "They're going to be pissed that they need a new drummer."

We ate and then drove her home. It turned out she lived in Diablo and her parents had been gone for the weekend, so, as she had predicted, no one even missed her.

Despite the nightmares I had that night, I knew I'd done the right thing. Was Fang a shitty excuse for a guy because of the vampirism in him? Or did power just make it easier for him to hurt people? And what did that mean for me?

Still, I promised myself I'd never take a life again.

I had no way of knowing how quickly I'd break that promise.

Chapter Fourteen

I'd overslept, so I bustled around, brushing my teeth and generally ignoring the dark circles and the residual terror that came with memories of being kidnapped by Fang.

"I'm ready," I finally said. "Let's get moving."

Vaughn, who'd evidently been up and dressed for some time, studied my face. "You all right?"

"Let's go and see if we can figure out where The Drainers are staying." I grabbed a hat and sunscreen, and we were on our way.

"They're probably sleeping," Vaughn said. "Sunset to sunrise is when vampires are out."

"That's true," I agreed. "But we have a better chance at convincing Skyler to come with us when Travis isn't around."

No luck. If anyone knew where The Drainers were spending their days, they weren't talking.

Without any other leads, we'd stopped for a late lunch at a cheerful-looking café. The restaurant was almost empty, so they sat us at a table looking out over the ocean.

The air conditioning was a relief, but the sour odor of my sweat clung to my body.

We ordered—ham and brie for me and a gigantic burger and fries for Vaughn. At the last minute, he added two slices of chocolate cake.

I was picking at Vaughn's fries when Rose and Thorn slid into empty chairs at the table next to us.

"What's the matter, little witch?" Thorn asked. Her head tilted to the side inquiringly. I was relieved to see that there was no sign of her dagger, but I was pretty sure she had it hidden underneath her clothes somewhere.

I glared at her. "Where'd you run off to yesterday?" I asked. "Did you set me up?"

The server came by to take their order, but Thorn waved her away.

"You think we would betray you?" Rose frowned.

I held her gaze. "I don't know."

"We were required to be somewhere else," Thorn said.

"You let Fang grab me and take me to his lair."

"From the look of it, you handled that just fine," Thorn said. "Apart from the cleanup, which *we* handled for you. You're welcome."

"Thank you," I said. "I'm sure vampire is hard to get out of…everything."

"We can help you find your friend," Rose offered.

"That's what you said last time."

"She'll turn up at one of their shows sooner or later," Thorn said.

Vaughn put a comforting arm around my shoulders.

"Friendship is a powerful bond," Rose said solemnly. "You should not discount its power."

"And you shouldn't feel guilty about killing Fang," Thorn said.

"Because he was already dead?" I asked.

She shook her head. "Because he was a monster. It was for the good of humanity."

"It doesn't feel like it," I murmured.

"That's because *you're* not a monster," Thorn said.

I looked down, overwhelmed by the fear she was wrong. My phone was on the table, so I picked it up and searched The Drainers' social media posts for clues. Rose and Thorn said they were needed elsewhere, and they left.

Natasha, the leader of the Bleeders, was someone I'd never met yet disliked intensely just from the content of her Instagram feed. She posted nasty comments about other Bleeders and took way too many selfies with the band, which usually featured one of them biting some part of her body.

I followed her anyway, because I was desperate for a clue about Skyler's whereabouts. She was either part of the problem—the problem being bloodsucking vampires who fed on and murdered girls—or a vain, clueless follower who was oblivious to the pain of other people.

It was worth it, though, because she'd also posted that The Drainers were holding auditions for a fill-in drummer while Fang "recuperated" from the flu. Could vampires even get the flu? And Fang wouldn't be "recuperating" from what I'd done to him. I was sure of that.

My mind flashed to that room—the kidnapped girl, the wall stained with blood—but I forced it back to saving Skyler. I wouldn't kill to rescue her, but maybe if we hung out with the band, we could get what we needed to break Travis's hold over her. I thought about trying to make her come with us, but she'd just go back to him the first chance she got.

Did their fans realize the boys in the band were real vampires, or did they think it was just a marketing ploy, like that son-of-darkness shtick that headbanging band Granny liked had done? In any case, The Drainers needed a new drummer—and I happened to know just the person.

"Vaughn, weren't you in a band?" I asked casually. I already knew the answer to my question. I'd mooned over Vaughn playing the guitar enough times. "Don't you also play the drums?"

"Yeah. Years ago." He was focused on his chocolate cake, but something about my question made him look up quickly. "Why do you ask?"

In response, I handed him my phone with the "Drainers need a drummer" audition notice.

He read it quickly and then practically shoved the phone at me. "No way, Tansy," he said, but I gave him a pleading look.

"We need to infiltrate the band," I said. "Then I'll cast a spell to break the hold Travis has on Skyler and we'll take her home."

"You know why I quit the band back in middle school?"

"I thought it was because you were too busy with sports and helping your dad," I said.

"Stage fright," he replied. "I felt like puking every single time I got onstage." He studied me for a minute. "But I'll do it for Skyler," he said. "And for you. I'd do anything for you."

And just like that, my little crush on Vaughn Sheridan turned into an avalanche of feeling. How could I keep resisting him any longer?

"What will you do while I'm off being a rock star?" Vaughn joked. "Assuming I get the gig, that is?"

I batted my eyelashes at him. "I'll be your devoted girlfriend."

"I like the sound of that," Vaughn said softly.

So do I.

"Now, finish your dessert," I said. "We have some shopping to do."

We ended up—despite Vaughn's protests—at Goodwill, searching for the perfect audition outfit.

"Remember, I haven't played the drums since middle school," he said.

I considered that for a minute. "Then you'll get the gig for sure. The Drainers sound like they haven't touched their instruments in years, despite all evidence to the contrary."

"What exactly are we looking for?" he asked while I thumbed through a rack of dress pants.

"I'm going for a pretentious-asshole vibe," I said. "So you'll fit in with the rest of the guys."

"You think they know Fang's"—he made an explosion motion with his hands—"or do they think he's holed up with a groupie somewhere?"

I wondered if The Drainers had any true fans or if every one of them had been compelled into their superfan status.

I shrugged. "Travis knows. You'll go in and chat up some of the Bleeders who're sure to be hanging around and see if you can find anything out about Sky."

Vaughn gave me a sarcastic thumbs-up.

"These look promising," I said, holding up a pair of synthetic leather pants.

He read the tag. "They're a size too small."

"Even better," I said. I draped them over my arm and then perused the men's shirts. There wasn't anything frilly enough there, so I drifted to the women's stuff. I almost collided with a life-size mannequin wearing a tight white bustier and black stovepipe pants. It looked like something Natasha would wear to show off her bite marks, and I made a face.

I found a white silky blouse, extra-extra-large with a bunch of ruffles down the front. Vaughn could leave it unbuttoned, which would be the only way it would fit his broad shoulders. I was going for Russell Brand circa *Forgetting Sarah Marshall*.

"Go try these on," I ordered.

"I'm gonna look like I flunked pirate school," he complained, but he went into the dressing room anyway.

I was checking for messages on my phone when Vaughn summoned me. "Tansy, get in here."

"Come out so I can see."

"There's no way I'm appearing in public in these," he said. "Help me. Now."

I knocked on the dressing-room door. "Are you decent?"

"Decent is a relative term," he said, sounding aggrieved. "I'm fully clothed, if that's what you mean."

I opened the door, then let out a low whistle, and he blushed. The pants clung to his long legs and tight butt.

"Tansy, my junk is somewhere near my kidneys right now."

There was a lot of tan chest on display, and I wanted to linger to appreciate every inch, but Vaughn really did look like he was in pain. "Okay, I'll see if I can find something a little roomier."

It took a few minutes, but I found a similar pair of pants in a larger size and brought them back to Vaughn. "Here you go," I said cheerfully. He huffed a little but grabbed the clothes and went into the dressing room.

After a few minutes, he called out grudgingly, "These will work."

"It's for Skyler," I called back.

"Then I'll wear whatever you want me to." He was a good friend. He came back out wearing his own clothes.

"The tryouts don't start until after sunset, right?"

"Right," I said.

"Then there's still time to shop for you," he said, heading to the women's section before I could open my mouth to protest.

"I can't go," I said. "Travis and the guys know what I look like."

He held up a long black wig. "Not if you wear this." He scanned the clothes racks, and I knew what he'd found when his face lit up with a grin. "And this."

He motioned to the bustier-clad mannequin I'd noticed earlier. "There's no way that will fit me," I protested.

"You never know until you try," he said. I thought about arguing until he threw my words back at me. "For Sky." I made a gimme motion and went into an empty dressing room. I changed and then sat on the little bench. Maybe if I was quiet, Vaughn would forget all about me.

"Let me see," Vaughn insisted.

"No way," I said.

"I showed you mine."

"Yes, yes you did." I giggled, and he let out a bark of laughter.

"I showed you my *outfit*," he clarified.

I sighed. "Come on in, then." The clothes fit, although the tight bustier made my boobs land somewhere near my chin, and I could barely take in a breath for fear of a nip slip.

"I look like Morticia Addams in this," I said. I tugged at the bodice, but it wouldn't budge.

"Exactly," he replied. "You'll fit right in."

"I guess," I said. I felt twitchy, though. These pants felt way too slippery.

Vaughn didn't say anything for a long minute. "You won't be able to run in that," he finally said.

"I can barely breathe in it, so no," I replied.

"Let's find something a little more comfortable," he said. "But keep the wig."

I smiled at him gratefully. Vaughn understood my discomfort but didn't tease me about it.

"I need something that will hide my necklace," I said. "I don't want any of the guys in the band to recognize it." Travis had reacted badly to it before.

We settled on short shorts and a silky top that, though it revealed more skin than I was used to, had adequate coverage and didn't put my nipples in danger of making a public appearance.

We started getting ready just before sunset. Vaughn even let me put a little guyliner on him.

For my own look, I went with red lips and lots of cat's-eye liner and darkened my eyebrows to match my wig. I even remembered to dab some concealer on my neck. The puncture marks had faded, but there was a tiny golden scar that I wanted to hide.

"You look like a different person," he said.

"That's the idea," I argued. "You have the whole hot-rocker thing going for you, too."

I'd slicked his hair into a fauxhawk and grabbed a couple of cheap leather bracelets and put them on his wrists.

"Do you think Travis will recognize me?" Vaughn asked. He started to run his hands through his hair and then seemed to remember I'd just styled it and stopped.

"It was dark," I said. "Plus, he was concentrating on me, and he probably only caught a glimpse of you before you threw that soda can at him."

"My pitching skills come in handy once again," Vaughn replied.

We studied each other.

"I prefer the way you usually look," he said.

"Me too," I said. Even though I'd opted out of the bustier, I still couldn't wear my necklace. The last time I'd been without it, Travis had taken a bite out of me, so I stashed it in a tiny clutch, along with a pair of folding travel scissors and some plastic baggies, in case I got close enough to give a vampire a haircut.

"I'd like to feed Travis a fistful of garlic," I said.

"With a stake chaser," Vaughn said.

I tugged on Vaughn's hand. "There's one other thing I need," I said. "We'll make a quick stop at the gift shop." In the elevator, I couldn't stop staring at him. He was my boyfriend, even if only a pretend one.

The gift shop had a small selection of high-end perfumes.

"I need your help to pick out the strongest perfume," I told Vaughn. "Nothing that smells fruity."

"Good call," he said. "I might put my fist through Travis's face if I hear him rhapsodizing about how good you smell one more time."

Jealous Vaughn was hot. He picked up a tester bottle and gave it a sniff, then reared back. "I think we have a winner."

Vaughn insisted on paying for the high-dollar perfume that smelled like eau de corpse flower, but it was a small price to pay if it meant we'd find Skyler.

I dabbed on as much as I could without choking from the fumes.

"Do you still have the charm Granny gave you?" I asked. He was going to jam with a band of vampires. I wanted to make sure he was protected.

"Yes," he said. "I keep it on me at all times."

"Close your eyes," I said. Another protection spell

couldn't hurt. He did as I asked, and I dug out the fennel oil I'd found at one of the little shops by the beach and applied it to the pulse points at his wrists and neck. I took his hands in mine and whispered a simple, "Protect him."

His hands gripped mine tighter.

"You can open your eyes." He did, but he didn't let go of my hands, just pulled me into a hug. We stayed wrapped together, not saying anything, until his phone buzzed.

He checked it. "Almost time."

He was nervous. Distraction time. "We need a few pics on our phones of the two of us."

"We have tons of pics of us together," he said.

"Not of us *together*," I said. "You know, all snuggled up."

"Good idea," he said. His dimples flashed.

We posed next to bougainvillea, avoiding the setting sun. Vaughn pulled me close, and I took a few shots.

He handed his phone to me. "A few for me, too."

He tilted up my chin and leaned in. I trembled. Was he going to kiss me? Instead, we stared into each other's eyes, lips almost touching, while the camera phone whirred.

"I think we should kiss," Vaughn said. "If we're pretending to be a couple, we won't want our first kiss to be in front of a bunch of vampires."

"O-Okay," I said, my voice trembling.

Neither of us moved at first, but then Vaughn's arms encircled my waist loosely as he leaned down. His lips were gentle against mine, both of us tentative, our eyes open, like we were both surprised we were actually kissing. I know I was.

When he deepened the kiss, my eyelids fluttered shut. I ran my fingers through his dark hair.

Someone honked their horn, and I pulled away.

"Th-That should be enough for now," I said. My voice

sounded breathless, shaky.

"We should remember to do that every day," he said, taking my hand like we were really a couple. I wasn't sure if he was talking about taking photos or making out. I knew we were faking a relationship to find Sky, but a big part of me wanted it to be true. Did Vaughn want the same thing?

Chapter Fifteen

We left the Deathtrap at the hotel and walked the six blocks to the tryouts, which were being held at the Diablo Community Center, of all places.

Vaughn didn't let go of my hand, and I didn't complain.

"You know, being a musician is really the perfect job for a vampire. If only Travis could sing."

"Hasn't stopped him so far," Vaughn deadpanned, and I giggled.

"The Drainers are awful," I agreed. "You'll probably be too good for them. And too good-looking. The groupies will be all over you."

"You can be my protection tonight," he said. "You know I don't like that kind of attention."

It was one of the things I liked about him. Some guys never seemed satisfied with getting to know one person at a time.

Vaughn was gorgeous, but he'd never been the kind of guy to hook up with anyone who batted her eyes at him.

Inside the community center, I spotted a vending

machine. I was thirsty after our walk.

I motioned to the machine. "Want anything?"

"No thanks," Vaughn replied. "There's always a lot of people at an open call like this. I'll get in line."

I put in my money and selected a Pepsi.

Vaughn was right—there was a line, but it was going quickly. As usual, I scanned the area for Skyler, but no luck.

I spotted Natasha carrying a clipboard and directing the people in line.

She was dressed in white shorts and a white shirt with *B Positive* emblazoned across the chest. I was surprised by such a cheery message until I realized it wasn't a message; it was her blood type.

Another girl near her was wearing an almost identical outfit with *B Negative* across her top.

Natasha bustled over with a supercilious air. "What do you think you're doing?" she addressed me.

"Waiting in line," I said. Vaughn nudged me, and I added, "Is there something wrong?"

"No sodas," she practically screeched. "Don't you know anything? The band doesn't allow carbonated drinks like that anywhere near them. It's even a rider in their contract."

I sighed and took one last sip before throwing the can in a nearby trash can.

"Satisfied?

She sniffed. "Name?"

Vaughn sputtered, so I answered for him. "Johnny Divine."

He smothered a yelp of laughter.

"And who are you?" she asked me. "Groupies aren't allowed inside."

"Then what are *you* doing here?"

She looked like she wanted to slug me with her

clipboard, but Vaughn stepped in front of me. "She's not a groupie; she's my girlfriend."

Natasha put a hand on his arm. "Are you sure about that? We could hold our own audition."

My fangs started to come down, but I forced myself to stay calm. It wouldn't do to blow our cover. And also, no fangs meant I could ignore that I was turning into a creature of the night. Besides, I'd noticed female vampires were a rarity.

The males liked keeping girls as their donors but not as their equals. Figures.

"Take your hand off him," I said. "Please," I added politely, but I let my eyes tell her what I'd do to her if she didn't let go of Vaughn.

She released her death grip on him and took a big step back. "This way," she said. "The drum kit's all set up."

As we approached, a cacophony came from the room she was leading us toward.

"Don't they sound great?" Natasha asked with every evidence of sincerity. Now, when I listened to Travis sing, I heard the deceit—the compulsion he wrapped in the music.

"What I wouldn't give for a set of earplugs," I said to Vaughn, but Natasha heard me and glared.

"Loud sounds are bad for your hearing," I added quickly. Her scowl remained, but at least she seemed to believe me.

"Do you read music?" she asked Vaughn. When he nodded, she thrust some sheet music at him.

"Take a look at this," she said. "You'll be next."

He glanced down at the music, and I noticed his hands were shaking. Damn. His stage fright must be kicking in. I had no idea what to do to take his mind off his nerves. Well, no *good* idea.

Which was why I tugged on his hand, pulled him toward

me, and said in my breathiest voice, "Knock 'em dead, baby." And then I leaned up and kissed him.

He froze, but then his arms snaked around my waist as he pulled me against his hard chest, his head slanting to get better access to my mouth. And just like that, I forgot why we were here, forgot we had an audience, and perhaps forgot my own name. Vaughn wasn't just a good kisser—he was an all-star.

The only thing I wanted to do was get lost in Vaughn's kiss, but someone let out a wolf whistle, and I forced myself to remember our goal. I gripped Vaughn's wide shoulders, then pushed backward and ended our kiss. He easily let me slip from his arms, but his gaze remained unfocused.

But then a grin slowly spread across his face as he ran his hand through his hair, then turned and strode toward the drum kit. My heart was pounding so hard, I didn't trust my legs to walk, so I just stood and watched him take his place behind the drums while the guys in the band drank something red out of clear bottles before joining him.

"So do any of the guys in the band have girlfriends?" I asked, trying not to sound like I was fishing for information.

"Why do you want to know?" Natasha asked.

I shrugged. "Just making conversation. If Johnny gets in, I'll want someone to hang out with. If the other guys have girlfriends, I'll have someone to talk to during rehearsals."

"The band doesn't do girlfriends. I'm their number-one girl," she said.

I narrowed my eyes at her. "Do you date one of the guys?"

She smiled. "I'm the leader of their fan club."

Oh, is that what they're calling it?

"I'm Tiffany, Johnny's girlfriend," I said. I was really

getting into the jealous-girlfriend act. Too bad I was afraid it wasn't just an act.

"Yeah, you said you were his girlfriend already." She gave me a catty smile. "But since I'm their fan club president, you'll have to get used to me being up close and personal with your guy."

We'd see about that.

Vaughn hadn't even glanced at another girl, but they were everywhere The Drainers went. The Bleeders consisted of girls of every ethnicity, shape, and size, but they were all beautiful, and they watched Vaughn and me like we were the latest episode of Skyler's favorite Korean drama.

Another girl came up to Natasha and whispered something in her ear. I heard the words "Sky" and "sick." Natasha frowned and glanced over at me. I pretended to be entranced by Vaughn's biceps, which were, in truth, entrancing, but I eavesdropped like a mom right before prom.

When the girl left, I started to edge away so I could snoop, but Natasha caught me.

"Where are you going?" she asked.

"Bathroom," I said. "Not that it's any of your business."

"But your boyfriend's getting ready to perform."

The Drainers sounded like two tomcats fighting in a burlap sack to me, but if I was posing as the drummer's devoted girlfriend, I couldn't say that.

I giggled. "Tiny bladder. I'll be right back." Then I blew Vaughn a kiss. "Good luck, baby," I cooed.

Travis lifted his head and sniffed the air.

I hurried from the room. Skyler was here, but where would they have stashed her?

I waited in the hallway until the other girl—the one

who'd been whispering Sky's name—left the community center, and then I followed her.

She hurried along, not noticing me in the crowd of summer people strolling along the streets of Diablo. She ducked into one of the nicer hotels along the boardwalk.

There weren't many streetlamps around, but I got out my phone and texted Vaughn my location while I tried to figure out if I should go inside or not.

When the girl didn't come out again, I went to the front lobby and pretended I was waiting for a friend. Half an hour passed, and then Natasha hurried in. I ducked down, but she didn't even look around, just headed for a bank of elevators. As soon as the doors closed, I watched to see what floor she got off on. The third.

She came back fifteen minutes later, loaded down with luggage, with the other girl trailing behind her.

They went straight to the front desk. "We're checking out of room 313," Natasha said. "Yes, under Mina Harker."

I rolled my eyes. Of course they'd use the name of a character in *Dracula*.

Still, why were they using an alias? Did they think they were celebrities or on a secret mission of some kind?

Something was wrong. The other girl's lips were trembling, and she looked seconds away from freaking out. A few minutes later, they loaded their bags into a newish white Mini Cooper and peeled out of there. I made a face when I saw her license plate was #1BLEDR.

My stomach was in knots. Natasha and her friend had fled like they were leaving the scene of a crime. What if something had happened to Skyler?

I decided to check out the room. Something had freaked them out. I didn't know how I was going to get inside, but fortunately the door to "Mina's" room was open a crack, so I slipped in easily.

The room seemed unoccupied, and nothing appeared out of place. I looked under the bed, but there were only a few dust bunnies hiding under there.

I found Skyler in the bathtub, cold and still.

The dread almost overwhelmed me, my heart threatening to jump out of my chest. She only wore a tiny thong and a stained T-shirt, and her skin was sickly white.

I rushed to her side, my hands roaming over her wrists, looking for a pulse. *Please dear God, please let her be okay.* At first, I thought I was too late, but then I saw a shallow inhalation of her chest.

"Skyler?" I begged, but she didn't answer. Her eyes were closed, and her breathing was so slow that I was worried if I called an ambulance, it would be too late. It was probably why the Bleeders had fled.

Nobody wanted to hear that vampires were real. Nobody wanted to know that vampires were using up girls and then throwing them away. But I wasn't going to let that happen to Skyler.

I lifted her out of the tub, careful and slow, and carried her to the bed. I yanked down the comforter and then found the spare blankets and pillows and covered her with all of it. She needed to warm up.

I knew of a healing spell, but it required a few ingredients and temporarily drained a witch's powers, which might leave me vulnerable to a vampire's compulsion. I couldn't protect Sky if I was vulnerable—but still, I had to try.

I didn't know where I was going to find the things I needed, but a good witch made use of the ingredients she had available. There was a little coffee and tea kiosk in the room, and I rummaged through it.

I found blackberry sage tea and tore the bag open,

emptying the leaves into a cup. I poured in a packet of honey and then searched the room for the last few things I needed. Even though the decor wasn't as nice here as the hotel Vaughn and I were staying in, there were still fresh roses in a vase by the window, and I tore the petals off three buds and threw them into the cup. Finally, I mashed it all together and recited, "Wrap thee in cotton, bind thee in love, protection from pain, free as a dove."

I repeated the spell over and over, until my voice grew hoarse and my energy began to fade. Finally, Skyler's breathing seemed to grow stronger, and her eyes opened. "Tansy, you found me." She inhaled. "I knew you would."

I slumped over, drained but relieved. She was awake, and her color looked better.

Then I heard footsteps in the hallway. Was one of the girls coming back? I froze when the handle to the door turned.

Dare I chance it? I rummaged through my bag, found my scissors, and snipped a lock of her hair, which felt brittle and dry. She didn't stir, but I whispered, "I'll see you soon, Skyler."

It was a promise.

I managed to shove the lock of hair in my pocket before Gary walked into the hotel suite. "Who are you?" he asked, giving me a suspicious look.

My mind went blank.

He grabbed my arm and hauled me to my feet. Exhaustion hit me, and I staggered. I tried to talk, but my throat had closed up.

"Time for you to go," he said. He shoved me out of the room and slammed the door.

I needed water. My throat was tightening, like someone was squeezing it in a vise. I started to wheeze, frantically trying to force some air into my lungs.

Black spots swam in my vision. I fumbled for my phone and typed out my location before I fell.

I woke to the sound of Vaughn's voice. "Tansy, I've been looking all over for you. Please, please wake up."

Where was I? My eyes snapped open to meet Vaughn's gaze. I was laying across his lap. We were on the floor in the hotel hallway, and he was cradling me in his arms.

"It's okay," he said. "Don't try to talk yet. Do you want some water?"

I nodded, and he held up an open water bottle to my lips. I drank greedily. The pain in my throat eased.

"How did you find me?" I asked. I sounded like I'd been sucking barbed wire lollipops.

"You sent me a text," he replied. "Don't you remember?"

I nodded again, not trusting my voice.

We sat on the floor until I finally felt like I could breathe again.

"I got the lock of Skyler's hair," I said. I told him what had happened, how I'd been too weak to fight when Gary had thrown me out of the hotel room.

He ran a comforting hand down my back. "We have time."

"We do?"

"I got the gig," Vaughn said. "You're looking at the new drummer for The Drainers."

"That's good news." I snuggled my face into his neck. "All good?"

"It will be," I said. "Once I give Travis a trim."

I needed to cast the spell as soon as possible. I wasn't sure Skyler had much time left.

Chapter Sixteen

I walked into Vaughn's first practice with The Drainers, trailing behind him. I tugged on my violet micromini, trying to make the hemline a little longer. I'd paired it with tall white boots, which concealed the drumstick I'd used to kill Fang. I felt safer when it was with me.

There was a long whistle. "Fresh meat," the keyboard player said.

Armando was the most traditionally handsome guy in the band, with high cheekbones and flirty brown eyes, but inside, he was as rotten as the other two.

Vaughn glared at him. "She's off-limits."

Travis jumped off the stage. If I had tried that move, I would have broken something. I blinked, and then he was standing in front of me. Incredible vampire speed, check.

"Who's this?" Travis asked. His gaze crawled over my body. Vaughn drew me closer to his side.

"This is my girlfriend," he replied. It sounded so right, him calling me his. "T—"

"Tiffany," I interrupted him.

Travis flashed a bright white smile and stared into my eyes. "Tiffany and Travis. Our names go together, don't they?"

A warm glow suffused my body. *I never noticed how beautiful his eyes are.*

But then I realized what was happening and forced myself to look away. Hypnosis wasn't going to work on me.

"They do go together," I said. "They sound like we could be siblings."

"Excuse me?"

"You know," I said. "I get that brotherly feeling from you."

"Brotherly?" Travis said the word like I said black olives. In other words, like it was something loathsome and wrong.

"Are we going to play or what?" Vaughn asked.

A group of girls walked in, snagging Travis's attention. "In a minute," he said. "I just want to go say hi first."

He called out something to one of the girls, who was almost as tall as he was with curly brown hair and amber eyes. She was stunning. At first, she tried to ignore him, but then he whispered in her ear, and her gaze snapped to his.

He stared into her eyes a long time and then took her hand. She gazed at him adoringly as they left the room.

I wondered if he'd replaced Skyler already, and anxiety and doubt crept into my thoughts. Maybe my magic hadn't been strong enough to heal her, or maybe she'd relapsed.

While the guys were practicing, Skyler showed up. She was with one of the Bleeders who spent a lot of time with Armando, at least judging by the band's Insta. They were giggling and swaying, arms wrapped around each other to keep upright.

My best friend was looking better than the last time I'd seen her. The healing spell had worked. I knew Vaughn had spotted her, too, when he missed a beat, but he tore his gaze away from Skyler and concentrated on the drums.

My heart pounded in time with Vaughn's sticks. I wanted to rush over and hug her, but instead, I took a deep breath.

I'd been reading on my phone with earbuds I managed to hide with my hair, but I removed them quickly and put everything in the pocket of my purse.

I strolled over to the other girls, trying to act casual. "Hey," I said. "I'm Tiffany." I knew Skyler would know me anywhere, even with the wig, but I also didn't want her to blurt out my real name in front of all the vampires.

"Alice," the tall, silver-haired girl said. The platinum hair contrasted well with her dark skin and gray eyes.

"And this is Sky." When Alice introduced her, Skyler's eyes roamed over me without a hint of recognition. I tried to swallow down the rawness in my throat.

It turned out I didn't need to worry that Skyler would greet me like her not-so-long-lost bestie. "Hey," she said before staring at the band members without blinking. Her lips were chapped and swollen.

I was desperate to do something, anything, to help her. "Want to try on some of my jewelry?"

Alice rolled her eyes to Sky when she thought I wasn't looking but agreed to try on a bangle. She probably thought I was the new girl looking to butter them up, but I had ulterior motives.

I gave Sky a necklace made of woven fabric that I'd soaked in rose petals and protection spells, and I gave them both bracelets decorated with some of Granny's charms.

"This is so pretty, Tansy," Skyler said. She touched the necklace. "You're such a good friend."

"Tansy?" Alice laughed. "You've got to stop letting

Travis bite you so often. Your brains are leaking out along with the blood. Her name is Tiffany."

It looked like Skyler was about to protest, but then her eyes went hazy. "Tiffany," she said.

Alice changed the subject, and I "forgot" to get the charms back. While they chatted, I watched Skyler, noting the pallor of her skin and the deep violet rings under her eyes.

The band roadie yelled "dinner," and Armando, Ozzie, and Vaughn joined us. I was pretty sure that Sky and Alice were the dinner Gary was talking about.

Travis came back with the girl, who now had a huge bite mark on her cleavage.

"What did I tell you about snacking before dinner?" Armando asked mockingly.

Travis sniffed the air like a coke fiend. "Something smells good." His eyes landed on me. "Really good." My stomach roiled, but I managed a tight smile.

Skyler tugged at his arm. "Come on, baby," she said. "Aren't you hungry?"

He turned his attention to her. "Famished. We're on break, guys," Travis said before she tugged him out of the room.

Armando and Alice left, too. I'd had all the interactions with The Drainers I could stand for a while. At least we'd made some progress. I'd seen Skyler, and she was alive, although it looked like she was in rough shape. I wanted to grab her and run but knew I had to break the hold Travis had on her first.

"Want to get out of here?" I asked Vaughn.

"Yeah," he said. "We can talk while we eat."

When we were walking to the nearest fast-food place, I told him, "I need to get some sort of vampire repellent.

I think Travis almost recognized me by smell."

The restaurant was empty, except for an employee mopping the floor. We ordered burgers and fries.

"I'll just have to wear even more of that perfume," I said.

"We're running out of time, Tansy," Vaughn said. "Skyler looked terrible."

"I know," I said. "But I can't just walk up to Travis at practice and cut his hair."

"The guys in the band aren't in a hurry to leave Diablo," Vaughn said.

"Why not?" I asked.

"They won't tell me anything else."

"Do you think they suspect you?"

"Nah," he said. "I'm just not one of them, you know?"

"The good news is that I managed to slip Skyler one of Granny's protection bracelets."

He brightened. "Do you think it'll work?"

"I don't know," I admitted. Frustration made my voice tense. "I've been reading up on protection charms in the book I borrowed from Granny. And when I gave Skyler a necklace full of protection charms, it seemed like she recognized me, but then it was gone."

"Do you think your necklace is why you can resist Travis and the music?" Vaughn asked.

"Not entirely," I admitted. "I do think the charms amplify a human's resistance to evil, which is why I've been handing them out, but some of the info in the file indicated Mariottis are resistant to vampire compulsion."

"Maybe if Skyler wears her necklace long enough, she'll see Travis for what he really is," Vaughn said.

Our original necklaces had contained the memories of our friendship. I hoped the substitute necklace would be enough.

...

B ut the next time I saw her, the necklace was gone.
      She seemed in a trance most of the time, and
nothing I did broke the spell she was under. She was so
thin that I could see her clavicles. Bite marks, old and new,
marred her tan skin. It killed me to watch Travis with her,
but I was even more worried about what would happen
to her after he lost interest.

We'd been stuck in Diablo for nearly a week. Fortunately
for us, Travis liked to throw money around and had given
Vaughn cash, since he was practicing with the band every
day, which meant we didn't have to rely on his dad's credit
card for everything.

"You ready to party?" Armando asked Vaughn. I
suppressed a yawn. Vaughn had been practicing with the
band until almost three a.m. I'd watched the other guys
carefully, but the girls who hung around seemed willing
blood donors—no compulsion required. Not like Fang. But
I remembered the dead girl from the cave. Maybe they'd
decided to be more careful. I hoped so.

We were hanging out in the tour bus, and it smelled
ripe. The space would have been luxurious if someone had
bothered to clean it occasionally. There were dirty clothes,
take-out boxes with half-eaten moldy food, and glasses
containing suspicious-looking liquid drying on the rim.

"You guys need to clean this place up," I said, then
wished I hadn't. Red eyes turned my way. "Or, I mean,
hire someone."

"Travis's dad will pay for it." Armando chuckled.

"Or we could just get a Bleeder to do it," Travis suggested. "Dad's already paying for the band to cut a demo."

I pitied the sound engineer on that project. And anyone else who had to listen to an entire album of The Drainers' songs.

I was sitting in Vaughn's lap while Natasha was making out with Ozzie at the small table. A couple of girls I didn't recognize sat on either side of Armando. He was feeding them appetizers from a take-out box like they were his pets.

Travis was alone for a change, but his knee jiggled impatiently.

"Travis, do you have a girlfriend?" I asked.

He glanced at me, and then his eyes narrowed. "No, I don't," he said. "Why do you want to know?"

I had hoped to ask about Skyler but didn't want to be obvious about it. Fail. "I—I…"

"She wants to set you up with one of her friends," Vaughn said, saving me.

Travis's attention was diverted when two of the Bleeders got into a fistfight over Armando.

"Why don't you guys quit it?" I asked. They ignored me, and I thought I was going to have to do things the hard way, but Travis stepped in between them, scooped them up, and threw them out the bus doors.

"Hey, I wasn't done with that," Armando said.

Travis lifted his head and inhaled. "There's something familiar in the air tonight."

I realized then I'd forgotten to reapply my perfume-slash-vampire-repellent. I needed to get out of there. Now.

"That's our cue to leave," I said. "Night, all."

When we made our exit, the girls Travis had thrown out were rolling around on the asphalt.

"Should we do something?" Vaughn asked.

"They're Travis's problem," I said. I was too tired to tell those girls they were wasting their time with The Drainers.

I yawned all the way back to the hotel. "These nights are killing me," I said. "I can't remember the last time I saw the sun."

"Me either," Vaughn said. "Maybe we should set an alarm for early. Aim for lunchtime?"

The last few days, we'd been getting up later and later. Yesterday, we didn't stir from bed until almost sunset.

"Can I even go out in the sun?" I asked, finally voicing the thing neither of us had really been mentioning lately. I knew Vaughn had noticed the changes in me, but he hadn't said anything. My stomach tightened, waiting to see what he'd say next.

"You're not a vampire, Tansy. You're a striga vie. A seriously badass striga vie." His warm eyes crinkled at the corners, and he laced his fingers with mine. Some days, it was almost impossible to remember we were just pretending to be a couple. Like now.

I swallowed and whispered, "Thank you."

Sensing the moment was getting tense for me, he changed the subject. "Did you come across any good intel?"

The other Bleeders gossiped a lot whenever Natasha wasn't around. They had scary things to say about girls who followed the band. Girls who disappeared one day. The more hopeful Bleeders thought it meant the girls were finally turned, but I had my doubts.

"Not really. I just have more questions."

"Like what?"

"Why have we never met a Sundowner? The file said they have yellow eyes, but I've never seen one," I said. "I've never even seen a female vampire." Except for Bobbie Jean, but I thought she was more like a half vamp. She'd had Travis's blood but hadn't been drained dry or killed anyone by drinking them dry. And I didn't count myself;

I wasn't a vampire. And I would never take someone's blood forcefully.

"Maybe we have seen one, and we just didn't know it," Vaughn answered.

I shook my head. "I'm getting really good at spotting vampires," I said. "Even when I can't smell them." I'd identified a famous fashion photographer, an ex-president (not one of the good ones, so not exactly a surprise), and a couple of personality-deficient reality stars. "Maybe we'll see a Sundowner at the show tonight."

"The show. Tansy, I'm not sure I can do this," he said. "Perform with The Drainers. The stage fright is better during rehearsals, thanks to your trick—" He cleared his throat. "But I don't think I can do a live gig."

"I know it's risky to go on the road with a band of vampires—"

"No, I mean perform in public. The waiting is only making me more anxious."

"How can I help?" I asked.

"Just stay close, okay?" Vaughn said. "I know you're worried about Skyler, and so am I, but I don't like the way the guys in the band eye you like you're their next meal."

"I don't want to hang out with them, either," I said. "They're ridiculous yet still dangerous. But we have to."

He nodded, then sighed. "Let's go."

I adjusted my black wig and grabbed his hand. Time to rock and roll.

Someone—probably Natasha—had posted that The Drainers would be introducing a special guest drummer while Fang continued to recuperate. When we got to the venue, it was another hole-in-the-wall bar with questionable ID policies, so the place was full of Bleeders.

Packs of girls went in, but I didn't see anyone I knew.

"What are we waiting for?" Vaughn asked.

"Travis isn't here yet," I said.

"Something's wrong," he said. "Travis loves to perform."

"Perform" was a stretch, but I didn't think the band would appreciate me calling him "the guy who made my ears bleed."

We watched the door for another hour, and then, at around one a.m., Natasha stormed in with Travis on her heels, right before the band was scheduled to go on.

"I won't do it," she shouted.

His face flushed with rage, and I thought he was going to hit her, but instead, he shrugged and went backstage.

"That's my cue," Vaughn said. He kissed me quickly. "Wish me luck."

His expression was calm, but when he grabbed his drumsticks, his hands were shaking. I put my hand over his. "You've got this, Vaughn."

The corner of his mouth tipped up, and then he strode onstage.

There was the shrill sound of Bleeders screaming when the band was announced, and then Vaughn started a slow beat.

"Is that a new song?" someone asked. "They sound different."

Yes, they sounded almost decent with Vaughn keeping everyone in time. Travis's lack of singing ability couldn't be helped, but I was surprised to notice that Ozzie and Armando both could play. Travis dropped chords, strutted all over the stage in tight leather pants, and sounded like my neighbor Mrs. Garcia's angry Pomeranian.

Their set consisted of a lot of semi-plagiarized lyrics about blood and death. I thought I recognized an Edgar Allan Poe poem in there somewhere.

And the whole time, I searched the crowd for Skyler, but I didn't see her.

Afterward, the band relaxed in the greenroom with several Bleeders while Gary loaded up all the equipment.

"You should stay on the tour bus with us," Armando said. "Take Fang's bunk."

"Yeah, he's not gonna need it." Ozzie snickered.

I flinched at the mention of Fang's name, but I didn't think anyone noticed. Except Vaughn, who rubbed my back comfortingly.

"Thanks, but my girl likes her privacy," Vaughn said.

That provoked some knowing snickers, but then a couple of Bleeders caught their eyes and the subject was forgotten.

"Where you stashin' that sweet little thing of yours, Trav?" Ozzie asked.

"She's the perfect blend of sweet and tart," Armando said. "Ah, Skyler."

The Bleeder sitting on his lap stood up. "That's what you said about me."

The rest of the band laughed. "Busted, Armando," Travis said. "You need to get some new lines."

Armando ignored the pissed-off groupie. "Where you keeping her?" he continued. "I wouldn't mind a bite of that."

Travis showed his fangs. "Skyler's off-limits." He *could* remember her name after all. "I have plans for her."

I didn't like the sound of that at all.

Chapter Seventeen

Vaughn was right — The Drainers didn't seem to be in a hurry to leave Diablo.

Instead, they rented the top floor of a beachside luxury hotel and then threw a party.

"I tried to get out of this," Vaughn insisted as we walked to the suite.

"Yet we're still headed to the debauchery," I replied. "Debauchery" was an understatement. "It's okay," I reassured Vaughn. "Maybe Skyler will be here."

When we arrived, Gary was at his post guarding the door as a stream of Bleeders walked through, all dressed in skimpy white outfits.

I was in a crappy mood. A party had been the beginning of my problems, but I highly doubted it would be the end to them.

It had been harder than I'd expected to get Travis alone to steal his hair. He was always with someone: Bleeders, the guys in the band, even Gary. And I couldn't just whip out a pair of scissors and aim them casually at a vampire.

Turned out they weren't exactly fond of long, pointy things.

Skyler wasn't in the common area of the hotel suite. She was probably back in one of the bedrooms with Travis.

Armando was behind the bar, mixing drinks with a liberal hand. "What can I get you to drink, my lovely Tiffany?" he asked me, ignoring the three groupies who stood there waiting.

"Just water, thanks," I said. He didn't ask Vaughn what he wanted, so I added, "Water for my boyfriend here, too, please."

Armando's fingertips touched mine when he handed me our bottles. There was blood embedded in his nails, and I repressed the need to wash my hands. "You smell delicious," he said, which I ignored.

Travis and Skyler emerged from one of the bedrooms. Her eyes were glassy, and there was a fresh bite mark on the upper part of her chest, which I could see, since Travis hadn't bothered to pull her top up.

I waited until Travis let go of Skyler, and then, when I thought no one was watching, I pulled her top back on.

When I looked up, Armando was staring at me.

"Vaughn, when are you going to let me take a bite out of your delicious girlfriend?" Armando asked, like I should be flattered.

"How about never?" Vaughn replied.

Ozzie and Travis chuckled like it was the funniest thing Vaughn had ever said. "Armando can be very convincing," Ozzie said. "And he doesn't mind sharing."

"Well, I do," Vaughn said firmly. He had been right about posing as a couple to protect each other from The Drainers and their hangers-on.

Vaughn took my hand and led me to one of the large sofas in the entertainment area. He sat and then pulled me onto his lap. I perched there awkwardly until Armando wandered over, and then I wrapped my arms around Vaughn and draped myself all over him.

I shivered when Armando's eyes met mine. "I think your girlfriend's cold," he said to Vaughn. "Want me to warm her up for you?"

Instead of answering him, Vaughn nuzzled my neck and whispered, "Remember what we talked about."

"You want to kiss me?" I asked in a whisper.

"Is that okay?"

"Yes." The word was barely out of my mouth before his lips were on mine. His arms pulled me tight against his body. As the kiss deepened, I forgot about the vampires who were watching, forgot that it was all for show, forgot everything except for the feel of Vaughn's body next to mine.

He kissed me breathless. We broke apart, gulping air, but seconds later, Vaughn went back in. This kiss went on until one of the guys let out a long whistle. "Get it!"

Even though I was blushing, I stayed on Vaughn's lap.

"I want a kiss," Travis said. "How about it, Tiffany?"

"No way," Vaughn said in a growl.

Travis growled back, low and menacingly. He looked like he would attack Vaughn just for the fun of it.

"Yeah, no way am I kissing you," I said. "I saw that bat video. I know where your mouth's been."

The guys in the band laughed, and the tension left the room, but Travis's eyes followed me on and off for the rest of the night.

• • •

Between practices and gigs, Vaughn was developing hard calluses on his hands. The Drainers had performances scheduled back to back. We didn't want to rouse their suspicions, so he'd made it to every gig.

"We're lucky you don't have to stay on the tour bus with them," I said.

Vaughn made a face. "You're lucky, too. That place is a pit."

Being a vampire-band groupie was nowhere near as fun as I'd imagined it would be. In other words, even more terrible than expected.

The guys talked about themselves. A lot. They reeked like a toxic waste dump simmering in the California sun. And their groupies were mean, probably anemic, and definitely fought constantly among themselves. Still, the girls didn't deserve the treatment the band gave them— especially Travis.

After tonight's performance, the venue had mostly emptied out, except for the band and a few chosen groupies, when Travis and Armando started to argue.

"Mine!" Travis growled, and then he and Armando were rolling around onstage, punching each other as they went. They knocked over a mic stand but kept going, and nobody tried to stop them. Gary scurried around loading the equipment and didn't even look over at the two fighting band members.

Vaughn and I watched them from the table where we sat with Natasha, Skyler, and Alice, who'd become Armando's new favorite.

Finally, the guys stopped fighting and lay on the stage next to each other, panting. One of them would occasionally kick the other one, but they seemed to be cooling off.

"Why do vampires have to be so dramatic?" I said,

yawning. "Anyway, it's past my bedtime."

The guys had gotten to their feet, and it looked like the show was over. "Were they fighting over a girl?" Vaughn asked.

Natasha snorted. "They'd never," she said. "There are too many of us."

"Take them off," Travis suddenly screeched.

"You want them so bad?" Armando asked.

"Yes," Travis said. "They're my favorite pair."

"Fine." Armando's hands went to his waist, and then he shucked off his black leather pants and threw them at Travis, which left Armando standing there in tight boxer briefs and a smile.

Vaughn caught me looking and clapped his hands over my eyes. Objectively, Armando was gorgeous, with long-lashed brown eyes, a square jawline, and a wiry yet muscular body. But he was a creep, and all the pretty in the world couldn't make up for that.

"They're fighting over pants?" I choked out, trying not to giggle.

"But they're leather," Vaughn mocked, quoting an old movie we'd watched a few months ago.

To my surprise, Skyler started to giggle. The dullness in her eyes cleared. "Remember that time my stepmother got into a fight at a Black Friday sale at La Perla?"

I smiled at her, and for a second, it was like we'd never become entangled with the vampires.

Chapter Eighteen

It was still so hot in the bar that my dress was sticking to me. I went outside for some fresh air and spotted the tour bus. There was no one around—not even Gary, who usually spent most of the performances guarding the bus. I wondered what he was guarding. It wasn't like The Drainers would complain if a groupie or ten snuck onto the bus.

Impulsively, I decided to do just that and snoop around. If Gary caught me, I'd tell him I was looking for "Johnny Divine" and hope that he wouldn't mention it to the other guys.

The bus smelled only slightly less disgusting than I'd expected.

I looked around, but I couldn't figure out what Gary had been guarding the last few nights during the gigs. I knew he stood watch over the band while they slept during the day, but they were up most of the night. Two coffins were out and open along the wall. Gary obviously thought the guys would be tuckered out tonight, because two of the coffins were already pulled from the wall recesses and ready for occupancy.

Travis probably stored his coffin in the bedroom in the back. I'd bet the sleek burnished mahogany number was Armando's and the one with all the band stickers was Ozzie's.

There were warehouse-size tubs of licorice and some goblets with dried flecks of something I didn't want to think about too closely, but nothing really stood out.

I was getting ready to leave when I heard a muffled sound. I froze and listened. It came again, louder this time. A cry for help.

I'd looked everywhere, except in a closet in the kitchen area that I'd assumed contained cleaning supplies that never left the shelf.

I was running out of time before the band got here, but something made me open the door. A terrified girl, her hands and feet bound and her mouth duct-taped, looked up at me.

I heard voices and knew I had to go, but I couldn't leave her.

She barely had room to move at all, and the closet was dark and smelly. The knots were so tight that I couldn't undo them. When my fangs extended, she started to thrash.

"Please," I said. "I want to help, but you have to hold still." I cut the ropes and then started to remove the tape. "This is going to hurt. I'm sorry."

She fell over trying to get away from me. I didn't try to touch her, even though I didn't like leaving her on the dirty floor of the bus.

"I want to help you. What's your name?" I asked.

"It's Ruth," she said. Her throat sounded sore. She'd probably spent some time screaming.

"How long have you been here?"

"A couple of days, I think," she replied. "I heard them. They were going to h-hunt me."

"Hunt you? Like for sport?"

She nodded. "The blond singer said he was bored, and that creepy roadie promised they'd take me to the woods and the band could hunt me." She paused, her throat working, then added, "They weren't going to let me go, were they?"

My stomach roiled, but I told her the truth. "No, they weren't."

Her shoulders shook from her sobs. I put an arm around her and helped her to her feet.

"Can you walk?" I asked. "We have to get you out of here."

We'd made it down the bus stairs when I heard footsteps. "Ruth, roll under the bus," I whispered. "Now!" Thankfully, she listened to me and was out of my sight in a flash.

"What are you doing?" Gary asked me.

"None of your business, Rennie," I said, playing the part of the uppity girlfriend. "But if you must know, I'm waiting for my boyfriend. The drummer, remember?"

"They're still finishing packing up," he replied. "Why don't you go wait inside?"

I did as he asked, but I couldn't help but look back. Gary stood in front of the bus, watching me.

I wasn't sure if Ruth was still under the bus or if she'd managed to get away, but the next day, there was a small article about an unnamed girl wandering Diablo, not remembering what happened to her—but the girl had bite marks on her neck and rope burns on her wrists.

Ruth had made it.

More girls always came, but I had helped one person, and tonight, that was enough.

. . .

We'd been cooped up in the hotel room for too long, so while The Drainers were tucked away in their coffins, Vaughn and I decided to enjoy some quality daylight.

"I need lavender oil and a few other things," I said. We'd been in such a rush to go after Skyler that I hadn't thought to bring anything I needed for a few of the spells.

"Think we should bother with our disguises?" he asked.

"I can't stand another minute of that wig," I replied. "It itches. We can buy some big hats at one of the souvenir shops."

After our hat purchases, I spotted an aromatherapy shop, and we found several of the items on my list.

Vaughn, who had insisted on paying for my supplies, had just tucked his wallet away when I spotted Gary walking into the store.

I grabbed Vaughn's hands and tugged him toward the back of the store. "Hurry," I hissed, but Gary headed our way.

Had he recognized us, or was he just browsing?

There was a door near the back that was either a bathroom or a supply closet. We hurried inside and closed the door. Clearly a supply closet.

Once we were out of sight, Vaughn said, "That was close."

Silence descended, and you could have cut the awkward with a knife.

I figured I should make conversation. Because if I didn't, my mind would start to think up all the other ways we could spend some time.

"You, uh… You never said why you and Ashley broke

up," I started. Segue Girl, I was not.

He didn't answer my question. Instead, he asked one of his own. "Why did you and College Boy break up?"

The question threw me for a minute, but then I realized he was talking about the guy I didn't like to talk about. Or think of.

"Do you mean Oliver?" I said. "We went on one date."

"Ashley said that you and College Boy were serious," he countered.

"Ashley and I aren't friends," I said bluntly. "Why would you think she knew anything about my love life?"

"She said *serious*," he said. His eyes didn't meet mine, though, and there was a flush on his cheeks like he was embarrassed. "You know…" he added.

"No, I don't know," I said. I scowled at him. "Why don't you explain it to me?"

"Ashley said that you and that guy had sex," he blurted out.

Ashley, the Queen of Passive-Aggressive Land, had lied to Vaughn. About me.

I narrowed my eyes at him. "And you just took her word for it? Didn't ask me?" I ran my fingers through my hair, wishing I could wrap them around her delicate neck and squeeze.

Or maybe around Vaughn's for listening to her.

"First of all, it's none of Ashley's business who I sleep with," I said. "Or yours."

He flinched at my harsh tone. "I didn't think she'd have any reason to lie," he said.

"You didn't wonder how Ashley knew this particular bit of information about my sexual history?" My voice was getting louder, even though we were supposed to be quiet in the closet. "Or why she felt the need to share such a personal tidbit with you?"

"I—I," he stuttered. "Tansy, I'm sorry."

"Gee, Sheridan, thanks. She told you I hooked up with a guy I barely knew, and you bought it. Didn't even ask me about it."

"But why would she do that?"

This guy. I couldn't even deal with him right now. I turned my back on him. "I'm tired—let's just go back to the hotel. Gary's probably gone by now."

"I want to talk about this," he said.

"Oh, *now* you want to talk?"

"What did I say that made you so mad?"

I still couldn't look at him. I was too angry. "You could have asked me," I said.

"No, I couldn't," he said.

"Why not?" I asked. I crossed my arms over my chest.

"Jesus, Tansy," Vaughn said. "I was *jealous*."

I stared at him, my heart pounding into my throat. "You never acted any different."

He sighed. "When Ashley told me about that guy—"

"Ashley's a liar," I said.

He looked down at his hands. "She manipulated me," he finally said. "I never thought—"

"Obviously, you never thought," I snapped.

"For the record, I don't care if you've hooked up with someone," he said. "I just...I just cared that it wasn't me."

What now?

"Ashley said you'd probably picked up on how I felt about you and were trying to spare my feelings."

"How you felt about me?" I repeated, stunned. This whole time, Vaughn liked me. He liked me the way I liked him.

"I know we've just been pretending," Vaughn started.

"But for me…it's real."

My heart felt like it was going to pound out of my chest. "Vaughn…if you liked me so much, why didn't you ever say anything before now?"

"Because I knew you didn't feel that way about me," he replied.

"You *knew*, huh?"

I'd spent all that time agonizing over his relationship with Ashley, and I'd done it secretly. I hadn't even talked to Skyler about it because I didn't want to put her in the middle. I would never have made a move on him when he had a girlfriend, either, but there'd been times when we were both single—like now.

There was no time like the present. While we were in a supply closet.

His gorgeous eyes were vulnerable, uncertain, and a little hopeful. "Was she wrong?"

"She was so, *so* wrong," I said.

The smile he gave me was so sweet that it made my heart hurt. Until Vaughn opened his arms and I went into them.

"Vaughn, next time you want to know something, ask me, okay?"

"Okay," he said. "I want to talk to you about everything. I should have told you how I feel. Do you want to go out with me?" he asked. "I want to be—real."

I took his face in my hands and kissed him. His lips parted, and I snuck my tongue in, a little oral exclamation point to illustrate how much I'd wanted to kiss him.

We eventually broke apart, both breathing heavily. Vaughn was smiling and a little flushed.

"Do you believe me?" I asked.

"Yes," he said, clearing his throat. "Your, ah, enthusiasm

convinced me." I punched him in the arm, but his smile didn't dim.

This next bit was bound to be a mood-killer, but I needed to get it out. "Not that it's any of your business, but I didn't have sex with College Boy."

He had a neutral expression, so I kept going.

"I want my first time to be with someone I care about and trust," I said. "He didn't see it the same way and tried to force the issue."

Vaughn's eyebrows were doing something weird. "He tried to force you?"

I wasn't sure I'd ever seen Vaughn this pissed off before. Grumpy, sure, but right now his face was pure fury.

I put a hand on his shoulder. "It's okay," I said. "I kneed him in the balls and broke his nose. That changed his mind." I was grateful for the self-defense lessons the Old Crones Book Club had given Skyler and me. And I was grateful I'd broken that college boy's nose. "The end."

Vaughn finally said, "I want my first time to be with someone I care about and trust, too."

Wait, what? I'd assumed that he and Ashley had been visiting the Trojan horse for a long time.

"You and Ashley didn't...?"

He blushed but shook his head.

I blushed, too. "We really should get back."

"You're right," he said. "And, Tansy, I'm glad we had this talk about us."

"So there's an us?" I asked. I knew he wanted there to be, but we hadn't defined the relationship yet.

He chuckled. "Oh, there's definitely an us. No more wasting time."

Chapter Nineteen

Another show was finally over. I'd learned the hard way that the band—except for Vaughn, of course—always fed before and after a performance. Beforehand in order to look humanish, and afterward because they were "thirsty."

I was in no mood for an after-party, but Travis had insisted Vaughn attend for "band bonding." I was hopeful that I'd see Skyler, so I'd agreed, which also had the added benefit that Travis didn't pout like a bloodthirsty toddler. I was tired of waiting. Tonight was the night I was going to cut that asshole's hair and get my best friend out of here.

Travis and the guys seemed to have finally forgotten about Fang. I hadn't wanted to kill him, but part of me thought that justice had been served. It wasn't like there was a jail for predator vampires.

At least I didn't think there was. It was hard enough to make sure the regular kinds of predators were locked up, which was made obvious by the number of creepers still walking the streets.

When we got to the party, everything felt wrong. There

must have been at least a hundred or so people there, but no one was talking. Travis and his band weren't even playing, just standing around on a makeshift platform. He was wearing a flowy white shirt, which was stained with either taco sauce or dried blood.

I scanned the crowd and finally spotted Skyler, her long dark hair in braids, which she always told me she hated because she said it made her face look too round. She was wearing a white sundress that fell to her ankles. Her only accessory was Travis, hanging on her arm, which was another thing unlike Sky. She never went anywhere without her diamond studs and her necklace that matched mine.

She didn't see me, but I couldn't keep my eyes from her. She had violet bruises under her eyes and was so pale, she looked see-through. She was like a Skyler-shaped husk, hollowed out and empty.

"What now?" Vaughn asked.

"We wait until Travis is distracted," I said.

"You have a plan?"

"I want to rip his heart out," I confessed. "But I'm not sure he has one. I need to be able to get close enough to him that I can steal a lock of his hair without him noticing. Do you think I could bribe a Bleeder to get it for me?"

Vaughn shook his head. "If you ask a Bleeder, they'll go right to Travis."

He was right.

Travis bent to whisper something in her ear, then nuzzled her neck. Her legs buckled under her, but he held her in one hand. Was he *feeding* on my best friend? Right in front of *everybody*?

I made my way through the crowd toward them.

"Tansy, there's no way we can get her out safely if you confront Travis right now," Vaughn said. "Look around you."

As I did, someone knocked into me hard. "Who're you?" she asked, looking me up and down. I recognized the intimidation tactic from middle school and put my hand on my hip.

"Who are *you*?" I asked right back.

Her eyes flared yellow, and I realized I'd finally met a Sundowner. She looked and smelled differently than the Bleeders, the humans who were in thrall to a vampire but who hadn't gone all the way over to the dark side. Sundowners had a just-starting-to-rot smell, like a refrigerator in need of a good cleaning instead of the totally rank smell the guys wafted my way.

She smiled at me, her fangs undersize and dull. "I'm Temple."

"Well, Temple the Sundowner," I said, and she flinched in surprise. "I'm Tiffany." I smiled back, and Vaughn nudged me.

"Tif, we need to get backstage now," he said, practically dragging me away.

"What's the matter?" I asked him as soon as we were out of earshot.

"Your fangs were showing," he said.

I slapped a hand over my mouth. "Oops," I said. "That Sundowner just made me so mad."

"Do you think there are more here?"

From what I could spot in the crowd, there were only a handful of them, but they were hollow-eyed and looked at Bleeders like they were a herd of cows and they were picking out which steak they were going to eat. Not all the way vampire, though. They didn't move as quickly as the guys in the band, and their fangs, which they flashed proudly, were undersize and duller than the vampires' razor-sharp teeth.

"I can try a quick healing spell on Skyler again," I said. "She doesn't look very good."

"Wait until she goes to the bathroom or something," he said. "Uh, there are lots of Bleeders here tonight, too. We'll wait until he's distracted."

Skyler and Travis headed for a roped-off area, clearly meant for VIPs only. When I got a few feet away, a couple of burly bodyguards growled at me, but then one of them seemed to recognize Vaughn.

I snapped "move" at them, and they did, shooting a look at Travis, who gave a short nod. I ignored him and concentrated on Skyler. She looked awful. Up close, I could see that her white maxi sundress was stained in places with dried blood. Her brown eyes were vacant. I wasn't sure she even knew where she was.

How long had Travis been stealing pieces of my best friend? Too long.

We sat at a booth. It was just Travis, Skyler, Vaughn, and me. Skyler was so out of it that she kept sliding down to the floor. Travis would remember to catch her before she fell—most of the time.

"Where are the rest of the guys?" Vaughn finally asked.

Travis smirked. "They'll be along. They're busy… making friends."

"I just threw up a little bit in my mouth," I whispered to Vaughn.

He slung a casual arm around me and pulled me closer.

Skyler's fuzzy gaze sharpened for a moment. "Tan?"

For the first time, I was grateful for Travis's inability to remember anyone's names.

"Uh, yeah. I'm Tiffany. Skyler, want to go to the little girls' room with me?" I asked, wincing inwardly. I'd never in my life called the bathroom that, not even when I *was* a little girl. "Please?" I added.

I didn't want to risk a direct order. Even a clueless wonder like Travis might notice someone doing a little witchcraft right in front of him. Or was it my vampire side? I forget.

I tugged on her hand, but she resisted. Travis whispered in her ear again, and she got up and followed me, like a good little girlfriend/groupie/blood bank.

Once we were inside the one-stall bathroom, which needed a serious cleaning, I asked her, "Do you even know who I am?"

"You're Johnny Divine's girlfriend," she said.

"Did he suck out your memory along with your red blood cells?" I asked. Harsh, but I was frustrated. We were surrounded by vampires and vampire wannabes, and Skyler showed no indication she would ever leave Travis.

"Jesus, Tansy, don't be such a bitch," she snapped.

My mouth opened. "You knew who I was?"

She nodded. "You and Vaughn. But Travis isn't happy with you—the real you, I mean."

"You were protecting us," I said, softening toward her. "Okay, I'm going to do one quick spell. It'll help you heal."

"You think you're smarter than he is," she said. "But you're not. After you healed me last time, he knew."

"How did he know?"

She shrugged. "My blood, I guess. It tasted different."

"You can't keep on like this," I said. "I'll do it anyway. Just avoid him for a few days." Or until I figured out how to get him alone. The idea sickened me, but I knew it was what I'd have to do. One bite from Travis had changed my whole life. What might happen if he got close enough to figure out who I really was?

"Forget it," she said. "Just go home."

"Not without trying to help you," I said. "Please, Skyler. You're my best friend. You know me better than anyone — you know I'd never leave without you."

Her gaze turned scornful. "I do," she said. "And that's why I know you won't do anything to stop me. You're still that scared little girl who got dumped off at your grandma's house. And that's all you'll ever be."

Hateful words poured from her mouth, but her eyes flickered, desperate and afraid.

"Let me help you," I said.

"You want to help me?" she asked. "Leave me alone. Quit acting like you know what I want."

I'd been raised by a tribe of strong women. Women who raised one another up instead of tearing one another down. That was the only reason the hateful, angry words trembling on my tongue didn't spew out of my mouth.

I wanted to blast her with all of them, but instead, I turned and left her there, surrounded by vampires.

I went back to Vaughn, who was sitting at the booth.

Skyler stumbled in behind me.

"We're leaving," I said sharply.

He stood. "What's wrong?"

At the last minute, I remembered our cover and decided on Jealous Girlfriend 101 to get us out of there. I may have channeled his ex a bit. "I saw how you were looking at her."

"Who?" Vaughn looked truly lost.

"Her," I replied, tossing my head at Skyler.

Skyler slid into the booth next to Travis and licked his ear, watching for my reaction the whole time.

I wheeled around so I didn't have to look at her. "Let's go," I told Vaughn and didn't even wait for his reply.

The sound of Travis's laughter accompanied our retreat.

As soon as I was out of their view, I was crying so hard

that I couldn't see in front of me. But then there were hands on my hips, guiding me through the crowd.

"Vaughn?" I sobbed out his name.

"Shh," he said. "Don't cry, please, Tansy."

"I-I'm n-not," I said, clearly blubbering.

Once we were outside, he hugged me for a long minute. Vaughn gave the best hugs, and no matter how scared and frustrated I was, it calmed me.

I told him what Skyler had said to me.

My tears were finally drying when he said, "You know she didn't mean it. That wasn't Sky."

"Then what was it?"

"She's lashing out," he said. "She's hurting, so she wants you to hurt, too."

"You're right. That wasn't Skyler. She'd never talk like that to me."

"Or to anyone," he added.

I nodded. Everyone liked Sky. She was one of the most popular people in school, and not mean-girl popularity. She was kind, thoughtful, and funny. I needed to remember that.

His gray eyes had turned storm dark. "Let's get out of here."

Angry Vaughn was hot. I'd never seen him like this before; he was the most even-tempered person I knew.

I'd known it would be difficult to convince Skyler to leave the band, but I'd never guessed it would be this hard. I'd underestimated the hold Travis had on her.

But I wouldn't make that mistake again.

When we were back at the hotel, Vaughn handed me one of his T-shirts and, because he knew I hated cold feet, a pair of comfy socks (and honestly, this hotel was nice, but who knew what bodily fluids had ended up on the floor).

I went into the bathroom, still hiccupping with sobs,

and changed. Then I splashed cold water on my face. Then I cried some more. I was sick of restaurant food, I was sick of The Drainers and their Bleeder groupies, and most of all, I was sick of my best friend who, poisoned or not, had said that she loved me and then ripped me to shreds.

Chapter Twenty

The next night, Vaughn drove us to a performance at a seedy club just outside of Diablo called Alexa's Bar.

Vaughn turned down a narrow two-lane highway until we reached the parking lot. We'd arrived early, but there were already a bunch of cars there.

I was wearing another one of my disguises, same black wig, different *dressing like the drummer's girlfriend* outfit.

"This is where you're performing?" I asked. The building looked like a strong gust of wind would knock it over, and the paint was faded and peeling.

There was a bouncer at the door. "Twenty bucks," he said in a bored tone. He didn't seem to know or care that we were underage.

"We're with the band," Vaughn said. The guy frowned, looking squinty-eyed at the both of us before waving us through.

The walls were wallpapered in red velvet, the carpet a faded red with unidentifiable stains. A scarred black bar ran along the end of one wall, and the place was ripe with perspiration and cheap beer.

There were a lot of people crammed into the small space. I recognized some of them as Bleeders.

The carpet felt tacky when we walked, and I was glad I'd decided against sandals and instead had paired low-top purple Converse with a black maxi dress. I looked like a crow in a sea of white doves, since there were a lot of Bleeders in their *let's get bloody* white outfits.

"I don't see Skyler," I said fretfully. I thought I caught a glimpse of Bobbie Jean in the crowd, but she disappeared before I could talk to her.

I was running out of ideas. I'd thought that being face-to-face with Skyler would have given me the opportunity to break the hold Travis had on her. Or that our friendship would be some magical cure. But it wasn't. Sometimes, friendship wasn't enough to save someone.

Part of me wanted to give up on my best friend—just go home and leave her to her fate. But I could never do that—not to her or all the other victims here—so instead, I followed Vaughn backstage, into a teeny-tiny dressing room marked with his name.

"Don't you have a show to get ready for?" I teased. "What's your pre-show process? Meditation?"

"Kissing my girlfriend," he said. There was barely enough room for the two of us, but he didn't seem to mind as he pressed up against me and kissed me. "For luck," he said.

When he released me, I noticed a package with a note on it on the only chair. "Looks like someone left you a present."

Vaughn reached for it and read the note before opening it slowly. "The guys expect me to wear this tonight," he said, unfolding a sleeveless black tee.

"It doesn't seem so bad," I said, but then I saw the lettering. *I DO bite* was written in block letters under the band's name.

"Ugh," I said. "Travis had to be the one who thought that one up."

"They've been making noises about how I'm the only human in the band," he said. "And how they should change that."

I sucked in a breath. "It's not safe for you to be alone with them."

Vaughn shrugged off my concern. "Anything for Sky." He stripped off the shirt he was wearing, and I zeroed in on his bare chest. Vaughn was so ripped. God, his body was a thing of beauty.

The door opened without warning, and Travis appeared. He put the STD in stupid, but he'd been paying attention lately. Too much attention.

"Am I interrupting something?" he asked with a sly grin that told me he'd hoped he was.

"Not at all," I replied at the same time that Vaughn growled, "Yes."

Travis inhaled deeply. "It smells good in here," he said. "Like a strawberry milkshake."

I flinched. Travis smiled at me, his fangs flashing.

"It's probably my shampoo," I said. "Lots of girls use strawberry shampoo."

"Not like this," Travis replied. "It's like strawberries and vanilla and—" His long pause made me shift on my feet, but the next word made me freeze. "Magic."

With that mic drop, he turned to Vaughn. "Get your ass moving. We have a show to do."

After Travis left, I met Vaughn's eyes. "I screwed up. I don't think my perfume is working anymore."

"You think our cover is blown?" he asked.

I nodded. "I'm afraid so."

But everything seemed normal at the gig. I left Vaughn backstage and joined the audience.

Predictably, there were a bunch of females gathered around an empty stage. Most of them wore white. And they were whispering about me. The words were clear over the clank of the busboys clearing dishes, the server who was chewing gum, and the roadie unloading instruments onstage.

"What's she doing here?" Natasha hissed as she stared right at me. I stared back.

She had her shiny black hair down but held away from her neck by two silver barrettes. Her outfit was the skimpiest I'd ever seen. Her white dress was basically two strips of cloth connected by a gold chain.

It wasn't my business what she wore, but it made me queasy when I realized she was dressed that way in order to show off her bite marks.

I shot a look at Natasha. "I can hear you, you know."

She smirked at me. "I know." And then she flounced away.

"Natasha's not happy with you," Rose said. I hadn't even noticed she was there. Spooky.

Bobbie Jean leaned in and spoke in my ear. "She and Thorn have been following you since you got here. Where's Natasha?"

"Don't know where the number one Bleeder is," I said. "She's probably doing something for The Drainers'

Instagram feed."

"I'll be right back," Bobbie Jean said, and then I lost sight of her in the crowd. I had to admit I was happy that Rose and Thorn were here because the Bleeders surrounding me looked like they'd rip me limb from limb and smile while they did it. Jealousy, I guess, because I was dating a band member?

Or something else?

Bobbie Jean appeared a few minutes later.

"Where were you?" I asked.

"In the bathroom," she replied. Something about the way she said it made me nervous.

"What were you doing in there?"

"The usual," she drawled.

"I thought you were trying to give us the slip." Stress was making me paranoid. Bobbie Jean had been completely forthcoming with me. Hadn't she?

She shook her head. "I just really had to pee."

I was sweating. The room was crowded, and as bodies pressed in, I felt light-headed.

"Why are you so consumed by that girl? Why do you want to help someone who doesn't want your help?" Bobbie Jean's voice was sharp.

"Because she's my friend—my best friend," I replied. "She needs my help whether she wants it or not. And maybe I can help some of the others, too."

"You can't save everyone, Tansy," she said.

"I can try," I replied.

The lights went off, and then a laser show started. The band took the stage to the roar of the crowd. Travis held up his hands, and two balls of vampire fire appeared to float in the air. As the crowd's cheers grew louder, the flames went higher. Then he clenched his fists and the flames went out, and another kind of noise began when the band started to play.

I stood in the front, surrounded by girls in skimpy white outfits, and admired the way Vaughn's arms flexed as he kept the beat.

After about an hour, the band took a break and disappeared into the back room.

"The new drummer's hot," one of the Bleeders said.

"He has a girlfriend," I snapped.

"So?"

"So that girlfriend is me," I said.

"Drummer's off-limits. Got it," she said quickly and dragged her friend to the other side of the stage.

The band came back onstage, and the screaming began again. And I wasn't talking about from the audience. The definition of a cacophony was taking place in front of me, and people were convinced it was music.

I watched Vaughn; he looked like he was in pain, but I couldn't really blame him.

Travis screamed into a microphone right next to him, so Vaughn was getting an earful of pitchy wailing.

"They sound worse than last time." I spoke in Bobbie Jean's ear, but the music was deafening, so I doubted she could hear me.

Thorn shoved her way next to me. "Maybe earplugs will help." I handed a set to her. "He mesmerizes them with music," I said. "Didn't you know?"

She frowned but took the earplugs. I put my set in. Immune or not, I didn't want to hear Travis making "music."

After I rescued Skyler, maybe she could help me figure out a way to stop the band for good. I adjusted them in my ears to make sure they blocked out most of the sound.

I thought I caught a glimpse of Skyler right by the

stage, but by the time I'd elbowed my way to the front, she was gone.

Travis almost dropped his guitar, which would have been a bonus, but he recovered quickly.

At every gig, I'd noticed the guys in the band—excluding Vaughn, of course—all picked out a few girls from the audience, and tonight was no exception. Gary scurried around to escort the twelve girls (blech, twelve girls for three guys) to the back.

The band left the stage, and I thought my ears might get a rest, but the girls in white started to clap and shout.

Please, no encore, I begged, but after a few minutes, Travis came back looking as engorged with blood as a summer tick. There was an encore. A long, loud, painful encore.

When it was finally over, I went to the bathroom and sprayed on a new cloud of scent-concealing perfume and took a few deep, cleansing breaths.

I headed to the VIP area, which was cordoned off by velvet ropes and guarded by a big guy with a judgy expression. The band was already lounging on some couches in the back. The bouncer stepped in front of me and tried to stop me from entering.

I heaved a long sigh. "I'm with the band," I said.

Chapter Twenty-One

When I finally made it through the velvet rope to the VIP section, the guys were all sitting around in chairs with various Bleeders draped over them. I tried not to grimace when I saw Ozzie nibbling on Natasha's neck.

My heart thumped when I realized it was Skyler on Travis's lap. Her hair was matted and tangled, and her body was a mass of bruises and bite marks even worse than the ones I'd seen before.

Vaughn sat at one end of a sofa. There was a girl at the other end, but she was inching closer. She had her neck tilted to one side, like she was offering it to Vaughn. Did she think he was a vampire, too?

I walked over and sat in his lap, really trying to sell the whole girlfriend thing. Also because I liked being close to him.

"Baby," he said. "What took you so long?" The panicked look on his face told me he was aware of the girl trying to get him to notice her.

I leaned in, nuzzled his neck, and whispered, "I'm going to try to get what we need tonight."

Vaughn's arms tightened around me, but Travis's loud voice drew my attention away. "Did I tell you guys that Johnny has been keeping something from us?"

Ozzie and Armando both stopped what they were doing. "Yeah? What?"

There was suspicion in their eyes, and it didn't lessen when Travis explained, "Johnny here knows my Schuler," he said. "She's been telling me all about it."

"I do know *Skyler*," Vaughn said evenly. "Tiff and I both do. We go to the same high school. There are tons of kids at our school, but I've seen her around." It wasn't a lie.

Travis deflated. He'd obviously thought we'd deny it or something.

"Did she say anything else?" I asked. *Like my grand-mother is a witch? Or that I am?*

"I don't pick girls for their conversational skills," he said, snickering.

I raised an eyebrow. "Then what do you pick them for?"

"For the way their blood tastes," he said.

I tried to keep any expression from my face. "There's a difference?"

"Hell, yeah," Ozzie said. "I'm a B-positive man myself."

"I like a good A," Armando chimed in. "But I'm not fussy."

"He's like a blood bank." Travis snorted. "He takes all types of donations."

"What about you?" I asked, then wished I hadn't when Travis said, "I like O negative. But I had blood from a redheaded witch once that was the most delicious thing I've ever tasted."

I froze. Had he figured out who I was?

"Jesus, Travis," Ozzie said. "Quit obsessing about the witch."

"I know a witch," Sky said drowsily.

His eyes gleamed red. "That's right, baby," he said. "Tell me all about her." He crooned it.

"It's Granny," Skyler said. "Granny used to make me apricot crostata when I was little and was missing my mommy."

Travis relaxed. "I've never bitten anyone's grandma."

"Ease up on your girl, Travis," Ozzie said. "I think she's a quart low."

I had to do something before Skyler started to tell Travis everything about my grandmother and me.

"Baby," I said loudly to Vaughn. "I want to be alone with you."

Vaughn's eyebrows rose. "I thought we were going to hang out with the guys tonight."

The band members were watching us now, but I didn't want them to remember what they'd been talking about moments before.

He'd ditched the gross vamp tee and changed into a navy shirt. I put my hands on the inside of Vaughn's button-down shirt and started undoing the buttons. "Now, baby," I pseudo-whispered. My fingers lingered because touching his smooth skin was exhilarating, even in a room full of vampires.

Our eyes met, and he must have seen the panic in mine, because Vaughn kissed me gently on the lips and stood, then hoisted me into his arms. "We'll be back." I wrapped my arms and legs around him.

Travis snickered. "We don't mind a little show."

He was so disgusting.

"She's shy," Vaughn said.

I buried my face in Vaughn's neck, just so I wouldn't say something I'd regret. Then it occurred to me what I had to do.

"Don't be mad," I whispered to him and slid out of his arms.

And then I asked Travis to dance. "I love this song," I said. "Come dance with me."

His brow furrowed before a slow grin covered his face. "Your girl's getting tired of you, Johnny. I told you, they can't resist me for long."

I dug into my purse and pretended to search for my lipstick, but instead palmed the folding scissors and slid them into the sleeve of my top.

I ignored Vaughn's pissed-off expression, and I led Travis onto the dance floor.

It was a risk getting this close to Travis, but I was desperate. "Thank god the DJ is on now," I said.

Travis frowned at me. "Don't you like our music?"

"Of course I do," I lied. "I just meant that since you're not onstage, it gives me the opportunity to dance with you."

A slow song started, and Travis grabbed me and held me in a tight grip. Up close, the smell of decay and old blood was overwhelming, but I tried not to let my distaste show.

I put my arms around his neck and slid the scissors from my sleeve but fumbled and almost dropped them. I caught them before they hit him, but it drew his attention. "What are you doing?" he said, shouting over the music.

Sweat poured off me. This was my only chance.

"I love your hair," I cooed, stroking a promising lock with my other hand and grasping the scissors with the other.

When Travis's hands started to wander, I snipped, catching the long strands. But now what was I supposed to do with them?

"Can I cut in?" Vaughn said.

"What? No," Travis said.

"Oh, but I have to give your other fans a chance," I said and moved quickly into Vaughn's arms.

Travis looked like he might argue, but the song ended, which seemed to galvanize him. Without another word, he strode off toward the DJ booth.

"What the hell were you thinking?" Vaughn growled.

"I was running out of chances to get a lock of his hair," I said. "But I did it."

"He had his hands all over you," Vaughn growled.

"It wasn't great," I admitted. "But now I have what we need for the spell, except for the filet of fenny snake." That had to be easier to get than a lock of vampire hair.

"If he touches you again, I'm going to knock him out," Vaughn grunted, but handed me my clutch, so I guessed he was done being grumpy. I grabbed a plastic baggie and placed the vampire's hair into it before shutting it back into my purse.

Travis said something to the DJ, and she handed him the microphone. "Baby, come up here," he said.

A couple of girls, including Natasha, started forward, but he waved them off. "Schuler, where are you?"

A spotlight panned over the crowd, and then I saw her. Skyler, looking like she was being held up by invisible men who were moving her arms and legs, walked to where the DJ booth was.

"What's he doing?" I asked Vaughn.

"He does this at special shows," a girl nearby said. "He performs a magic trick."

"Magic? What kind of magic?"

"He really likes fire," she said. "He calls it vampire fire."

Sky was now standing next to Travis.

He waved his hand theatrically, and then a small blue flame danced in the palm of his hand.

There was no expression on her face—not even when Travis snapped his fingers and ordered her to touch the flame. Sky's hand passed over the flame, and her mouth opened in a silent scream, but she didn't say anything.

"That had to hurt." The girl next to me winced. "At the last show, the girl ended up in the emergency room."

I had to do something. I had to put the fire out.

What was Travis doing?

My mind went blank. I couldn't remember anything Granny had taught me. Instead, *Expecto Patronum* ran through my brain on repeat. For the first time, I regretted my love of Harry Potter.

"Enough!" I finally shouted, trying to clear my brain of my childhood favorite.

Then the overhead sprinklers went on and everyone started screaming and running. The only light was the red EXIT sign, but I didn't move toward it.

Enough was enough. I wasn't leaving without Skyler.

Vaughn used his phone as a flashlight. "C'mon, Sky has to be around here somewhere."

He was right. "You look upstairs," I told him.

"We shouldn't separate," he said.

"There's no time," I argued. "We'll cover more ground if we go in different directions."

He nodded and then merged into the crowd. He made it to the stairs and then disappeared.

I pushed against the exiting crowd, but apparently

Bleeders, Drainers, and baby vamps didn't like to get wet. They were stampeding toward the exit.

Bodies flowed past me. Someone stomped on my foot, and I swore. I shoved a guy out of my way and managed to jump on top of the bar to scan for Skyler, but I didn't see her.

A girl let out a long scream. She'd fallen, but another girl yanked her up and helped her move out of the way.

Before long, the club had emptied out. We were too late.

Chapter Twenty-Two

Vaughn made his way back downstairs. We searched the entire first floor, but it was empty.

I wanted to punch a wall. I couldn't stand the thought of Skyler with him.

"Maybe Sky's still here," Vaughn said.

"We'll search the rest of the club," I decided. "You stay down here this time."

Upstairs, I searched until I found an unmarked door open just a crack.

Inside sat two guys, one with a hipster mustache and too much cologne, the other an acne-faced teen. And they weren't alone. I'd finally found Skyler, but she was in bad shape, with several fresh-looking bite marks. There was new and dried blood all over her clothes.

It made me want to gag.

She sat on a crusty-looking sofa between the two vampires.

They'd hurt my best friend. Turned her into the scared, quivering thing before me.

I took her into my arms and rocked her gently, trying not to touch the bruises and bite marks on her body, but there were so many of them.

I closed my eyes, but all I could see was my best friend's pain. The sight of her made me want to scream the house down.

"Travis said we could," Mustache muttered. My eyes snapped open, and whatever he saw in them made him cower. "Sh-she wanted it," he added.

I put Skyler down on the couch gently before I advanced on him. "Say that again," I said.

There was a tornado in my mind, whirling and destructive.

"She—" But he never got the rest out, because I stabbed him in the heart with Fang's drumstick.

I stared down at his unmoving form. "That's the last time you'll listen to Travis."

I didn't expect the dead man to turn to ash, like in the movies, and just like Fang, he leaked black goo all over the tacky carpet. The smell was horrific, so I put a hand over my nose and tried to breathe through my mouth.

I turned to the remaining vampire. "What's your name?"

"My n-name?" he asked, like he'd never heard the question before. My eyes narrowed, and he added quickly, "It's Leonard."

"Well, Leonard," I said. "Skyler is off-limits. Upon pain of death. Spread the word. You understand?"

"Yes," he replied.

"Don't move," I said. I took my phone out of my back pocket and texted Vaughn, who was searching the kitchens and storage areas. I stared at them while we waited. Soon enough, I heard Vaughn's footsteps pounding up the stairs.

"Thank god," he said. Then he saw her and swore under his breath. "What did they do to her?"

Leonard didn't answer the question. He just grabbed his keys. "Good luck. From the look of her, she only has a few hours."

"A few hours before what?" Vaughn asked.

"You bunch truly are babes in the wood," Leonard said. "You have a few hours before she goes apeshit and tries to eat one of you."

My wig itched, and I ripped it off my head. There was no sense in hiding behind my groupie-girlfriend disguise anymore. We were busted anyway the second I used my power to kill Mustache.

"Now, Leonard." A voice like a cat's claw, swift and bloody, interrupted our conversation from the doorway. "Why don't you introduce me to our guests?"

I didn't think the vampire could get any whiter, but the sound of the voice turned him even paler.

We all swiveled and stared at our company. The newcomer stood in the doorway, flanked by Travis and the rest of the band members. He looked like a fifty-five-year-old accountant, dressed in a neat suit and tie. Except for his deathly pallor and his tie printed with what looked like little bats, he resembled Granny's favorite beau, who was a CPA.

"K-Kral?" Leonard stuttered out.

"Who are you?" I asked.

"Jure Grando at your service," the man said. His eyes were like a portal to hell, all flames and screaming and the torture of dead souls. I forced myself not to shudder.

"What do you want?" I snapped.

"Are you a vampire, too?" Sky asked. "Like Dracula?"

It was the first thing she'd said since we'd found her.

Jure's lip curled. "That poseur? Never. He was a pale imitation."

"See what he did there?" I snickered sarcastically until his black eyes turned to me.

"I thought Leonard called you Kral," Vaughn said.

Jure kept his black eyes focused on me but answered the question. "Kral means king."

"You're king of the vampires?" That meant Travis was his son, since Rose said he was the prince.

Papa Vamp gave me an "obvi" look. "Would you like to be my queen?" he mocked me.

"I wouldn't if I were you, Dad." Travis sneered.

Lightning fast, he grabbed his son by the back of his head and slammed his face into a table. Over and over. Each sound was like an explosion, but Travis didn't make a peep. Jure's anger was so strong, it pushed everything else out of the room. Everything except fear.

The other band members looked like they wanted to run, but no one moved. No one even breathed until Jure stopped rearranging his son's face.

Travis lay there with blood leaking from a few orifices. He finally lifted his head.

"Don't *Dad* me," Jure said. "I am your king."

Leonard looked at me. "Come with me," he said.

I raised an eyebrow. "No."

"N-no?"

Leonard looked confused, but Jure cleared it up for him. "She's a striga vie, you fool."

"You're going to let all this food go to waste?" he whined.

Jure grabbed him by the neck and lifted him off his feet, one-handed. "Do not touch them. The redhead is a witch, and my son, who thinks only with his fangs, bit her."

"What about the other one?"

Jure shrugged. "No matter to me."

Leonard moved toward Sky. I stepped in front of her. "Try it and see what happens."

"Enough, Leonard," Jure said. "You are wasting my time."

"My king," Leonard said. "I was going to—"

"Shut up," Jure Grando said.

Leonard's lips snapped shut, and then black blood started to seep from his closed mouth. His eyes bulged, and he let out terrified little squeaks as his lips melted until they were just mangled flesh.

Gross.

"Who died and made you king?" I asked.

"Several people, as it happens," he replied.

"So you're Travis's daddy," I said. I'd had enough of bloodsucking losers, and this one looked like the worst of all. "He's kind of an asshole."

Papa Vamp didn't look like he disagreed with me. He sighed. "He is my son. My *only* son."

"You're the guy in charge," I said. "Numero Uno. The big cheese."

Jure nodded coolly.

I could feel anger moving its way up my spine, through my jaw, and into my throat. I was so mad, I could taste it on my tongue.

"You do not treat women like your personal sippy cups," I screeched. My face went numb. I looked at Vaughn, panicked. "What's happening to me?"

It felt like I'd just gone to the dentist—my mouth was numb, gums sensitive. I was pretty sure I was drooling a little.

"Tansy, I don't know how to tell you this, but your fangs are golden," Vaughn said.

Leonard started bowing and scraping.

I felt my incisors with my hand. "Those are some pointy suckers."

"You're a *Mariotti* witch," Jure said. There was just a hint of awe in his voice.

How did he know that? "You say that like it's a bad thing," I said. Though it wasn't like Granny Mariotti ran around hiding it from everyone. The people who knew about her knew the truth, and everyone else probably thought of her as the friendly librarian who always seemed to know exactly which book they needed. Nobody had ever called *me* a witch in that tone, though.

He snarled at me, and I jumped back.

Jure snorted. "Only my son is that stupid."

"You said it," I replied.

"You have a smart mouth for someone in your position," he countered.

I shrugged. "Not the first time I've heard that."

"I'll let you live if you kiss my ring and swear fealty." He lifted his long talons. I wondered briefly if my fingernails would eventually turn into claws. An enormous signet ring was on the third finger of his right hand.

I wrinkled my nose. "Hard pass. It looks like I could catch the plague from it."

He waited, hand in the air, but I didn't move.

"If you're the one who lets vampires do this to girls"—I gestured at Sky—"I'd rather die."

"As you wish." That bloodsucker had just used my favorite quote. He'd ruined *The Princess Bride* for me.

He waved his beringed hand, and the doors closest to us slammed shut.

"Burn the witch," Jure said. "Burn them all." Then he vanished.

"And I thought Travis was a pain in the ass," I said, just before smoke filled the room.

Chapter Twenty-Three

I stood frozen at the sight of billowing smoke. I knew we had to get out of there, but I couldn't leave without the locks of hair or this nightmare would never end.

I dropped to the floor and crawled around, searching for my clutch.

"What are you doing?" Vaughn asked.

"My purse," I said. "I have to find it."

"We need to go." His voice snapped me out of my frantic searching just as my hands touched my clutch. I tore it open and took out the baggies filled with hair.

"Hold these," I said. I'd need my hands free, so I had to leave my purse behind. I shoved the baggies into the front pocket of his jeans.

"Let's move," he said. Vaughn picked up Sky over his shoulder. I didn't know what would happen if she started to struggle.

I tried the only window. The lock was sealed shut.

"I can't open it," I choked out. "We're trapped."

"You can do this," Vaughn said, but then he started to

cough from the black smoke.

I grabbed a chair and threw it at the glass with all my strength. The chair ricocheted without doing any damage.

"Again," Vaughn said. The smoke was so thick now that I could barely see his face.

I tried to remember what my granny had told me as my eyes streamed with tears. Something about humming? I took a shallow breath, trying not to inhale the thick-as-tar air.

I hummed a few bars of the "Moonlight Sonata." Granny had told me that for some witches, music helped to focus the magic. I didn't feel anything magical, but my hand did start to tingle and then throb. It hurt so much that I thought I'd been burned, but when I checked, my skin was untouched.

I muttered, "Break, damn it," and the window shattered. *Thank god.*

I started to rush toward the fresh air but noticed Vaughn was bent nearly double from coughing. I grabbed his shirt front and held on. "Follow me and don't let go of Skyler."

"Never," Vaughn croaked out.

By the time we made it outside, someone had already called the fire department, because I heard the wail of sirens in the distance.

We'd escaped, but Sky had gone limp and quiet, and Vaughn had an angry-looking burn on his arm. I'd coughed up so much smoke, I thought I was at a Miley Cyrus concert.

A fire truck arrived, and firefighters started doing what firefighters do. I wished I'd thought to try telling the flames to stop. Maybe I wouldn't have lungs that felt like a dirty ashtray.

An ambulance pulled up, and emergency responders

started checking us out.

"What happened?" Skyler asked. Her smoke-smudged skin looked pasty.

"You're safe," I said.

"It's so bright out." She shielded her eyes from the rising sun.

"Do you know how the fire started?" a firefighter asked her.

"I don't even know where I am," she replied.

He hustled her off to check her out.

Vaughn came and sat next to me. He gave me a quick kiss. My mouth probably tasted like ash, but I kissed him back.

Then I realized that Travis was gone. "Do you still have the hair?"

Vaughn's face paled, and he searched his pockets. "Got it."

I exhaled in relief. "I have to cast the spell *now*."

He handed me the baggies. Skyler's hair was already mixed with lavender and rosemary, but I didn't have any juniper or fennel. Or the filet of fenny snake.

There was a fast-food restaurant across the street. I started jogging. "I'll be right back," I called to Vaughn.

I burst into the empty restaurant. "I need a frozen fish," I said. "Now."

The cashier gaped at me. "You don't want me to cook it first? The microwave only takes a second."

"Now," I replied. "It's life or death."

"Okay, okay," he said. He disappeared into the back and returned with a small container.

I gave him a twenty. "Thanks for this."

When I returned to where Vaughn stood, I held up the frozen brick. "I'm improvising."

A eucalyptus tree was nearby and went over and pulled off a few leaves. It would have to do.

I mingled Skyler's and Travis's locks and the other ingredients. "Release her," I said in my most commanding voice.

"Now what?"

"We cross our fingers and hope it worked," I said.

"I know it did," he said. "We make a good team."

I smiled at him. My throat was still burning, but I managed to get out, "We are. And now I'm ready to go home."

But even as I said the words, I knew I wasn't going to be able to leave and forget those other girls, even if I wanted to. We'd drive Skyler home, where she'd be safe with Granny, and then we'd figure out a way to stop these monsters, even if it meant telling Granny the truth.

That I knew she'd lied. That I knew my mother was alive.

But none of that was going to happen. Because when I looked around to tell Skyler it was time to go, I couldn't find her.

"Where is she?" I asked. The last time I'd seen her, she was being examined by a cute EMT. But the EMT was talking to a firefighter now.

"Maybe they put her in the ambulance?" Vaughn suggested, but when we asked around, nobody seemed to know anything.

I slumped over, shivering in the night air. The spell hadn't worked.

Of course it hadn't. I'd used a frickin' Filet-O-Fish.

I wanted to scream.

"Don't cry," Vaughn said. "Maybe there's another explanation."

I brushed away the tears. "I'm not crying. Smoke got into my eyes."

"What now?" Vaughn asked, taking my hand.

I looked at him pleadingly. "She couldn't have gotten far."

"Maybe we shouldn't…" Vaughn trailed off when he saw my face.

"Don't say it, Vaughn," I warned. "She's our best friend."

"You almost died."

"But I didn't," I said. "I won't."

We searched the entire city, but Travis and the rest of The Drainers had vanished. We returned to the hotel, smelling of smoke and adrenaline. My phone rang while we were still in the parking lot. My grandmother was calling.

"I thought you were going to check in with me," she said.

"I've been a little busy," I said. "What do you know about Jure Grando?"

There was a pause, and then Granny replied, "Why are you asking?" Her voice was sharp.

"He's Travis's dad," I said. "And he just tried to burn me alive."

"You need to come home right now," she said.

"I'm okay," I said. After I managed to calm her down enough that she wasn't jumping into her car and coming to Diablo, I asked again, "Have you heard of him?"

"Yes," Granny said. "He's the king of the vampires."

"And he's a shitty one," I said.

"So I've heard," Granny said.

"Tell me everything you know."

Granny sucked in a breath. "Are you sure you want to hear this?"

"I don't have a choice."

"The vampire world is divided up into realms," Granny said. "Kingdoms. Jure's in charge of the California realm. And he has a bad reputation, even in the vampire world."

"Bad how?" How much of an asshole did you have to be to get a bad rep with *vampires*?

"He'll kill anyone who gets in his way," she said. "Supposedly, he killed his own mother. The only things he cares about are wealth and power."

"Granny, I know now that the monsters in the dark are real," I said. "I need to know how to fight them."

She sighed. "I just... I wanted to keep you from all this."

"I know," I replied. "But you can't. I have to help those girls."

I heard Vaughn shouting my name.

"I'll call you back later, Granny," I said and hung up.

"Look." Vaughn pointed to the side of the hotel, and there it was: the tour bus was parked a block up. I never thought I'd be so happy to see that mobile petri dish.

"Quick, they're pulling out," I said. "We need to follow them."

Bobbie Jean and her white pickup screeched around the corner of the hotel parking lot and pulled to a stop beside us. "Get in," she said.

"What?"

"You're chasing after your girl, aren't you? I know where they're heading. We'll talk on the way." Bobbie Jean's blond hair was frizzy and unwashed, and her clothes were wrinkled like she'd worn them for a few days. "Get in or I'm leaving without you."

What was the real story between her and Travis? I had a feeling she wasn't telling us everything. I didn't trust her, but what choice did I have?

Vaughn looked at me, and I nodded. I took the middle while Vaughn slid in next to me.

"I saw Travis hustle her into the tour bus," she explained as she started driving. "The rest of the band was with them. But that's not the bad part."

"Bobbie Jean, just spit it out," I said on a sigh.

"Jure was with them, and they're headed for the ranch," she said.

"A ranch? Where?"

"North of here," she said.

"How do you know all this?"

She wouldn't meet my eyes. "I told you," she said, "I've been tracking Travis since the band left Texas. I found out a whole lot about his daddy, too. None of it good."

I caught Bobbie Jean checking Vaughn out and wanted to growl "mine" like some Neanderthal. Or maybe lick him. Skyler's brother, Davis, used to lick the cookies so nobody else would want one.

Instead, I let my incisors go down and flashed my gold fangs at her. She nodded once, like I'd said what I'd been thinking aloud, and returned her eyes to the road, where they belonged, instead of all over my guy.

"Tell me more about this ranch," I said.

"Jure's place, real private," she said. "It's up north a way. Where he takes the girls."

"You mean the Sundowners? Or maybe the Bleeders?" I was trying to ignore the ominous way she said it.

"Not them," she said. "The other girls."

"Don't they have enough?"

"I don't want to worry you—" she started to say, but

I interrupted her.

"That phrase has never made anyone worry less," I said. "Please just tell us."

"The ranch is where the girls go in, but they don't come out. And we only have until sunset to get there."

There was something she wasn't telling us, but I didn't have time to push her right now. Sky needed us.

Bobbie Jean drove with her knuckles white on the steering wheel. "The ranch is a long way north," she said. "You two may as well get some rest."

Vaughn wrapped an arm around me. I snuggled in. "You make a good pillow," I told him.

Vaughn and I had been up all night, and though I was too amped to fully sleep, I did doze.

It was already dark again by the time Bobbie Jean eased her truck onto the shoulder. "We have to walk the rest of the way," she said.

"There's nothing around here," I said. We'd stopped along a desolate part of the road, with nothing to see except a few horses and cows grazing in the fenced-in pastures. "Except endless space."

"In space, no one can hear you scream," Vaughn quipped.

I nudged him. "You're not helping."

"Follow me," she said. We hopped a fence and then started walking. It seemed like we walked for miles without seeing anything but ancient oaks, tall grass, and placid bovines, but we finally came to a long driveway. An iron gate guarded the entrance. There was a mailbox next to it, but you couldn't see the house from the end of the drive.

I dropped back, and Vaughn did the same. "Do you think it's a setup?" I grabbed his hand.

"Nothing would surprise me now," he said.

"Stop talking," Bobbie Jean said. "Any closer and they'll

be able to hear us."

She seemed so different from the bubbly girl I'd met in Los Angeles.

"Is something wrong?" I asked.

"Yes, many somethings are wrong," she said.

Through the trees, a Spanish-style mansion came into view. We were still far away, and there were only a few security lights on, but I made out a red tile roof and an enormous fountain near the crescent driveway.

The structure was luxurious, but it looked odd to me; lopsided, even. Then I realized there weren't many windows, and the ones it did have were disproportionately small for the size of the house. It looked like…a prison.

The house itself was shrouded in darkness. But in the driveway were several black limos.

"Looks like Jure's having a party," Vaughn commented.

Bobbie Jean flinched.

"What do we do now? Walk in the front door and say hey?" I didn't really have a plan, but I couldn't leave Sky.

"I know another way in," Bobbie Jean said.

"You seem to know a lot about this place," I observed.

"I was here with Travis once," she said.

"I thought you said you met him in Austin?" I asked.

"Something like that," she hedged. "Anyway, the kitchen has a back door. Nobody ever uses it."

"Vampires don't eat?" I asked.

"They don't *cook*," she corrected. "Jure prefers his blood fresh."

I could smell the blood. It saturated the air. The house, the grounds, and the entire ranch were soaked in blood and pain.

The back door was unlocked. Vaughn and I exchanged a look.

We crept through the immaculate designer kitchen and down a long hallway. I could smell vampire, but it wasn't The Drainers' scents. It didn't reassure me that I was able to tell their terrible vampire smell from other, equally as terrible, but different vampire stenches.

We were walking into a trap. We all knew it. I turned to say something to Bobbie Jean, and that's when our suspicions were confirmed.

"I'm sorry," Bobbie Jean whispered, right before someone put a gun to my back.

We were led into a huge great room, which was decorated in southwest style with a dash of toxic masculinity.

Oh, wait, that was just Jure and his cronies.

"Someone had a free hand with taxidermy," I said, staring at the stuffed heads of dead animals.

"I enjoy dead things." Jure smirked at me from his leather chair, which was as big as his ego. In other words, ugly and oversize.

Clustered around him was a group of men holding glasses filled with blood.

I recognized a Chicago-based rapper, an A-list actor, a famous quarterback, a musician (not Travis—one who could actually sing), and another man who, although I didn't recognize him, wore the unmistakable air of self-importance. And to round things off, the boys in the band stood awkwardly by the fireplace. It was weird to see the band without a couple of Bleeders hanging off them like human fast-food meals.

The men all wore expensive cologne, applied with a liberal hand—perhaps to mask the stench of vampire, but I could still detect it.

Travis made the rounds, handing out something small and silver. He was passing out demo tapes like it was 1995.

Why had Bobbie Jean brought us here?

I scanned the room, but Skyler wasn't there. In fact, there weren't any girls in the room except for Bobbie Jean and me. I didn't like where this was going.

The Chicago rapper held up his glass. "There's nothing more refreshing than the blood of a young girl."

He would be the one I killed first. As soon as I figured out exactly how to kill a vampire. It had been nothing but luck both times I'd managed it. Luck and my trusty drumstick.

Travis glared at me. "What's she doing here?"

The guys in the band looked over at me. "What's the problem? She's cute."

"Cute?" Travis said. "She's the reason we needed a new drummer." Then he looked over at Vaughn. "Why is our temporary drummer here? This is a vampire-only party."

Jure scowled. "You let the witch's consort in your band?"

"What?" Travis replied. "He's good with the sticks."

Jure didn't even look at Travis when he backhanded him.

"Is Skyler actually here?" I asked Bobbie Jean. "Or did you lie about *everything* just to get us here?"

She didn't answer me, but Jure said, "My son's little friend is currently my guest."

"Let her go, Jure," I said, but he didn't even flinch. My command voice bounced right off him.

He smirked at me. "That only works on young fools like my son."

He motioned to someone sitting in a little alcove. "Get their rooms ready." An older woman in a severe black uniform stood and then left the room. From my brief glance, I couldn't tell if she was a vampire or human, but I thought she was human.

His stare forced me to look up, but I remembered to

focus on something over his shoulder and avoided his direct gaze. I was astonished by the sheer rage coming off him in waves. One wrong word, and he'd snap my bones and rip out my heart to serve it in a stew.

I'd never had anyone hate me like this. Terror made it hard for me to think.

I wasn't sure if he hated me because I was a Mariotti witch or simply because I was female.

"Don't look in their eyes," I whispered to Vaughn, but Jure heard me. He let out a laugh that sounded like it had been kept in a vault and only taken out for special occasions.

"That might work with my pathetically weak progeny, but I'll bend you to my will as quickly as you bend a straw."

Arguing with him would only sap my strength, so I tried ignoring him.

"Take off your necklace."

My hand raised against my own volition, but I managed to stop it with enough concentration. "No," I said. "If you want it, come and take it from me."

"You won't be so disrespectful soon," he managed, but he looked shaken. He recovered quickly and snapped his fingers at The Drainers' piano player.

"She's wearing a necklace," he told him. "Take it off her. She'll be more…compliant without it."

Armando approached me slowly. "I don't suppose you'd take it off for me?" he asked.

"Must have flunked Vampire 101," Bobbie Jean muttered. "Vampires don't ask; they tell. That's why Jure's so pissed at you. You resisted his compulsion."

Interesting. I turned my attention to Armando, who was still watching me hopefully.

I shook my head. His hand inched closer to my neck,

where the chain showed. I snapped my teeth at him, and he jumped.

"Remember Fang?" I asked him.

"Fang's dead," Armando said.

"Yeah, I know," I replied meaningfully. "I killed him."

Now if I could only figure out how I'd done it and repeat the effort.

He studied me for a second and then shook his head. "Anything you could do to me, Jure would do worse."

He wrapped his hand around the chain and started to yank but let go almost immediately when his skin started sizzling. The smell of burned vampire flesh filled the air.

The guy howled with pain while I gagged from the odor. Still, I smirked at him as he writhed on the floor.

"Leave it for now," Jure said. I noticed *he* didn't try to take my necklace. He smiled at Vaughn. "We have other ways of making Ms. Mariotti cooperate."

That *asshole*.

"You've done well, Bobbie Jean," Jure said.

Bobbie Jean squared her jaw. "I brought her here like you asked," she said, confirming she'd double-crossed us. "Now give me my sister."

"You'll be reunited with the girl soon enough," Jure said. His eyes gleamed, and I realized he was getting a sick pleasure from playing with her. If it were up to him, Bobbie Jean and her sister wouldn't be leaving here.

At least not alive.

Bobbie Jean seemed to realize the same thing. She took a swing at him, but Jure's body moved at an incredible speed, and when he stopped again, he was on the other side of the room.

I'd been so naive—too worried about Sky to worry about myself. Or Vaughn.

"Please show our guests to their accommodations," Jure said blandly, like we'd been invited for a sleepover. His lips were wet with blood from his goblet.

I held out a cross, which Edna had given me before I left, and Jure laughed in my face. "I'm afraid we've built up quite a tolerance to the more traditional vampire repellents," he said. "We have coexisted with humans for hundreds of years."

That probably meant holy water wouldn't work, either, and I'd read that the strongest ones could even walk in daylight, as long as they avoided direct sun.

The housekeeper returned, stone-faced. "The rooms are ready, sir."

"Thank you, Hilda," he replied. "My friends would enjoy a little playtime, I think." The other vampires laughed, which sent a shudder down my back. I didn't think we had the same idea of "playtime."

She nodded once and left the room. The guy holding a gun at my back prodded me with it until I followed her.

They took Bobbie Jean and Vaughn somewhere else and then led me upstairs to a bedroom and shoved me inside. Now that I was here, "room" wasn't exactly the right description. Holding cell? Prison?

There were bars on the window, and after the door slammed, I heard the distinct *click* of a lock from the outside.

Bobbie Jean could rot after betraying us, but I would find Vaughn and Skyler and get us out of here. I wished I knew how I'd managed to kill vampires before, but it had just happened. I hadn't even meant to do it. But now, when I really, really wanted to kill one, my powers had deserted me.

I still had my trusty drumstick. I hoped that would be enough.

Chapter Twenty-Four

I was in a high-end bedroom. It looked like something a ten-year-old girl might like. There was a white canopy bed piled high with a frilly white comforter set and pillows. A painting of a little girl with enormous eyes hung above the bed. Her solemn gaze made me walk away, out of the direct line of her fixed gaze, but I still felt like she was watching me. The room was big enough to contain a fireplace—unlit—and a small table and chairs.

Strangely, there were plenty of snacks on the table. My stomach growled, and I reached for a piece of red licorice.

"It makes the blood taste sweeter." The voice was low, rusty, but with a hint of a Southern accent. "They love it. I'd rather starve."

I hadn't noticed her. She was thin to the point of emaciation and had light-brown hair instead of Bobbie Jean's platinum blond, but I could tell immediately that this was her sister. She had the same-shaped eyes and soft accent. She looked out the bay window, sitting on the window seat, staring at nothing.

"Who loves it?" I asked, but I already knew the answer.

She ignored my question. "They'll come for us soon," she said.

"I'm Tansy," I replied. "What's your name?"

"Opal Ann," she whispered.

"How old are you, Opal Ann?"

"I'm sixteen." She paused. "Unless I had a birthday since I've been here. I've kind of lost track of time."

Sixteen? She's still so young. No wonder Bobbie Jean was willing to betray us.

"Are you Bobbie Jean's sister?"

She nodded once.

"She's looking for you." I didn't feel any satisfaction that Jure had double-crossed Bobbie Jean after she'd double-crossed us. After getting a closer look at the girl, I'd do whatever it took to get her out, too.

There were thick bars on the window. Opal Ann was back to gazing out of it.

"What are you looking at?" I asked.

"If I sit just right, I can see the ocean."

She was basically one big bruise. Her hair was matted, and she gave off a distinct odor.

"How long have you been here?" I asked.

She shrugged. "I think about six months."

I gasped and couldn't mask the horrified look on my face.

"It wasn't all bad," she said. "If Jure was in a good mood, sometimes he'd take me to a party."

"A party?" I asked, shocked by the idea that people had seen Jure with a teenager and hadn't done anything.

"Sure," she said. "Sometimes, there were good things to eat." But then her smile fell.

"People saw you? With bruises like those? Did they

try to help?"

She shook her head.

"*I'm* going to help you," I said. "You'll see Bobbie Jean soon. I promise."

"Bobbie Jean is here?" She looked like she was about to cry. "I told her to go home and forget about me."

"She didn't."

Opal Ann closed her eyes briefly. "They'll never let us go."

There were no clocks in the room, and my phone was nearly dead, so I'd powered it off. But it felt like they left us there for a long time.

"Any minute now," she said dully.

Footsteps sounded loud in the silence. I tried to drag the bureau in front of the door, but it was bolted down. All the furniture was secured to the floor.

"Hurry, tell me something. Anything that you think might help," I urged.

"There's nothing," she said. "You can't fight him. Jure's too powerful." The hopeless tone nearly wrecked me, but then she said, "Except…"

"Except?"

"Except," she said again, her lips turning up so slightly that it barely qualified as a smile, "I know how to kill vampires."

The footsteps were closer now.

"This one girl, Sarah… She's gone now," Opal Ann said. "She got all funny toward the end. Started chugging Diet Dr Pepper. She'd down a couple of those liter bottles before lunch. And Jure had a party…"

"What happens at these parties?"

"They leave just enough blood in you. Just enough. But when they're done with you, you wish you were dead."

I wanted to purge the picture she'd painted from my mind, but I couldn't. "What happened with Sarah?"

"When this disgusting old vampire drank her blood, it killed him." Her eyes gleamed with satisfaction. "He had a bad reaction to the soda, I guess. After that, they were dragging her off, but she managed to grab a liter of the stuff and throw it at one of the vampires. His face bubbled up like she'd thrown acid on him. That's the last time I ever saw her."

"Seriously?" I couldn't believe it. "Crosses, holy water, none of that stuff works, but it's as easy as *soda*?"

"It worked," Opal Ann said.

The undead were vulnerable to soda. That explained why The Drainers had banned it from all their shows.

The door opened, and a guy in Wrangler jeans and a T-shirt came in and grabbed Opal Ann by the arm. He was in his mid-twenties, just a few inches taller than me, and prematurely balding with a droopy mustache and eyes to match.

"Let go of her," I said, trying to use my power. "I command you."

He let out a short laugh. "That magic stuff won't work with me." He started to drag Opal Ann out.

"Why are you doing this?" I asked.

"Jure lets me have his seconds," he said.

Opal Ann's face went white, and I could see her shoulders shaking. "Don't bite me again," she whimpered.

Rage started as a ripple in my belly or maybe a little lower, like period cramps. Then the ripples spread throughout my body, but still, my power didn't come.

If my witch side wasn't working, maybe my vampire side would do the trick. I let my fangs descend and my nails turn into long golden claws.

"Let her go," I said.

He smirked at me. "There's enough of me to go around." He held Opal Ann tight but made a grab for me.

I jumped away from him, and when I looked again, he had a long, pointy knife in his hands. "It's my pig sticker," he said, laughing when he saw my face. He swiped at me, and I felt a burn in my upper arm.

He'd cut me.

I went woozy at the sight of my own blood but took a deep breath. I couldn't faint.

I remembered Granny's advice to "aim for the squishy parts" and rammed my fist into his Adam's apple. He let go of Opal Ann.

"You are going to regret that," I said.

Then I reached out and used my hard, pointed fingernail to rake a line across his throat. I was hoping to cut his carotid artery. Blood sprayed from his neck, and I had to resist the urge to vomit as he tumbled to the floor.

"How many people knew you were kept here?" I asked Opal Ann.

"A lot. Vampires. Humans too. The humans mostly looked the other way."

"Let's go," I said.

"Is he dead?" she asked.

I shrugged. "I don't know, but we need to get out of here."

She nodded and then kicked him in the crotch as she went by.

I liked this girl.

We started toward the door, but then she went back and yanked something off his belt.

She jingled a set of keys in her hands. "*Now* we can go."

I *really* liked this girl.

"Great idea," I said with a smile.

"Follow me," she said.

As we crept along the hallway, I asked her, "Where would they have taken my friend Vaughn? He was with Bobbie Jean when they brought me to your room."

"We don't get many guys here," Opal Ann said, avoiding my eyes.

I tiptoed to the head of the stairs, but I didn't hear anything.

"I think they're still having drinks," Opal Ann said. "Dinner's usually not until nine."

Dinner. It's people.

To the world, they were famous and influential men, but to the girls upstairs, they were dangerous predators.

"If you did happen to get a male 'guest,' where would they put him?"

Opal's face went blank. "Nowhere good."

Damn it. I needed to find Vaughn and Skyler and get out of here. We'd escaped Jure once, but I didn't want to take any chances.

"He might be in Mr. Small's room," she finally said.

"The actor from that historical drama?" I was astonished.

"You don't believe that a vampire can be an actor because of the reflection thing?" Opal Ann asked. "The mirror thing is true, but they do show up on film."

I'd seen enough of the band's photos/videos/Instagram posts to know that. I didn't have time to ask if this actor guy could walk in daylight, but I really wanted to know. Otherwise, wouldn't auditions be a pain?

"Do you know which room is his?" The place was huge.

Opal Ann shook her head. "But I know he liked the third floor."

We made a detour to the kitchen to look for diet soda. The refrigerator was empty except for a can of beer and a bottle of vodka.

"Jure must have gotten rid of it," she said. "And the vodka's for Marisol. She gets a little uncooperative if they don't sedate her first."

I liked the sound of Marisol already.

"Where else can we look?" I asked.

"Maybe the housekeeper's room?"

"Show me where it is," I said. "And hurry."

Jure struck me as the kind of man who didn't have much patience. He'd come for me, and I needed to be ready for him.

How was I going to get my friends out of here? There were at least seven vampires in the living room, not including Jure, who was the most powerful one of them all.

Then I realized what Opal Ann had said. "Are the other girls still here?"

She shrugged. "Probably. I think I heard Marisol the other night, but she was screaming a lot." Her voice was flat, but her hands shook as she said it.

"We have to check all the bedrooms."

We moved slowly and carefully. I opened each bedroom door with the keys Opal Ann had stolen from the guy probably bleeding out in her bedroom. I felt a twinge of remorse, but then I remembered what he'd done to a sixteen-year-old. Only a year younger than me.

I stuck my head in a bedroom, but it was empty.

There was no sign of Skyler. I heard a creak and turned, fangs bared, but it was Vaughn. His shirt looked like it had been ripped from his body, and there was blood all over his arms and legs. He gave me his *don't worry* look, which made me really freak out. The last time he'd used that look, he'd broken his ankle while we were hiking. I didn't trust Vaughn's *don't worry*.

"I'm okay," he said.

"Sure you are," I said. "You're bleeding."

"It's not my blood," he said. "I killed one of them."

"What? How?" I said. It was bad enough that I was a killer, but now Vaughn had taken a life, too. It had been in self-defense, but that didn't make it easy.

"I found this mounted over the fireplace," he said. He held up a sword, its blade still wet with blood. "It was bolted to the wall, but I managed to pry it loose."

His hands were bruised and bloody. He caught me staring at them.

"I was...highly motivated."

"How did you get away?"

"I used it on the vampire who came in." He made a slicing motion across his throat. "Off with his head." His words sounded glib, but his face was sweaty and pale. He looked like he was one good exhale away from upchucking all over my Chucks.

"At least we know one thing that will kill them," I said. "I don't suppose you saw any more swords lying around?"

"Just this one," he said.

"Why would they be stupid enough to leave a weapon in plain sight?"

"They kept us so weak and scared, they thought we wouldn't fight back. And we didn't." Opal's voice was weary. "Except for Sarah, and she's probably dead."

I sent a sharp glance her way. "That's not your fault. Everything that happened to you isn't your fault. It's Jure's."

Bobbie Jean stepped into view, arms raised. "Don't shoot! It's me!"

I ran up to her and punched her right in her backstabbing face.

"I said it was me," she groused but stayed on the floor.

"I know," I said. "That's why I hit you."

"Fair," she said.

I grabbed her hand and helped her up.

When she saw Opal Ann, her shoulders relaxed, but she didn't smile. It was too early for smiling.

"I've been looking for you," Bobbie Jean said. She hugged Opal Ann so tightly that the other girl nearly fell over.

"We would have helped you," I said. "Instead, you led us into a trap."

"He had my sister," she said. "That's why I cozied up to Travis. He told me where she was."

"Well, now he has all of us," I said.

"I know a way to get us out," Bobbie Jean added.

"Oh, so now you're suddenly on our side?" I'd had a plan, but it hadn't included Bobbie Jean sharpening her knife on my spine.

"Less talking, more moving," Bobbie Jean said.

"We're not leaving those other girls," I said. "We're not leaving Sky."

"He knows she's your best friend," Bobbie Jean said. "He'll try to use that against you. She'll be safe as long as he thinks she's an asset."

I glared at her. "You better pray she's still alive."

It was too much to hope for that they kept diet soda around, but maybe one of the humans had a secret stash.

I didn't have much time. Jure and the others would wonder where their meal was, and he seemed like the type to get hangry.

"Where's Skyler?" I asked Bobbie Jean. "And don't you dare tell me you don't know."

"There's a bedroom in the attic," she said. "She might be there."

"You take Opal Ann and get her out of here," I said. "Vaughn, you go through the house and search every room. Except the living room, where I'm sure the vampires are still drinking cocktails and thinking about their dinner."

He started off but came back and kissed me quickly. "Be careful."

"You too."

"I'm not going anywhere," Opal Ann said. "I want to help."

We all looked at Bobbie Jean, who said, "Okay, but the second the rooms are unlocked and we find your friend, we're out of here."

"Agreed," I replied.

Vaughn came back with four girls trailing him like little ducklings to his mama duck. There wasn't time for introductions.

I thought the attic bedroom was empty at first, but I found Skyler hiding in a closet. She had her arms wrapped around her legs and the frightened look of a child who'd just woken from a nightmare.

Finally. My emotions seesawed between relief and anger. Was it wrong that I wanted to smack her and then hug her? I'd found my best friend again, and this time, I wasn't letting her out of my sight.

I slipped a protection necklace around her neck. "It's me, Sky. I'm here."

Her eyes had that same scary, blank look they'd had the last few times I'd seen her. She stared at me like I was a stranger.

I whispered stories to her of our childhood, of summer at the beach, of the fall when we had watched Connor play football, of the time in the sixth grade that Sky TPed Tamala Decker's house because she'd called me fat. Of the time in middle school that I thought Vaughn liked me. Of the time that I finally found out he did.

It took a long time—time we didn't have—but her eyes eventually cleared. "Tansy?"

"We have to get out of here, Sky."

"They scared me," Skyler sobbed.

"Shh, it's okay," I said, wrapping my arms around her. "We're leaving, okay?"

She nodded. We tiptoed down the attic stairs to where Vaughn was waiting.

He carried Skyler, who seemed to sink into an exhausted stupor as we moved through the mansion. The other girls weren't in much better shape. Opal Ann could barely walk, so Bobbie Jean carried her.

Jure, because he was a rich asshole, had separate quarters for the hired help. They were in the same building but in a much less plush part. The carpet was brown, and the walls were beige. Stock artwork, like the kind you saw in hotels, hung on the walls. This part of the mansion looked like an upscale prison.

Hilda the housekeeper was human. It was possible she didn't drink soda, but it was also a possibility that she hid her stash from her boss.

We didn't have a lot of time, but we needed a defense against the vampires or we'd never get out the door.

I felt weird rummaging through some stranger's things, but then I remembered how the housekeeper had shown me to a bedroom and locked the door. She wasn't innocent.

I finally found her stash in her closet. There were two liters of off-brand soda wrapped up in an ugly sweater. I found a couple of minis in her boots and, when I looked under her bed, a six-pack of Diet Dr Pepper.

"What are you doing in my private chamber?" I hadn't heard the housekeeper come in. She was light-footed, but maybe she had to tread warily around a house full of vampires.

She looked like she was going to scream, so I clamped a hand over her mouth.

"Tie her up," I said. I didn't feel too bad about it. After all, she had to have known what the vampires were doing to all the girls locked away in this mansion.

"You make me sick," I hissed at her. My fangs had distended. "If they let you live, you better hope I never see you again."

I handed out the sodas. Bobbie Jean was wearing a pair of shorts and a halter top, so she didn't have many places to conceal her weapon.

Opal Ann was shivering, so I took a long gray cardigan off the chair and passed it to her. She took some of the soda. Vaughn loaded up the pockets of his jeans, and I stuffed a couple of cans in my back pockets.

"Tansy, you're bleeding," Vaughn said.

"J.T. stabbed her," Opal Ann said. My throbbing arm confirmed Jure's human servant had taken a slice out of me.

"Let me see," Vaughn insisted. I batted him away, but he caught my hand in his. "I want to take a look at it before I go kick his ass."

"Too late. He's already gargling in his own blood."

"You *killed* him?"

"Hey, you killed someone, too," I said defensively.

"Don't get judgy."

Vaughn frowned. "It's a nasty cut."

I glanced at my arm, which was a mistake. My blood looked thick and crusty. Dizziness threatened to overcome me.

"Put your head between your knees," Vaughn said, steering me to a bench in the hallway.

"What kind of vampire faints at the sight of blood?" Bobbie Jean asked.

I glared at her, but her words did the trick. "I'm not fainting. I just don't like to see it. We need to get out of here."

I remembered I was mad at her and glared.

"Y'all were so worried about your friend, but he had my sister," she said.

"Which you could have told us about," Vaughn pointed out. "Instead, you let us walk into a trap."

I shot her a look. "Bobbie Jean, we're going to get everyone out, okay? Not just Sky. Not just your sister. Everyone."

We were going to get *everyone* out of there. I had no idea how, but I couldn't bear the thought of those girls, locked up and terrified.

"Skyler, when I tell you to run, you run," I said. "Don't look back and don't stop, no matter what."

"But—"

"No. Matter. What."

She nodded.

"I'll go first and make sure the coast is clear," I said.

I moved quietly to the door, but before I could open it, there was a rushing sound, and a blob of gray smoke materialized into a man. Or a monster shaped like a man.

"Where do you think you're going?" Jure stood in front

of the door, blocking our escape.

The civilized businessman facade was gone, torn away by the vampire underneath.

His talons were long and yellow-looking. His breath was so foul, I could smell it from three feet away, a rotten-egg sulfur belch of breath. Did vampires even have lungs?

I tried not to flinch when he stepped closer to me. "Someone needs a Tic Tac," I said, fanning the air dramatically.

He hadn't called his cronies yet—probably because he was more powerful than the rest of the vampires combined, and he didn't think he needed backup.

He'd kept these girls shackled in his house for months, and nobody reported it. Nobody noticed, or they were too afraid. But what I worried about the most was that everyone knew and they just didn't care.

I had to distract him. Vaughn and the others needed a few more minutes to get free.

When Jure reached for me, I panicked. My mind went blank. I'd forgotten not to look into his eyes. I'd forgotten everything.

"Yes, that's it," he said. "Come closer."

I strained to keep my feet from moving, but they did. His hands were so cold.

He held me by the arm with one hand and used the other to brush the hair away from my neck. He reached one talon under the chain of my necklace. I flinched when it snapped and fell to the floor, but I didn't move.

I couldn't move.

His fangs grew longer.

There was death in his eyes, but I couldn't look away. He'd drink me dry. My hands fumbled for something, my brain not able to remember what it was. Soda?

Why was I thinking about caffeine at a time like this?

But my hands knew. They opened the tab top of the Diet Dr Pepper and threw it in his face.

Intentions plus actions, I remembered. I wanted the soda to be like acid on his skin, to melt away the smirk — the knowledge that he was stronger than me, able to overpower me.

And it did.

He screamed.

I'd never heard a sound like that of an injured vampire before. He was only injured, not dead, which was unfortunate, and judging by his roars of pain and rage, I would be dead if I didn't get out of there. Plus, his cries were bound to alert his pointy-toothed friends.

While Jure screamed and staggered around, I shouted to the others. "Run!" And then I ran.

I almost collided with Vaughn as I rushed out the front door.

"I thought you were going to the car," I said.

"I wasn't about to leave you here," he said. "I'll never leave you."

"I appreciate the sentiment," I said, "but less talking, more running."

We darted through the trees until a sharp ache in my side made me double over. I looked back, but as far as I could tell, no one was pursuing us.

"Why aren't they following us?" I huffed out the question, vowing I'd start running more once I made it back home. Or at least get on the elliptical Granny kept in the spare room that we mostly used as a giant clothes hanger.

Vaughn wasn't even breathing hard.

"It's after sunrise," he said. Hopefully Jure wouldn't risk going out when he was injured, and the rest of the vampires probably weren't daywalkers.

I realized he was right and lifted my face up to the sun's rays. The warmth reminded me I was still alive. We started moving again, slower this time. I ached all over, but we had to keep going. We wouldn't be safe until we were out of Diablo—maybe not until we were back home, out of harm's way with Granny Mariotti.

Chapter Twenty-Five

We'd planned to drive straight through until we were home, but a summer storm was brewing, black clouds filled the sky, and the girls we'd rescued were tired and hysterical, so we stopped before night fell. We were safer in a hotel room than on the road, where a hundred terrible things could happen to us after dark.

We'd used Vaughn's credit card to rent a three-bedroom hotel suite—the kind that had a little kitchenette, meant for vacationing families trying to save a buck. We all crowded into it. Somehow, without saying anything, they'd given Vaughn and me one of the bedrooms while six girls shared the other two. Bobbie Jean chose to sleep on the couch where she could watch the door.

Vaughn and I were unpacking in our room. I hadn't anticipated that we'd be gone for as long as we had, and Opal Ann's outfit was little better than rags.

"What are we going to do with them?" Vaughn asked. "Long-term."

"We'll take them back to Granny Mariotti's," I said.

"She'll help us figure it out."

"In the meantime, we need to feed them," Vaughn said. "Opal Ann looks like she could use a few hot meals."

We went into the common area to ask about food, and Bobbie Jean was sprawled on the couch, watching the television intently.

I cleared my throat. "It seemed like earlier, you wanted to talk to me about something."

"Yeah, I did," she said, but she didn't take her eyes from the screen. She cleared her throat. "I just wanted to say thank you for getting my sister out of there."

I was still angry at her betrayal, but I understood it. I'd done plenty of things I wasn't proud of to save Skyler.

We ordered groceries to be delivered. We couldn't risk anyone seeing the emaciated, bruised girls and asking questions. Not before we made it back to Granny Mariotti's, where we would be safe. Where she could help us contact the authorities to help the girls we'd rescued.

"I need a shower," Opal Ann said. "I feel like I'll never get clean, no matter what."

"It's something that happened to you, not who you are," I told Opal Ann. "You can be whoever you want to be."

"He thinks no one can stop him," she said.

There was a burning in my chest when I thought of Sky and all the other girls he'd hurt. "He's not unstoppable."

All those girls were dying, and no one seemed to care. But *I* cared.

She shrugged. "You're probably right, but no one bothered to try. Not before now."

It was almost too much for me. I was seventeen years old, and I had no idea how to help them.

"You've already helped them," Vaughn said, and I realized I'd spoken aloud. "I'll make us something to eat," he added. "These pans are worse than I expected, though. The best I can do is veggie omelets."

"Sounds great," I said. "Keep at it—I'll be back in a few minutes." At least I could find them some T-shirts to sleep in. I'd been doing all the shopping at hotel gift stores lately, but this time, I went to the souvenir store I'd spotted on our way in. My debit card winced when the clerk ran it, but it went through, and at least the girls would have something clean to wear.

When I got back to the room, Vaughn was pacing.

"Opal Ann fainted in the shower," he said. "Bobbie Jean's with her now." He held up a plate. "I made her something to eat."

I took it from him. "I'll go see if I can help," I said.

The door to their room was closed, so I knocked softly. Bobbie Jean opened it and peeked out.

"I thought I could try a healing spell for Opal Ann."

"She's sleeping," she said. And then shut the door quietly in my face.

I knocked again. "Vaughn made her some eggs. And I think I can help her. Please let me try."

Bobbie Jean opened the door and motioned me through. "Fine. But not too long," she warned.

Opal Ann was sleeping on one of the queen-size beds but opened her eyes when I entered the room.

"I'll be back in five," Bobbie Jean said, then left.

Opal Ann seemed better after I managed to coax her into eating a few bites of the omelet Vaughn had made. He was a good cook. More than good—great, actually. He'd been helping at his dad's catering company since he was big enough to hold a spatula.

I cast the same healing spell I'd cast for Skyler, but there was a strange resistance when I tried it with Opal Ann.

"Opal Ann, are you feeling better?"

She was already out again. I wasn't sure if the spell had worked, but I couldn't bear to wake her up. She needed the rest.

I tucked the covers in around her and left the room.

Vaughn was sitting in the common area, watching TV with Skyler. "How is she?"

"Better," I said. "I tried a healing spell, but I'm not sure it did any good."

"It helped me," Skyler said. She hadn't been talking to me very much, but I hadn't had much to say to her, either.

"Tomorrow, we'll be home, and Granny Mariotti will be able to help her."

Skyler lifted her head and looked at me. "Let's just have something to eat and then get some sleep. We'll deal with everything in the morning." She sounded incredibly weary. "It's my mess. The least I can do is help clean it up."

She was blaming herself instead of the vampires.

"Skyler, you didn't ask for any of this," I said. "You aren't responsible. He is. They all are. It'll be okay."

She didn't say anything else, but she didn't look like she believed me.

"I'll figure out how to fix this," I said. "I promise. We'll talk to Granny, and she'll tell me how to undo the whole undead thing, and then everything will be back to normal."

"That's tomorrow. For tonight, let's head to bed," Vaughn suggested, giving me a warm grin.

"I thought I'd watch a little TV," I said.

He came to sit next to me. "What's wrong?"

"What if I lose control?" I finally said. "What if I bite you?"

What I couldn't say aloud was, *What if I turn into a monster who uses people for their blood?*

"You're not anything like Travis," he said, seeming to read my mind.

He had a point.

It wasn't like we could get down and dirty in a hotel room with a bunch of other people in it anyway, but he held me until I fell asleep. I could get used to this: Vaughn and me, safe and warm. Together.

I woke to the delicious smell of frying bacon and the even more delicious smell of freshly brewed coffee.

Vaughn was taking a pan of bacon out of the oven when I entered the kitchenette.

"Morning," he said cheerfully. He poured me a cup of coffee. "How would you like it today? Bitter and black like Travis's heart?"

"It's like you don't know me at all."

"You're a grump in the morning," he said. "You'll feel better after you drink your coffee."

I took a sip and then noticed he'd added cream and sugar. I smiled at him when I realized he *did* still know me.

"One sugar and a splash of cream," he said. "You really didn't think I remembered how you take your witch's brew?"

"You're in a good mood," I observed.

His lips tipped up in the smile I only saw him give to me, then he wrapped his arms around me and pulled me close before he whispered, "Who wouldn't be in a good mood with you as his girlfriend?"

I blushed, and Bobbie Jean let out a chuckle as she came into the kitchenette.

After breakfast, we packed up to head home. After a quick stop in Diablo to pick up the Deathtrap, we headed through L.A. In the middle of the usual traffic, we caught sight of Natasha, of all people. The #1BLEDR license plate was hard to miss.

"There's Natasha," I said. "I want to talk to her." Natasha and I weren't friends, but I had to try to make her understand that The Drainers were exploiting her.

Vaughn was driving, so I nudged him to follow her.

She was weaving as she drove, obviously upset about something. She pulled into a diner and went inside. Bobbie Jean had been following us in her car with Opal Ann and the others, and they met us in the parking lot.

"Anybody hungry?" Bobbie Jean asked. We grabbed a booth, and Vaughn stayed with the girls while I went to talk to Natasha. She was alone, which surprised me. No Bleeders or boys in the band in sight.

Natasha gave me that up-and-down look mean girls everywhere had perfected. I'd dealt with plenty of her kind before, but mean girls with fangs were a different story.

The head of the Bleeders wasn't technically a vampire, but she hated me, and I wasn't fond of her, either, especially when she eyed Vaughn like he was a delicious dessert instead of my boyfriend.

I made myself take a kind tone with her. "Natasha, I would like to discuss something with you, if you have a moment."

Surprise flashed in her eyes, but she gestured to the chair across from her. I hadn't really thought I'd have this conversation at a twenty-four-hour diner, but I'd take what I could get.

"Did you know I found a dead girl? Someone in the

band drained her dry and just left her in a cave," I said bluntly.

I watched her closely. Surprise, anger, and pain flashed across her face before her expression went blank.

"You're lying," she said. "Travis would never do something so horrible. None of the guys would."

She laughed, but she sounded more like an irritated seagull than an amused girl.

"Wouldn't he?" I asked softly.

"The Bleeders are all willing participants," she said. "There's a wait list to donate."

"Some might be willing, but not everyone is," I said. I studied her for a minute. "Do you know I'm a striga vie?"

"Travis told me," she said.

"How do you think that happened?"

"You're a witch, and then a misguided vampire bit you," she replied.

"Without my consent," I added. "And that 'misguided vampire' was Travis."

Somehow, I had to stop him. Me, the girl who couldn't even raise her voice in class, who hadn't been able to tell Vaughn how I felt, who hadn't been able to save Skyler before she got hurt.

"Come with me and help us defeat Travis," I offered. And then quietly, "Please."

As she seemed to consider my words, there was a sudden commotion when a group of women walked through the door. I glanced over and recognized them.

"Think about the offer, Natasha. Please," I urged, then waved Granny over. God, it was good to see them. "Granny Mariotti, what are you doing here?" I beamed at her as she approached the table.

The rest of the Old Crones Book Club waved at us as

they found a booth and quickly picked up menus. Probably to hide their shame. But I couldn't be mad that they were checking up on me, because I was too happy to see them.

"We were on our way to the Getty when we saw the Deathtrap," she said.

"You were going to the Getty this early in the morning?" Vaughn asked.

"And it's in the other direction," I said. At least I thought it was; my directional skills left something to be desired.

"Okay, she was worried about you," Evelyn said.

"Tansy, aren't you going to introduce me to your friend?" Granny asked, eyeing Natasha curiously.

"We're not friends," Natasha and I said at the same time.

"Introduce me to your *acquaintance*, then," Granny said.

"Natasha is the leader of the Bleeders," I said. "They let vampires use them for their blood."

Natasha glared at me. "Harsh."

"But true," Granny said, taking note of Natasha's healing bite marks.

Natasha hung her head, but Granny put a gentle hand under her chin and tilted it up. "Child, I have some lotion in my purse. It'll help those marks heal. You want them to heal, don't you?"

"Yes, ma'am," Natasha replied.

"And, Tansy, what do I always tell you?" Granny asked.

"Not to be all judgy," I said.

Where Natasha was concerned, I wanted to judge her. But the look in Granny's eyes made me ashamed of myself.

"Natasha, I'm sorry for the way I spoke to you," I said.

Her mouth hung open. The apology had surprised her.

Granny put a hand on my hair. "Why don't you join us when you're finished?"

I nodded, then turned back to Natasha, careful not to

phrase anything as a command. "I need your help," I said. "I don't want The Drainers to keep taking advantage of girls."

She didn't say anything, so I continued. "I know the Bleeders think that the girls who disappear get to become Sundowners, but I think when the band is tired of them, Travis ships them off to his father, who lets his friends feed off them until they're almost dead. Not undead but lights out."

"I don't believe you," she said.

I gestured to my traveling companions. "We rescued them from Jure's ranch."

"Travis invited me there once. He said it was like a resort."

"I know you don't like me," I said to Natasha. "But I'm asking you, whatever you do, please don't go there."

She studied the group. "Is that your friend? The one you've been looking for?"

A wide smile escaped me. "Yes, that's my best friend."

"She talked about you sometimes," she said. "When she was coherent, that is."

"So?"

"So Travis knows a lot about you," she warned. "Where you live. That your grandmother is a witch."

"That's good information to have." I nodded once. "And could you please think over my offer? We could really use you on our team. It's only a matter of time before he hurts you, too."

Chapter Twenty-Six

The car turned in to my familiar driveway, and for the first time in weeks, I felt safe.

We were home.

We piled out of the Deathtrap. It had broken down twice after our stop to eat, and I was sure Granny Mariotti had beaten us home from the diner. I stretched, my muscles aching. It was bright out, and I raised a hand to shade my eyes.

I caught Skyler looking at me. "I forgot my sunglasses," I said.

"It's not that sunny out today, Tansy," she replied. "Are you sure you're not...?" She made little fangs with her pointer fingers.

"Stop worrying," I said. She bit her lip but didn't say anything.

"Rose and Thorn say that I'm different than a regular vampire," I added. "There have only been five striga vie before me. One of them could walk in full sun."

"And the others?"

I didn't answer her. I didn't want to tell her about the striga vie I'd read about in Rose's file—the one who'd gone full vamp and killed an entire city.

Bobbie Jean and Opal Ann pulled up behind us a few minutes later.

"Have you heard from Rose and Thorn?" I asked.

"They said they had to report back to the Paranormal Activities Committee," Bobbie Jean replied. "I'm sure they'll be in touch."

Everyone but Skyler stared at their feet. "What are you waiting for?" I asked. "Let's go inside. I'm sure Granny will know of a concoction to help."

"Is she really a witch?" Opal Ann asked.

Skyler gave her a hug. "She's not that kind of witch," she assured her. "Granny M is the best."

Best at lying, I thought, then scolded myself. No matter what, I knew my grandmother loved me. I hadn't confronted her, but I also hadn't forgotten how she'd lied about my mother's death. And I wanted to know why.

"Granny, we're home!" I hollered. She wasn't in the kitchen or living room.

"I'm in the back," she shouted.

Granny was on her knees, wearing gardening gloves and a big straw hat. The Southern California sun was no joke this time of year.

We brought Granny six shell-shocked girls and Bobbie Jean, who couldn't stop fussing with her sister's hair.

"Come inside," Granny said. "I'll make a pitcher of lemonade." She grabbed several lemons from the tree and ushered everyone in.

She bustled around the kitchen, getting out a plate of cookies and the lemonade, plus water in chilled glasses. Granny Mariotti's lemonade was the perfect mix of sweet and tart. The taste always made me think of home—of long summer days reading in the hammock in the backyard.

This summer was different. I gripped the glass tightly and wished for the time that an overdue library book was the most I had to worry about.

I told Granny our entire story, Vaughn chiming in with his own bits. Skyler stayed quiet, and I caught Granny shooting worried glances at her.

We had to figure out sleeping arrangements. Our tiny bungalow was too small to host everyone, at least long-term, but nobody wanted to leave, so we decided everyone would bunk down on the floor in sleeping bags.

I grabbed a few out of the storage container in the garage. Those sleeping bags had been stored there since the Old Crones Book Club's Winter Solstice campout.

"Need some help?" Granny asked.

"I thought we had more sleeping bags," I said.

"I'll ask Edna," Granny said. "There are some clothes you've outgrown in that bag. I've been meaning to donate them to Goodwill, but the girls seem like they'd appreciate a change."

They were all still wearing the souvenir shop T-shirts—I was *sure* they'd appreciate a change.

Granny hugged me tight. "I'm so proud of you, my special girl."

"I'm not special," I replied. I was a killer, and if Granny knew, she wouldn't be proud of me at all. Witches, at least Granny's kind, believed in nonviolence, in harmony with nature.

I knew I'd have to tell her eventually, but I wasn't quite ready for the look of disappointment I'd see.

Her eyes were sharp as she gazed at me. "Everyone is special to someone. But more importantly, you are brave. Most people would have looked the other way—pretended not to notice someone else's pain."

"Those girls are the brave ones," I replied.

"It's not an either/or kind of thing," Granny said. "Those girls survived, and so did you. You helped one another do it."

I looked away, scared to see condemnation in her eyes. Granny had taught me the peaceful way. And I had failed her.

In the morning, Evelyn would take two of the girls, who we found out were called Marisol and Kylie—no last names given—to stay at her house. Bobbie Jean and Opal Ann would stay a couple more days at our bungalow so Opal Ann could get her strength back before they headed home to Texas.

Skyler and Vaughn would stay with us, too—at least until Granny could figure out how to protect them.

Granny wasn't in the mood to cook, but Edna made us some delicious roasted veggie tacos and fresh guacamole.

"Go easy on the garlic," I said.

Edna said, "Those girls aren't vampires."

I didn't look at Vaughn. I'd been thinking about kissing him when I said it. Nobody likes making out with garlic breath. "That's not why I said light on the garlic."

Granny and Edna laughed while I tried not to blush.

After dinner, Vaughn and I slipped outside.

I breathed in the familiar scent of fragrant orange and lemon trees, the sweetness of jasmine, and the fresh ocean breeze.

It soothed me. We sat in our backyard and just settled into the quiet. Until Vaughn's phone let out a shrill chirp.

Vaughn looked down at his phone, frowning.

"What's wrong?"

He hesitated. "Ashley texted me a bunch of times."

"Why?" My head was throbbing. The heat was suddenly oppressive, and I felt sticky from my own sweat.

"Because she's used to getting her way."

I didn't know what to say to that, so I didn't say anything. But I thought a bunch of things. Mostly swear words.

"Tansy, don't look at me like that," he said. "I'm not interested in her. At. All."

"Really?"

"I was as plain as a Taylor Swift song."

I quirked an eyebrow.

"We are never ever getting back together," he quoted.

I choked out a laugh. "An oldie but a goodie," I said. "And I didn't know you were a Swiftie."

"You and Skyler listened to that album nonstop for an entire year," he replied.

"That's classic Taylor," I replied.

Skyler came outside to join us, and for a second, it felt like none of the nightmares had really happened. Like we'd wake up tomorrow and worry about normal things.

But she had a fake smile plastered on her face. I hugged her. "I'm glad you're back home."

Skyler had been wearing the same perfume since she was eleven. Her mother had given it to her, an expensive special blend from Paris. The musky scent had been way too sophisticated for an eleven-year-old, but she loved it.

She never went anywhere without dabbing it behind her ears and on her wrists. She even put it on before she brushed her teeth in the morning. But when I hugged her, she didn't smell like Skyler. The odor coming off her was like rusting metal and decay.

"Are you sure you don't remember anything else?"

"I don't remember," she said, but she looked away. She didn't want to remember, and I didn't blame her.

"Sky, it's important. If you know anything about Travis and the others that might help protect those girls, we really need to know."

Her face tightened. "I said I didn't remember." But I knew when my best friend was lying.

"Let's talk about something else," Vaughn suggested.

Sky's face brightened. "Let's talk about the two of you," she said. "Is it official?"

"Yes, it's official," Vaughn said. "Boyfriend, girlfriend, the whole deal."

"Like social-media official?" she asked. "Because that would get your ex off your back."

"We've been a little busy," I said, but Vaughn got out his phone, pulled me close, and kissed my cheek.

Then he snapped a pic. "Done!" he said. "We're Instagram official."

"That's serious," she replied.

"I even asked her to prom."

"When exactly did you do that?" I asked.

He started to stutter, and I continued, "I do recall you talking a lot about taking the Deathtrap to prom. Maybe you asked my car instead of me?"

Skyler burst out laughing and slung an arm around Vaughn. "You, my friend, have zero game."

Vaughn turned to me. "Tansy, will you do me the honor of accompanying me to our prom? I promise I'll do the big ask later, but for now, please put me out of my misery and say yes."

"Yes," I said, grinning at him. "And I don't need a big, splashy, public promposal."

Skyler clapped her hands.

Even though I laughed and joked with them, I couldn't stop thinking that it wasn't over. Not yet.

Vaughn excused himself to call his dad, and I took the opportunity to ask Skyler a few questions. I could tell Vaughn wasn't in the mood to talk about it, but I needed answers.

"Can you tell me anything about vampires?" I asked her.

"They can't stand pumpkin spice lattes," Skyler revealed.

"That won't do us a hell of a lot of good in the middle of summer," I said. And I was kind of with the vampires on the pumpkin-spice thing. "It's just not right," I said. "Coffee and pumpkin in the same cup."

The limited-run drink came out in September or October, which meant the temperature was in the eighties when Skyler was sipping a festive fall favorite meant for getting out your turtleneck and watching the leaves change colors. It was like the devil's armpit in October in Southern California.

"It's so wrong, it's right," Skyler replied.

Skyler was able to confirm some other things vampires couldn't stand, like garlic, rose petals, and Diet Dr Pepper. She also warned us never to look into a vampire's eyes because they could hypnotize you in seconds, but I'd already figured that part out.

The Old Crones Book Club had done their homework, too, and reported that a stake through the heart really did kill a vampire, but, as Granny said, "It'd kill anybody else, too."

A lot of ways to kill Travis would also kill a human: the aforementioned stake, chopping off his head, burning him alive. After spending time with The Drainers and knowing the things they'd done to other girls, any of those options sounded not only doable but necessary.

"What are my other options?"

"You don't really have any, unless you're willing to let Travis keep sucking girls dry—their blood, their will, and, eventually, their lives."

"I'm not willing to do that," I replied.

"Then it's kill or be killed, I'm afraid," Skyler said. "Vampires don't play by the rules."

Chapter Twenty-Seven

Everything slowly went back to normal. The Drainers' website carried an announcement that they were on hiatus "indefinitely" due to the sudden death of their beloved friend and drummer Fang.

Vaughn was worried that Jure might retaliate, but as the days went by and there wasn't any sign of trouble, we all started to relax.

I'd convinced Granny to let me return to work because I needed the money. I'd picked up a shift at Sheridan Catering, and it had been…normal.

Opal Ann and Bobbie Jean were still staying at our bungalow, but the whole gang was all hanging out in the backyard of my house.

Bobbie Jean and I watched as Opal Ann picked daisies from the bushes and made them into flower crowns.

"Are you guys headed back to Texas soon?" I asked her.

"My parents want us to come home," she said. "But Opal Ann doesn't want to leave. Says she doesn't feel safe except when she's with y'all."

"I can understand that," I said. "Give it time."

But it turned out we didn't have much time left.

We were having a big family dinner with the Old Crones Book Club and all the girls who were staying at Edna and Evelyn's, plus Skyler and Vaughn.

I picked out black jeans and a summer top. It was light as air but long-sleeved, which meant it would conceal my so-pale-I-glow skin.

Vaughn and I set up everything under the pergola and may have exchanged a few kisses while we were working. Until Skyler arrived and caught us.

"Don't you two ever let up?" she said.

I took a step away, but Vaughn pulled me back again. "No. No, we don't."

After everyone got there, we sat down to fresh fruit, shrimp salad, and crusty bread, and the conversation flowed around us like waves. It felt like such a relief to be normal for an evening.

When dinner was over, I went into the kitchen to help with the dishes, but Granny was stirring something in a big copper pot.

She turned off the burner. "It needs to cool for a few minutes." She studied my face, then gave me a stainless-steel flask engraved with the tree of knowledge on it. "Drink it every day. It'll help with the symptoms. I'll give some to all the girls. Just in case."

"Just in case what?" I asked.

She hesitated. "You know with vampires, it's never that easy. It's not over. You need to figure out a way to stop them permanently."

"Whatever it takes?"

She nodded. "Whatever it takes."

I was shocked my peaceful granny seemed to be

advocating violence, even toward soul-sucking vampires. I kissed her cheek. "Thanks, Granny."

"You know, Tansy, if you're really serious about stopping them, you'll have to go into a vampire's nest. I think you'll need some added protection."

She handed me a silver charm that looked a little bit like a chili pepper.

"It's a horn, a *cornicello*," she said. "A protection from evil. It belonged to my grandmother."

"Thank you, Granny," I said before adding it to the charms I already wore. Her grandmother's jewelry was special to her. "I'll take good care of it."

We joined our guests, and for the rest of the night, we talked about everything *except* vampires, witches, and striga vie.

It was a good night.

My grandmother had somewhere to be, but she was dragging her feet. She and her coven were supposed to be headed to San Francisco for the weekend for an inter-coven conference.

"Granny, go to the coven meeting," I said. "Have a good time. I'll be fine."

"I hate to leave you alone," she said.

"I won't be by myself," I said. Bobbie Jean and Opal Ann were spending the weekend with the other girls at Evelyn and Edna's place, and truthfully, I wanted to be left alone. Since we'd returned with Skyler, Granny had been hovering, and she never hovered.

"I just want things to get back to normal," she said.

"And they will," I said. "If you go to your coven meeting. Besides, I have a date with Vaughn tonight." Vaughn and I grinned at each other.

Edna shoved a package wrapped in brown paper into my hands, and a couple of other ladies who I didn't know as well handed Vaughn and me various poppets, posies, and protections.

"I guess this is it," I said.

"I wouldn't go, except my friend Miriam will be there," Granny said. "She's bringing some ancient texts from Italy, and they might contain information about the striga vie."

"We can talk when you get back," I assured her. "And I'll call you with updates."

She caught my arm. "I have to go but remember this. When you need to summon your powers, the important thing is intent into action. You easily resisted a vampire's compulsion," she added. "That makes you unique."

"Until this summer, I didn't even know there were vampires," I said.

"If you're having trouble, close your eyes and hum your favorite song."

Her advice was sound. Humming and a huge dose of panic had worked to break the window when we were trapped.

She chuckled. "Don't look so doubtful. It'll clear your mind. Remember: intent into action. Be careful."

"I will." I hugged her tiny frame, reluctant to say goodbye. "You too."

She hugged me back for a long time and then handed me a gift bag. "Open it later," she whispered into my ear.

The book club had Vaughn surrounded, so I tugged on Granny's hand. "Time to go."

"Have fun, you two, but be safe." She waggled her eyebrows at me, and then it sank in.

"Grandma!" I said. My face flushed, and I couldn't look at Vaughn, but I heard his chuckle.

She ignored my tone and grinned at me. I only called her "Grandma" when I was ticked off at her.

She hugged me goodbye, her arms wrapped around me so tight that I could barely breathe. After a bit, I tried to wiggle free, but she only held me tighter.

A horn honked. "Let's get a move on!" Edna cried.

We waved them off and then headed back to the house hand in hand. This thing between Vaughn and me was so new, which meant I got a secret thrill when I held his hand and his ex didn't jump out of the bushes screaming.

"Let's get out of here," Vaughn said. "Why don't you put on a swimsuit and plenty of sunscreen? It's a perfect day for the beach."

I didn't know why I was hesitating. I'd been in the sun several times since I'd been bitten.

Vaughn studied my face. "Or would you rather do something else?"

"The beach sounds great," I said, forcing a smile.

"Tansy, it's okay if you're nervous about the sun," he said. "I was just reaching for something familiar."

"I know," I said. "We're going, and you're going to buy me a lobster roll at the snack shop."

"I have something else planned," he said. "Don't forget your hat."

I grabbed my bag, which contained sunscreen, waters, a magazine, and an inflatable beach ball, and Vaughn took it from me.

I stepped outside, realizing it had grown warmer while we were inside. Little beads of sweat formed on my forehead. My eyes hurt from the glare, and my skin felt prickly and hot. My stomach lurched, and I ran back inside.

Vaughn said something, but I couldn't make it out. My entire focus was reaching the bathroom before I lost it.

I threw up, thankfully making it to my intended destination, and then lay on the cool tile, dizzy and disoriented. I didn't know how long I lay there, but I heard a tap on the door.

"Tansy, can I come in?"

I dragged myself to a sitting position. "Give me a minute." I brushed my teeth and rinsed my mouth with mouthwash, then opened the door.

Vaughn pulled a lock of my hair back from my face. "You okay?"

I gave him a wan smile. It was safe to say that I wouldn't be doing much sunbathing the rest of the summer—not unless I wanted it to be the last thing I ever did.

Chapter Twenty-Eight

We sat in the living room, not talking while Vaughn rubbed my back.

"Maybe we should stay home," he said.

"I'm feeling much better," I said. I wanted to spend time with Vaughn that didn't involve The Drainers leering at me or the Bleeders trying to grope my boyfriend.

Vaughn didn't look convinced, but he grabbed our stuff. I'd managed to persuade myself that it was just my imagination, but as soon as I stepped foot outside, it happened again.

When I came back from the bathroom, Vaughn was reclined on the couch, his phone in hand, but he put it down once he saw me. He didn't say anything. He just held his arms open wide, and I flew into them. He held me while I cried out my hurt and fear onto his T-shirt.

"We'll figure it out," he said. He punctuated his words with little kisses, along my jawline, down my throat, and across my clavicle. And then below. "Your skin is so soft," he murmured.

I burrowed into him, trying to absorb his warmth.

Vaughn's hard body became harder, his muscles straining against me. I pressed into him. "Kiss me."

We kissed for a long time, but then Vaughn sat up. "I packed a picnic," he said. "Let me go get it. You should probably eat something."

I turned on the TV and searched for a show for us to watch. When Vaughn came back with the food, he also had a bouquet of flowers in his hand.

We had an indoor picnic and watched movies all afternoon. It didn't seem to bother Vaughn that I couldn't go outside without blowing chunks...but it might not always be that way.

"What if I'm an actual vampire?" I asked. "The creepy kind, like Travis or even that Sundowner we met, Temple."

"You aren't," he said. "And even if you are, you won't be anything like them. You'll still be Tansy."

I couldn't help it. I launched myself at him and kissed him while I tugged frantically at his T-shirt.

"What do you want?" Vaughn asked. I accidentally touched my tongue with one of my fangs and drew blood. I hadn't realized that they'd come out.

"You."

"Tansy, you're upset," he replied. "I don't want to take advantage of that."

"You're not," I said.

"Ashley was right about me, you know," he said conversationally. "I was too scared to reach for what I wanted. For who I wanted."

I looked up at him. "And now?"

"I'm not scared anymore," he replied. "Are you?"

I shook my head.

"Say the words," Vaughn said. "Say what you want."

I pulled his head down to mine. "I want you."

He was smiling as he kissed me, and somehow, that made it even hotter.

"Take this off," I said, pulling again at his tee.

Vaughn yanked at his shirt one-handed, but it got caught on his chin. I started to giggle, then my laughter stopped quickly at the sight of his bare chest. My face felt hot as I stared at his sculpted body.

"Let me help," I said. I snagged his shirt and carefully lifted it the rest of the way off before I threw it over the back of the couch. I kissed the hollow of his throat. He smelled like the ocean, sun, and sweat. I breathed it in.

He put his lips over the little golden fang mark. It felt so good when he touched my neck, not anything like when I'd been bitten. I didn't want to think about how it had happened, so I concentrated on the feel of Vaughn's callused fingers sliding over my skin.

I was going to get undressed in front of Vaughn. We were best friends, but I'd never taken my clothes off in front of him before. I sucked in a breath.

He picked up on my nervousness. "You don't have to do anything you're not ready for," he said. "We don't have to." His voice shook just a little. Someone who didn't know him as well as I did might not have even noticed.

"I know," I replied. "But I want to." I took off my shirt and sent it sailing. Part of me wanted to hide, but instead, I relaxed my shoulders and wiped my sweaty palms on my shorts.

I slid my hands down his chest to where his heart thrummed against my palms. It helped somehow that Vaughn was as nervous as I was.

That we were both new at this.

. . .

Everything looked different in the morning. Sunshine streamed into the bedroom through the open curtains. I yawned and stretched before I realized that I wasn't alone. Vaughn was asleep beside me, lying on his back with one hand flung over my stomach.

I stared at him long enough to veer into creeper territory. When he and Ashley were dating, she'd marked him with a clear "You Shall Not Pass" sign, and I wasn't going to lust after someone who had a girlfriend—even someone with gray eyes and the best smile I'd ever seen. Now I looked my fill: dark-brown hair cut short on the sides but longer on top so a tiny bit of curl came out to play. Deep tanned skin, gray eyes—erp, gray eyes staring back at me.

Vaughn was awake…

He smiled at me, and my heart stuttered. "Morning," he said, low and rumbly.

I could feel the mascara crusted around my lashes, and my breath probably smelled like a goat's butt. Yet Vaughn looked fresh as a flippin' daisy.

He leaned in to kiss me, but I jumped and covered my mouth. "Morning, and I have the breath that goes with it." I needed mouthwash, stat, but I also had to pee, which was something that always happened when I was jittery.

"I don't care," he said but moved aside to let me up.

I hurried into the bathroom and closed the door. I brushed my teeth, took care of my bladder, and then tried to regroup. I'd spent the night with Vaughn.

"Couldn't sleep, babe?" *He called me babe now?*

"I've been thinking about last night," I said, coming

back out to the bedroom.

His smile grew wider. "Yeah?"

"About what you said about Skyler," I clarified, feeling the blush creep up my neck.

We were quiet for a minute. It was sinking in that Vaughn and I were a couple. The hottest guy in school was my new boyfriend, but also, of course, still one of my best friends. What did we do now? I'd never had to maneuver a relationship before.

"This is weird," I said. "Isn't this weird?"

"This is wonderful," he countered.

While I stood there fidgeting, he got up and took his turn in the bathroom. As he came back out, the muscles on his bare chest flexed when he stretched and yawned.

He caught me looking and grinned. "C'mere," he said. "I haven't had my good-morning kiss."

He didn't wait for me but wrapped an arm around me and pulled me close. His lips trailed along my neck. "We could go back to bed," he said.

I tilted my head to give him better access. "I wish I could call Sky to tell her about last night."

"You want to tell her what happened?" Vaughn stopped kissing my neck. I glanced up at him and saw his expression.

"Not a play-by-play," I assured him. "Maybe just the highlight reel."

"What were the highlights?" His lips curved upward a tiny bit.

"All of it."

His smile grew and grew until it turned into a full-on laugh, and I couldn't help myself—I started to laugh, too. When I finally could control myself enough to speak, I said, "I know what we did is private. I just wanted to tell her that it happened and that we're…"

"Happy," Vaughn said. "Together. You're my girlfriend."
He nuzzled my neck, which sent shivers through my body.

B ut in the middle of the night, my stomach started cramping again. I slid out of bed, careful not to wake Vaughn, and tiptoed to the kitchen. I grabbed a glass and filled it from the tap.

I guzzled the water, but I was still thirsty, so I drank another glass, then another. When I shut the fridge, Vaughn stood there, wearing only black lounge pants. I stared at him—all that smooth, tanned skin on his chest. I wanted to sink my teeth into him.

My stomach cramped, and when I bent at the waist from the pain, the glass flew from my hand and shattered on the tile floor.

"Are you okay?" Vaughn started toward me.

"Be careful," I said. "The glass."

"Stay there," he said. "I don't want you to cut yourself." He bent and started to scoop up the shards but then let out a short grunt of pain.

Drip. Drip. Drip. My hearing was suddenly amplified, and I could hear the drops of blood as they hit the tile.

"Did you cut…?" A delicious scent wafted through the kitchen. Vaughn crossed to the sink and put his fingers under the water. He let it run for a second, then dried his hand on a paper towel.

"It's just a nick," he said. "Where are your bandages?"

My eyes were focused on the drop of blood welling on his finger. My jaw tightened. My teeth elongated. I wanted that blood more than I'd wanted churros from

Alvin's churro stand. More than I'd wanted Vaughn to break up with Ashley. More than I'd wanted for my mom to come back. I was sure at that moment I would have done anything for it.

"The t-tonic," I managed to say. "I need the tonic Evelyn left."

Vaughn caught on right away. "Shit, Tansy, I'm sorry. I forgot that..." He reached into the fridge and handed me the container of tonic. I chugged it until the fog lifted from my brain.

"Sorry," I said.

"Are you okay?" he asked.

I nodded, even though I was pretty sure that what I had, even a tonic couldn't fix.

Chapter Twenty-Nine

The day Granny was due back from her conference, Skyler and I were hanging out at my house. It was starting to feel like we might be getting back to normal. Or as close to normal as we'd ever be. I was having a hard time with the fact that she'd brought a vampire into my life and the consequences of that.

"Thanks for inviting me over," Sky said.

Since when did she thank me for hanging out? Since the vampires.

"You're welcome," I said, a little stiffly. Then, "It's what we do, right?"

That got a real smile from her. "Right."

Skyler was teaching herself to crochet and swearing every five seconds while I tried to finish a novel that I'd started at the beginning of summer.

"I'm hungry," Sky said. "How about you?"

Famished, I thought.

She went to the pantry and got out ingredients. "I feel like making brownies."

But there was more than chocolate and sugar on the kitchen counter. My stomach gave a weak gurgling noise when I saw the blood. "None for me, thanks."

"It's pig's blood," she said. "Granny M got it from the butcher."

I wanted to be grossed out, but instead, I watched those brownies bake like a dog watched a bone.

When they were out of the oven, the treats were a pretty reddish-brown color, like red velvet cake.

Skyler snickered at my hungry look. "They need to cool for ten minutes or so." She wandered into the backyard, but I sat at the kitchen counter and watched.

The smell of blood was overwhelming me. I reached over and scooped out a handful before bringing it to my lips.

"The brownies should be…" Skyler stopped when she saw me with brownies dripping from my mouth. "Jesus, Tansy," she said. "Get a plate."

"More," I growled. "More blood."

She edged away from me. "What's wrong with you?"

I growled at her. "Blood. Now."

"I don't think that's a good idea," she said. "Maybe have some water?"

"I want blood," I wailed.

She edged closer to the door. "Granny left you something," she said. She went to the fridge and rummaged in it before pulling out a different silver flask.

"Is that the tonic?"

"Yeah," she said. "Just like the one she gave me."

She handed it to me, and I unscrewed the cap, sniffing it. "It smells different than the one Evelyn gave me. This one's more like honey and flowers."

The scents of orange blossoms and honey fresh from

the hive and something I couldn't describe wafted out of it. I took a sip, the taste lingering on my tongue. I drank it slowly. It made me want to laugh and to cry. It made me want to live. It tasted like hope in a silver flask.

I felt calmer afterward. "Sorry about the brownies," I said, studying the mess I'd left.

"I can make more," Skyler said. "You know, there's probably a market for edibles like these."

"A market?"

"Did you see how many sick and hungry girls there were at The Drainers' shows?" I nodded, and she continued. "He doesn't feed them well. He likes them hungry. When he's the only one who can give them what they need, he can use it against them."

Despite the coldness between us, I was touched.

"This is really good. Maybe we could sell it to the ones who could afford it. Kind of a pay-what-you-can plan." We'd make it for free to help those who couldn't. But I was broke after not working for so many weeks, and selling something like this would be a way to make money.

"Don't take this the wrong way," I started to say, but Skyler stiffened.

"When someone says that, there's usually only one way to take it," she replied.

"I was just trying to understand what you saw in Travis," I said. "When you first met him, I mean."

"He's tall, good-looking, and a musician," she said. "There's something about a guy and an instrument." Truth. Vaughn was living proof of that, but he and Travis were polar opposites.

"And after that, you heard him play live, and the music compelled you," I said. "I understand that. Even I had a hard time resisting it." I thought of the way my heart sped whenever Vaughn picked up an instrument and nodded. "And musicians are sexy."

"He made it seem like he couldn't live without me," she said. Then we both snickered. "Not like that," she continued. "After Connor broke up with me…"

"Via geographical relocation," I said. "Like a big ol' chicken."

"'Geographical relocation' sounds so much better than 'he bailed,'" she said. "Maybe you should start writing books instead of just reading them."

I laughed. Now *there* was a way to make money. Or maybe I could go back to being a cater-waiter, where the real money was.

She continued. "Travis was so take-charge. He knew what he wanted. It was powerful. He was powerful."

"Power," I said thoughtfully. "He has the power. And we need to take it away."

"Exactly," she replied.

"We need to hit up another one of his shows."

"Vaughn won't like it."

"Vaughn's not here," I said.

"We can talk more about it later," Skyler said.

"Later?" I asked.

"Opal Ann and I are going to the movies," she replied. I waited for an invitation, but it never came.

Finally, I said, "Okay, have fun." I smiled, but inside, I was hurt.

I walked outside with her, squinting in the bright sunlight before waving goodbye. Thankfully, I managed to keep my lunch where it belonged.

I dropped the smile I'd been faking and went back inside. My best friend and I did almost everything together. I wasn't jealous that she was making new friends, but our friendship was in need of repair, and hanging out, doing normal things, would have helped.

I decided to curl up and read. It seemed like it had been months since I got lost in a good book. I fell asleep halfway through it.

When I woke up, my head was throbbing.
        I sat with a groan, an army of steel-toed ants crawling through my brain.

My mouth was dry. I wanted more blood. I started for the fridge, but dizziness made me stop, and I gripped the countertop so I wouldn't fall over. It finally passed, and I reached into the fridge, grabbed a bottle of water, chugged it, then rummaged through the fridge until I found more elixir.

Granny came home, her arms loaded with book bags. "Where's Skyler?"

"She said she was going to the movies with Opal Ann," I said. I checked the time and frowned. "They should have been back by now."

I explained about the blood cravings. Granny nodded. "I did make that elixir for you," she said.

I snorted in frustration. "It doesn't work for nearly long enough."

"Probably," Granny agreed.

"I have to find Sky," I told Granny. "She needs me."

She shook her head. "Tansy, I know you love Skyler," she said. "But you've got to stop hovering. And there are other girls who need you, too."

She was right. No matter how worried I was about

Skyler, I had other people to think of, too.

But no matter how much I tried, I couldn't stop worrying about Skyler. If we all worked together, we could triumph over the vampires. I knew we could.

My phone chimed with a text from Skyler. At first I was relieved. Until I read it.

Went to find Travis. I have a plan.

No. No, no, no. I'd been so naive. My best friend had lied to me.

While I was making plans on how to defeat Travis, she was just playing along, waiting until my guard was down, so she could go back to the guy who considered her little more than an appetizer.

Another chime. *It's not what you think. Opal Ann and I are going to stop him. Permanently.*

They were going to get themselves killed.

I slipped out of my room and knocked on Granny's door.

"I need your help."

Skyler hadn't gone to face the vampires alone. Opal Ann was with her, but I wasn't sure either of them would make it out alive.

Chapter Thirty

After I texted him with the latest, Vaughn met us at our bungalow.

"Skyler and Opal Ann went to find Jure," Vaughn said, the incredulity clear in his voice. His face was red. I'd rarely seen Vaughn lose his temper, but it looked like I was going to get a front-row seat.

"We have to find them. The vampires will rip them apart," I said. "What was Skyler thinking?"

"She was thinking that it was all her fault, and she was trying to make it right," Granny replied.

"I don't blame her," I said, ashamed of how I'd scared Skyler by almost vamping out—especially after what she'd been through with Travis. "But I still don't understand why she'd do something like this," I added. "We risked so much to get her away from him, and then she runs right back?"

"I think she may have heard Edna and me talking," Evelyn admitted.

"What about?" I asked her.

"How it might be possible to reverse vampirism," she said.

"Rose and Thorn's folder said it was possible," I agreed. "But they also told me it was dangerous."

"We were talking about how killing your maker—the one who turned you into a vamp—would reverse the process," Edna said. "And that if Travis was dead, you'd go back to a Mariotti witch, instead of a striga vie."

Granny quirked an eyebrow. "And?"

Edna looked at Granny with a guilty expression. "I only made one batch."

"One batch of what?"

"We're calling it Sunburn," Evelyn replied. "Skyler took it."

"So Skyler thinks she has what it takes to kill Travis?" It was reckless, but it reminded me Skyler would do anything for someone she loved. Even if it meant facing a predator like Travis. Despite it all, my heart warmed.

"We think so, since he's the one who bit you," Edna said.

"I'm going to find her," I said.

"I'm coming with you this time," Granny added.

While Vaughn drove, I searched social media for clues. It was already after seven p.m. Not long until sundown. The Drainers were playing in Huntington Beach, at a venue ten blocks from my house. Those vampires had a lot of nerve.

I gave Granny Mariotti the name of the place. "That used to be a bookstore," Granny said sadly.

"I can't believe Skyler and Opal Ann are going to try to take on a band of vampires," I said. "How reckless can they be?"

"Reckless? I think they're brave," Granny Mariotti said.

"Travis is a waste of space, but Jure is attached to him," I said. "Or as attached as a vampire can get. It won't go well for them."

"You think Jure will show up?" Granny asked.

"I know he will," I said. "Travis had Sky in thrall to him for weeks. Do you think she's strong enough to resist him?"

I was so angry at my best friend for going back to him, even if it was to trick him into drinking the Sunburn drink the crones had cooked up. But at the same time, I was also incredibly touched by Skyler's loyalty.

But when we got to the venue, it was clear we were walking into a trap. The only vehicles in the parking lot were The Drainers' tour bus and Skyler's red convertible.

The front door was open, so we went inside. It didn't creak ominously, but maybe it should have.

The main part of the restaurant was empty, so we headed backstage.

"Travis must really be pissed off," Vaughn murmured. "He canceled a gig just to lure you here."

"He does love the sound of his own voice," I said. "But that doesn't make any sense. How did he know we'd show up?"

"That part was easy," Travis said. "I just scheduled a show in your hometown and waited."

I whipped my head around. Travis stood near an amp, and he had Opal Ann in a cinch. The image of her clutched in Travis's hands made my heart pound in desperation. I scanned the area, but I didn't see Skyler anywhere.

Where could she be? I wanted to cry when I saw the tip of a shoe peeking out from behind a couch. I wanted to run to her, but I couldn't. Not until I got Opal Ann away from Travis.

He grinned at me before he sunk his teeth into her and took a long drink.

"Let her go," I commanded. He didn't. Why wasn't it working?

Blood was spilling from her, running down her neck as

Travis scooped it up. "Finger-lickin' good," he said. He put each bloodstained digit in his mouth and slurped.

I gagged, and he laughed.

"It's about time you got here. I've been waiting."

"Waiting for what?" I didn't stop to hear his answer, just raced toward them. I was too late. He let go of Opal Ann, and she dropped to the floor, her eyes unseeing.

He'd killed her. He'd killed sweet, innocent Opal Ann.

He needed to pay, but first I needed to get Skyler, Vaughn, and my granny out of there.

"You're a little old for a groupie," Travis said to Granny Mariotti. Then he took a good look at me. "You're not a groupie at all," he growled.

I fluffed out my hair. "No, genius, I'm not a groupie."

"You're that witch. My dad's been looking for you."

"And I've been under your nose the whole time."

"He's really pissed about his face," Travis said.

"What?" I asked. "He's not going to be voted prom king anymore?"

Travis sneered at me. Then, out of nowhere, he lifted his guitar and smashed Vaughn in the face with it. Vaughn went down.

"Vaughn!" I ran to him. "That's my boyfriend, asshole."

Relieved when Vaughn sat up, I stalked toward the vampire.

"I'm okay," Vaughn said. There was blood running down his face, but I ignored it in favor of cornering Travis.

"P-please don't hurt me," Travis said.

I made a mistake when I hesitated. Vampire fast, he reached Granny and backhanded her so hard that she flew against the wall and lay there.

I ran to her. She was awake and breathing okay but dazed. Her arm was at a funny angle, and I was pretty sure it was broken.

"You are going to pay for that," I said.

Before I could wrap my hands around his throat, he snapped his fingers, and a woman came into the room. I recognized her—but it wasn't possible.

Even though I hadn't seen her since I was five, I immediately knew who she was.

Granny had given me a photo of my mother and me. I'd been sitting on her lap; she was looking at me, but the expression wasn't one I'd ever seen in the eyes of a young mother.

I hadn't liked looking at that photo. Whenever I did, something cold and dark rose up in my mind. A memory just out of reach. Why did I hate looking at that moment in time?

Granny seemed to realize the picture distressed me and relegated it to the guest bedroom, which she used as her office.

Looking at my mother in the flesh gave me that same cold, dark feeling.

She had red hair like my own, but it was darker. Her eyes were hazel, not green, and she was slender.

Apart from her bloody fangs, she didn't look that different from those old photos. She wore nicer clothes— the kind of stuff a high-end clothing executive might wear. Tasteful jewelry. Her ageless beauty wasn't due to the miracle of Botox but to something much darker.

My mother was a monster. And not a cute made-for-TV/Disney version.

"Meet the Executioner," Travis said.

"The Executioner?"

He didn't know who she was to me. I wondered if she'd told Jure that I was her daughter. Or maybe *she* didn't even know who I was, but I was certain she knew my grandmother by the way her eyes sent laser beams of hate at Granny Mariotti.

"You told me she was dead." I whispered the words to my grandmother, but the betrayal was clear in my voice. I'd already known it, yes, but now the proof was right in front of me.

When I'd first come to Granny's, I hadn't talked much. Until Skyler had fought with me during that library story time, I don't think I'd said more than two words.

Granny had always said that Skyler talked enough for the both of us back then.

"Technically, I *am* dead," Vanessa said flatly.

Travis snickered. "The old woman is a liar."

"The old woman is my mother," the Executioner said.

Travis laughed at the way Vanessa said it. "Really? Since when?"

She shrugged.

"Are you a striga vie, too?" I asked Vanessa. Might as well know what she was working with.

She didn't answer me, but a flash of some emotion crossed her face—embarrassment, resentment, embarrassed resentment. Finally, she said, "Teenage witches are the absolute worst."

I sneered at her. "Worse than dumping your baby daughter and pretending you were dead?"

Travis replied, "No, your mom isn't a striga vie." He gave Vanessa a mocking glance. "But she wanted to be." Underneath my mother's icy composure, I caught a glimpse of emotion. She hid it quickly, but Travis saw her reaction. "She didn't have what it takes."

"What it takes to be a vampire?" I didn't hide my contempt.

"Again, I am dead," Vanessa said. "There's nothing wrong with it."

"You're not dead. You're undead."

I wanted to ask her who my father was, but before I could get the words out, she looked at me with her bright, wicked eyes. "He didn't want you," she said. "*I* didn't want you."

"Don't listen to her," Granny said.

I shook my head slowly. Nothing could protect me from this.

"*I* wanted you," Granny said. "From the moment I saw you, you were mine to take care of."

"I know, Granny," I replied. I knew she loved me, but I didn't know why my mother didn't. It didn't matter, anyway. The woman she used to be was gone, and only the monster remained.

"Leave it to your reckless son to screw up," Vanessa said to someone behind me. I hadn't even realized Jure had arrived. Maybe I was getting used to his vampire stench.

"Enough, Executioner," Jure snapped. I sucked in my breath when I realized he had Skyler by the elbow. Her eyes were wide and frightened.

There was a lump of something fleshy caught in one fang. I gagged, and he smiled wide.

"Tansy is my daughter," Vanessa replied.

"I'm *not* your daughter," I said. "You may have given birth to me, but that doesn't make me yours."

That shut her up, but only for a second. "Travis goes around biting girls without a care," she said. "How many Sundowners did he create unintentionally? He needs a muzzle."

I really hated that I agreed with the woman who gave birth to me, but she had a point.

"Make sure you get her face," Jure told Travis. He ran

a hand over his pustule-marked cheek.

Travis sent a ball of flame toward me. I'd been so naive; I'd underestimated Travis and his love of vampire fire. I darted out of the way, but I wasn't quick enough, and fire licked up my cheek. My nerve endings screamed, and I had to bite my tongue not to do the same. What kind of mother would let this happen?

My biological mother caught me staring at her. "Just wait until the first time you drain one of your little humans dry," she said. "There's no thrill like it, when you feel their heart slow and then stop."

"I won't kill anyone," I said. "Else. I won't kill anyone else."

I'd killed, but I hadn't drank any vampire blood — especially not Travis's. Rose had told me that it was possible to reverse the effects of vampirism as long as I hadn't had my maker's blood. I really hoped it was true. And I really wished there was a better term than "maker."

"Bloodsucking predator" had a nice ring to it.

She snorted. "You are a vampire. Vampires are predators who drink blood."

"I won't drink human blood."

"You won't be able to help yourself."

"I'm *not* you," I said.

She turned her back on me, ignoring me. "I'll kill the old lady first."

"If you even breathe on her, you'll be sorry," I said.

She looked at me over her shoulder, not even bothering to fully face me. "Oh, I'm so scared," she mocked.

"Oh, I'm so scared," Travis echoed her.

"Shut up, Travis," I said. And he did.

Too bad Rose and Thorn weren't here. They had the worst timing ever. I could have used Thorn's pointy dagger to stab Jure in the ribs or Rose's vials of perfumed poisons to shove down his throat.

I realized a second too late that Jure had chosen not to believe me and had lost patience. He jerked his chin once and turned. I ran toward him and Skyler, but it was too late.

Vanessa grabbed Granny by the hair and bent her neck back, which exposed a vein in her throat. She made the same sound I did when I saw a triple scoop of Baseball Nut ice cream.

"Don't!" I shouted. I ran forward, but Jure's voice stopped me. He put a single finger on my arm. His flesh felt spongy and moist. I shivered.

"Tansy Mariotti, do not move." His eyes. I'd looked into his eyes. A mistake that might cost Granny her life.

I tried to force my feet to obey me, but I was rooted to the spot.

"Do it," Jure replied.

"Vanessa, I— You can't kill your own mother," I said. For a moment, I thought I'd gotten through to her. She hesitated, and the red left her eyes.

"I command you," Jure said. And she sank her teeth into my grandmother's throat.

When Jure's attention was on my mother, I was able to inch forward, but Travis grabbed me by the arms and stopped me. I clawed and scratched at him, but he held me tight. I tried to summon my powers but failed.

Jure smirked at me. "You've never been compelled by a truly powerful vampire." I hadn't looked into his eyes last time.

My mind was a blur. I struggled to think, to override Jure's command. My brain settled on one thing: love. I loved my grandmother, and I wasn't going to let her die.

And then he made me watch as my mother fed on my granny.

Vanessa turned and smiled at me.

I was starting to understand why Granny had lied about her being dead.

Something built up in me, and I sent a howl of rage her way. It manifested as a lightning bolt, which went through her body. I knew it had to hurt like hell, but she barely even flinched. She took a step forward and then another before she crumpled. I sent a second bolt Jure's way, and it caught him in a sideways blow but didn't slow him down. I'd brought my drumstick and a can of soda, which I shook up and then popped the top. He screamed as the soda splattered his skin.

"Let's go," I said.

Granny's dress was slick with her own blood. She looked like she was sleeping, but I knew better. Vaughn picked her up. "We need to get help."

As we ran out of the restaurant, Skyler sobbed beside me. "I'm so sorry, Tansy."

I didn't know what I would do if my grandmother died. She was all I had.

I couldn't speak, but inside, I was howling, screaming, enraged. But Opal Ann was dead, and Granny was dying. I knew it in my bones. I could feel her spirit slipping away from me.

Chapter Thirty-One

When I woke, I was in my own bedroom, lying on top of the covers. I was sticky with blood. Granny's blood. My shirt was coated with it.

For a brief second, I thought it was just a terrible dream. But then Vaughn entered the room, and I could tell by his face that everything I remembered was true.

"Granny," I said. That was all I could say. I couldn't ask the question.

"Tansy, you're awake," Vaughn said.

"Where's my grandmother?" It hurt to talk. My face felt hot, the skin tight.

"She's okay," he replied. "What do you remember?"

"He tried to burn me," I said. "Jure tried to…" I put a hand to my cheek. It felt smooth, except for a ridged spot near my jawline. If I hadn't turned my face, the ball of flame would have hit me straight on. "He told Travis to aim for my face. Where's Granny?" I didn't care about how I looked right now. I needed to see my grandmother.

"When you fainted, I called Edna and Evelyn. They're

in with Granny now."

"Help me up," I said. "I need to see her."

"Tansy, maybe you should wait," Vaughn said. "You're still healing."

It must be bad if he didn't want me to see her.

"Please," I begged him. "Please."

"What do you remember?" he asked.

"I...I sent out lightning bolts. They hit Jure and Vanessa—"

"They survived," he admitted. "Jure and Vanessa *and* Travis—they're still out there. But we managed to get Skyler out safe. She's here."

I couldn't think about that right now. "I want to see my grandmother." I threw back the covers and stood, but dizziness hit me, and I fell back on the bed.

"Later," Vaughn said. "You need to rest. So does your granny. She's lost a lot of blood."

"Will she be okay?" I tried again, closing my eyes against what I might hear.

"She's resting," he said.

Resting—not dead. It took a minute for the news to sink in. The crushing weight on my chest lifted. She was alive.

Granny was alive.

"Please, Vaughn. I need to see her," I said.

He must have heard the conviction in my voice, because he said, "In her room."

I started to get out of bed, but Vaughn scooped me up.

"I'll carry you," he said gruffly.

I wrapped my arms around his neck, and he took me to my grandmother's room. She was in bed, covers to her chin, her eyes closed. Edna and Evelyn were watching over her.

"Granny," I said softly, but she didn't move. "How is

she?" I asked, but I already knew.

"She'll live," Edna said. "I'm not sure, but I think your mother held back."

"Maybe," I said doubtfully.

Evelyn nodded. "I think so."

"If I kill Jure, we'll all be free," I said.

Her lips set in a thin line. "About your mother…"

"I don't want to talk about her right now," I said. "I might never want to talk about her."

I would kill Vanessa, too, I knew, for what she'd done to my grandmother.

Edna gave a short nod. "I understand." She stood and then said, "I'm going to see if I can rustle up something for your grandmother to eat. She'll probably be hungry when she wakes."

I paced for an hour, only stopping to check on my grandmother.

"It's not working," I said. "She doesn't seem any better."

Vaughn smoothed a hand over my hair. "Give it a little more time."

Granny woke up with a groan.

"Can I get you anything?" I asked.

Edna came into the room, carrying soup. "She needs to eat."

"I'm not hungry," Granny said.

"It's your favorite," Edna coaxed. "Homemade chicken noodle."

"It smells good," she said. "I guess I could eat."

That had to be a good sign.

"You need your rest," I said. "We'll come back later."

Edna fed my grandmother because she was too weak and my hands were still shaking. Evelyn went to open the curtains and let in some natural light. I saw Granny looking intently at my face.

I immediately tried to hide it from her sight. She didn't need another thing to worry about right now.

"Don't," she said, her voice scratchy. "Tansy, you're beautiful to your very soul."

I couldn't answer because my eyes were leaking tears. "I haven't looked in the mirror yet."

I wasn't the vainest person in the world, but I was nervous to see what damage had been done.

I thought about Jure's face and what I'd done to it, and then I felt a little better.

Edna handed me a heavy antique hand mirror. "Tansy, it will fade."

"That sentence isn't reassuring me," I replied. I took a deep breath and then looked.

The scar was ugly and deep—melted-looking in some places, raised and angry in others. I sucked in a breath. There were worse things than a scar, but right now, I couldn't name them.

"Edna tells me she's working on a skin cream," Granny said. "But wounds caused by vampire fire are tricky."

I nodded before her friends started shooing me out of the room.

"She needs her rest," Edna said. "And so do you." She herded me back to my room and tucked me in.

There was a new charm necklace by my bed. She helped me put it on, and then I slid into sleep.

• • •

When I woke up, the house was quiet. The shades were drawn in my bedroom, and it made me wonder if I'd be stuck inside until dark—alone. Most vampires couldn't walk during daylight hours, and Vaughn hadn't been turned. Would I be forever banished to the night while he led a normal life? And how would I manage my senior year?

When I turned over, Granny Mariotti was sitting in a chair by my bed.

"You didn't eat dinner," she said.

"I'm not hungry." There was an acid pit in my stomach, so there was no room for food. "I want to be alone, Granny." I turned on my side and kept my eyes closed.

Sometime later, Skyler tiptoed into the room.

"What were you and Opal Ann trying to accomplish?" I demanded. "Did you suddenly develop superhuman strength when I wasn't looking?"

She didn't say anything.

"No? Super hearing, then? The ability to compel someone to do what you want them to do? Vampire fire?"

"We were trying to stop a predator," she finally said. "We failed."

"Opal Ann is dead, and this is your fault," I said, the words vicious and unfair, but I couldn't stop them.

Skyler went still. "You're right."

"Opal Ann wouldn't have died if it weren't for you," I continued. "If you hadn't gone back to Travis."

"I wanted to help you," she said. "I wanted to make up for getting you involved in all this."

"You could have told me the truth," I said. "But you didn't. Again. Instead, you snuck off on your own, and now people are dead, and it's your fault."

Skyler looked like I'd put a stake through her heart, but then she nodded once and left the room.

I stayed in my bed a long time, thinking about the mistakes I'd made. I was pretty sure I'd just lost my best friend, too.

I didn't know how they explained Opal Ann's death in a way that anyone would believe, but the news story didn't mention vampires once. I felt like it was a secret I should be shouting at the top of my lungs. *Vampires exist! Run!*

Those good-looking guys with fangs? In reality, they're vicious predators who kill for something to do on a slow Saturday night.

Jure wasn't the real problem. Silence was the real enemy. Indifference was the real enemy. But that didn't mean I didn't have to kill him.

Chapter Thirty-Two

Opal Ann was dead. Granny almost died. For a week, I sat in the living room, brooding, while the Old Crones Book Club members fussed over Granny's amazing recovery. I was relieved she was better, but I had places to go and vampires to kill.

I had to kill Jure Grando, and I had to do it alone. I couldn't put the others in any more danger. It bothered me a little how much I *wanted* to kill him.

Travis hadn't needed to kill Opal Ann. He'd done it to prove a point. To show me that he was more powerful than I was and to let me know that I couldn't stop him.

But I *would* stop him. And the point I would make would be with the end of a stake to his heart.

Opal Ann's body had already been sent back to Texas.

Bobbie Jean was driving home to mourn her sister with her family. She'd stopped in to say goodbye. I knew Bobbie Jean was hurting from Opal Ann's death; I just wasn't sure who she blamed more, Skyler or me. But definitely Travis and his father.

"I'm sorry about Opal Ann," I said.

Her eyes were red and puffy. "You did your best to help," she said. "It wasn't enough, but you tried. That's why I'm warning you."

"Warning me about what?"

"I'm coming back," she said. "And when I do, I aim to kill every vampire in this state."

I narrowed my eyes at her. "I'm a vampire."

"I know," she said.

"Well. Until we meet again, then," I said forlornly.

There wasn't anything else to say. After Bobbie Jean pulled away, I went inside and found Granny sitting at a barstool with a plethora of ward ingredients spread out in front of her.

"What are you doing?"

"Vampires are vindictive creatures," Granny said. "We need to prepare."

"Prepare for what?"

"Retaliation."

I sat next to her and reached for the garlic. We wove the cloves into garlands and then boosted their effect with protection spells.

Vaughn wandered in at some point during our witchy craft project, but I ignored him.

He wasn't in the mood to be ignored. He leaned over the back of my chair and watched me, not saying anything.

"If you're going to just stand there, you might as well help," I said.

He sat next to me, our legs bumping. "Show me what to do."

The three of us made garlic garlands, not speaking, until Granny sent us to pour a line of salt on every entryway.

"It's more of a demon thing," Granny said. "But it couldn't hurt."

We spent the day putting wards around the house, in front of every window and door.

Then we took some to Skyler's and Vaughn's. "Where's your dad?" I asked Vaughn.

"He's at work," he said. "But he knows I'm back and that Skyler's okay."

"I wish Skyler's dad cared about her as much as your dad does," I said.

"Tansy, you're a good friend," he said. "I don't think Skyler even knows everything you did for her."

"Everything *we* did for her," I said. "You were there, too. I mean, you had to fight off all those Bleeders on a daily basis."

I was trying for a teasing note, but Vaughn didn't even crack a smile.

"What about Edna and Evelyn's place?" That's where the other girls were staying. Kylie and Marisol were runaways Jure had lured to the ranch with promises of work. They'd turned eighteen there. I shuddered to think of what their birthdays had been like.

"Evelyn has it handled," Granny Mariotti said.

"But…"

"She would never let anything happen to those girls," Granny said. "Trust me. They are safe there."

She didn't say it, but I knew she meant safer than here. Where Jure would eventually come to find me and pay me back for scarring his face. For humiliating him in front of the other vampires.

It didn't take long. The next night, vampires had our house surrounded, but they couldn't come in without an invitation.

I peered out the window at them. "You think they'll just stay there until they get bored or until the sun comes up?"

"Or until an innocent person strolls into the middle of them and gets eaten," Granny Mariotti replied.

"That's likely," I said. "Since the Executioner's out there and she looks a bit hangry."

"I wish you wouldn't call her that," Granny said gently.

"What should I call the woman who gave birth to me and now wants to kill me?" I asked. "Mom? Maybe Mommy Dearest?"

"She's still my daughter," Granny said. "She's still your mother."

"That person is gone, Granny," I said. "How can you say that after what she did to you? I begged her not to hurt you, but she did it anyway. She knew it would hurt me. I think she *wanted* to hurt me. Who does that?"

"Send the girl!" Jure shouted from outside the window. "You know the one we seek."

There was no way I was letting Skyler step foot out of my house. She was hollow-eyed and shivering, even in the hot summer night.

"You can't have Skyler," I shouted back.

"Not the blood donor," he replied. "Send out the witch." He meant me.

"Never," Granny said.

Jure said something to one of his vampires, who went somewhere out of my eyesight. He returned, dragging someone with him. *Vaughn.*

No. No. No, no, no.

"Come out or we will drain him dry," Jure said.

"Don't do it, Tansy," Vaughn shouted. Jure backhanded him. I couldn't let Vaughn die.

"I'll come out if you promise to let him go," Granny said.

There was a short silence.

"You're not the witch I'm looking for," he finally said. Tricky vampire.

"I'm coming out," I yelled. "But you have to promise not to hurt Vaughn."

"Jure Grando never kept a bargain in his entire life," Granny M said.

I gaped at her. "You know Jure? Like, personally?"

Granny clenched her jaw.

"Do we have a deal?" I yelled.

I thought Jure was trying to figure out if I was really that gullible or if I knew it was a trap. I wasn't gullible. I was desperate.

Granny's breath hitched. "Tansy," she said.

"I have to," I replied.

"I know," she said, but she didn't move from where she blocked the door.

"Give me a minute," Evelyn said. "I think I found something that will help."

She left for a moment, then came back into the room and handed me a sharp wooden stake. "It's made of rowan. Aim for the heart," she said. "And don't miss."

Instead, I dug out my trusty drumstick, still caked with black blood. "I've got it covered."

Granny handed me the stake anyway. "It doesn't hurt to have a backup."

The coven huddled together with a stack of dusty books.

"No matter what, Tansy," Granny said, "I want you to keep fighting. Until you can't fight any more."

I kept my eyes down, the tears in them making it impossible to look at her.

"They'll kill him if I don't," I said. "I love you, Granny."

I couldn't bear to say goodbye to her, even though part

of me knew that was what I was doing. I kissed her cheek.

And then I walked out the door into a nest of vampires.

It was still dark outside, but morning was coming soon. The sky had that purplish tinge. Maybe Jure wasn't going to kill me himself. Maybe he'd leave me outside until the sun did the job for him.

Someone—probably one of the younger vampires, since I couldn't see Jure doing anything he would consider a menial task—had knocked out the streetlights.

I didn't see Vaughn but wasn't going to draw attention to his absence. Travis, Jure, and Vanessa stood there with a bunch of vampires I didn't recognize.

"Looks like the gang's all here," I said. What was a group of vampires called? A gang? A bite? A bite of vampires. I liked it. Fear was making me silly.

Some of the acid/diet soda injuries on Jure's face had healed, but others looked raw and full of pus.

"I didn't want to have to do this, Vanessa," I said.

I thought she expected me to use my witchy powers or even vamp it up, but instead, I fought like a girl and headbutted her.

I grabbed Jure, but his hand wrapped around my throat, and he forced me to meet his eyes. I squeezed his face until his eyes started to bleed, but he wouldn't let go. My fangs came down, and I bit off his ear. Travis sent ball after ball of vampire flame at me. He didn't miss me, but I didn't stop fighting his father, even when my skin started to sizzle.

"Let go of me," I gritted out. I could feel myself getting weaker, our wills battling each other. He tried to get me to look into his eyes so he could compel me, but I wouldn't.

Instead, I took one long fingernail and raked it across his cheek, digging deep until I struck bone. That did the trick. Jure finally loosened his grip, and I fell onto the ground with a thump.

Desperation turned me into something unrecognizable, all sharp teeth and claws, but it was no use. I was outnumbered, and if I didn't kill him, they'd never stop until they'd killed everyone I loved.

"Come here," he said. I was too weak to fight him this time, and my feet went. I tried to slow them down, to resist, but it was no use. They carried me to him.

He ignored my struggles and went for my neck. I tried to block it, but his voice in my head kept telling me not to fight.

He tore at my flesh, going for an artery. Making sure the damage was permanent, fatal. I finally gained control of my mind, but it was almost too late.

Intent into action. Intent into action. Intent into action. The words slowed down in my mind as my heartbeat slowed to match.

Somehow, I found the strength to wrench myself away, to fight, but he was so strong. *Intent into action.*

One of the other vampires laughed, sounding like a happy little psychopath. "She's not so tough now."

What was Jure's only weakness? His son? Yeah, right. His *pride.*

"What kind of king are you? You let your son turn me into a striga vie. Even powerful vampires like you are afraid of my kind."

I grabbed the garlic in my pocket and pressed it to his flesh. He screamed, but his lips still dripped blood. My blood.

Black spots were dancing in my eyes when he leaned in and whispered, "I'm going to kill them all, even your precious granny. And there's nothing you can do about it."

Just watch me, asshole. I took the drumstick and shoved

it into his ribs. It missed his heart, but he let out a hiss of pain.

He bit me again, his long fangs latching on and not letting go. I could feel my blood pumping out of my body, faster and faster the longer he held on.

I pried his fangs from my neck and then gripped him tightly around the throat. I could have killed him by drinking him dry, but I didn't want his disgusting blood.

He was so strong. He tried to shift, but the chanting from the Old Crones Book Club inside the house prevented it. Silver spots swam in my vision now.

I just needed to hang on to him, to keep him from escaping. It was almost sunrise.

I could feel the warmth gathering in the sky. I needed to hold on for just a few minutes longer.

Spittle flew from his mouth.

I heard the other vampires retreating, seeking a dark place to hide. Jure was desperate now, punching the side of my face, kicking me, his face white. He knew what was in store for him.

He still wouldn't die. Why wouldn't he die? I took the rowan stake and shoved it into his heart.

Jure started to shake.

I covered my eyes until I felt a pop. When I opened them, something slimy and black dripped down my face, but the loss of blood made me dizzy.

I'd gotten Jure Grando all over my clothes. It probably would stain.

I was weak and oh so tired, and I hurt all over. The sun was warm on my face when my grip loosened, and everything faded as I went under the dark.

...

Someone was screaming. It made my head hurt.
My mouth was open, and I realized the screams were coming from me. My body was fire, then ice. It hurt to breathe.

I was fading in and out of consciousness, but I heard Vaughn swearing under his breath. "Please, Tansy, hold on," he said. I felt him pick me up. Even his gentle touch hurt.

I woke in agony.

Cold. I was so cold. There was something heavy draped over me, but it wasn't enough. My teeth chattered. I didn't remember getting home, but I knew I was in my bedroom.

I was safe.

"What happened?" My voice was so hoarse, I barely recognized myself.

"Later," he said. "I'll explain later."

"What about Granny? Skyler?"

"Granny and Skyler are okay," he replied.

It was agony to move enough to speak, but I had to know what had happened to them.

He shook his head. "No more talking."

He took my hand in his and then guided my mouth to a vein on his wrist.

"Vaughn, no," I said.

"There are third-degree burns all over your body," he said. A pulse beat in his wrist. I could smell his blood. He smelled so good. Like my favorite beach day. Like delicious kisses and hot summer nights.

My pulse went double-time, and my mouth watered. My entire focus was on the vein in his wrist.

The pain was so intense, I was about to pass out.

"You're sure?" I asked, my voice a raspy sound I barely recognized as mine.

"Yes, I'm sure," he said.

"Get my drumstick," I said. "Just in case you need to use it."

"I won't," Vaughn said.

"Vaughn, you have to be able to stop me."

He gave a jerky nod. "Not that, but I'll stop you. I promise."

I was weak—so weak.

I kissed his lips softly. Then he sliced open his wrist and held it up to my mouth. His blood tasted so good, so sweet, just like Vaughn. Like honey and sunshine, like the salt of the ocean. Like love.

I drank, and drank, and drank, and didn't want to stop, but this was Vaughn. I had to stop. I had to.

Chapter Thirty-Three

A few days later, I sat on my grandmother's couch, my head in my hands, fully recovered. Vaughn's blood had done the trick. He sat next to me, his arm around me. I winced at the sight of his bandaged wrist. Rose and Thorn sat opposite us.

Yesmyqueenyesmyqueenyesmyqueen. The sound was like the buzzing of a mosquito, but the twins wouldn't stop saying it.

I didn't look up until Vaughn gave me a gentle nudge. Rose stood in front of me.

"McQueen," she said, bowing low. I gave Vaughn a puzzled look. What was Rose trying to say?

He snorted. "She's saying *my queen.*"

"Why is she saying that?" I asked him. He shrugged. I turned to Rose. "Why are you saying that?"

"My queen?" she asked, bowing low. "Jure Grando is dead."

I just stared at her. "I know, but why are you calling *me* that?"

Her mouth opened a little, and she glanced at her twin, who stepped forward. "Your Highness," she said. "You are now the queen."

It was like that time in advanced calculus when all the numbers suddenly looked like little squiggles. I didn't understand what she was getting at.

"Queen of what?"

"Queen of the vampires, of course," she replied. "Tansy Mariotti killed the King of the Vampires, Jure Grando. She is the new king. Or queen, whichever title you prefer."

"I don't want to be queen of the vampires. Or a vampire at all."

How could I figure out how to rule a vampire kingdom and protect my subjects? No, thank you.

"The strongest wins the crown," Rose said. "It is done."

"Well, undo it," I said, but it was too late, and I knew it. I had to face the consequences.

"Queen Tansy," Thorn said. "We can help you."

I sighed. Vampire queen.

What would the rules of my reign be? I was queen of a kingdom I didn't want. One full of monsters.

"Okay, so I'm queen of the vampires. Exactly how many 'subjects' are we talking about here?" I asked. "It's not like I can post something on social media telling all the vampires in California to check in with me."

"Jure must not have been Travis's maker," Thorn said. "Our reports indicate Travis and the rest of the band are still vampires. The good news is that you have two less vampires in your kingdom."

"Why's that?" I asked.

"Jure Grando was their maker and they hadn't killed anyone in vampire form," she said. "Therefore, they reverted to human."

"That's great news," I said.

"One of them was over three hundred years old," she added. "And immediately turned to dust."

"That's not so great," I said. "But still better than being a vampire."

Because of Travis's inability to keep his fangs in his mouth, I was a vampire witch. A striga vie, caught between two worlds.

Witches were human. Vampires were not. Then what was I? I still looked human, but so did vampires—at least humanish, until the bloodlust hit.

I comforted myself that I wasn't a true vampire, since I hadn't gone through the transformation, but I still had the pointy fangs and blood cravings.

The Old Crones Book Club called out suggestions of ways to contact my new subjects. I hadn't had a mother or a father, but I had a surplus of love from these women. They would help me figure out how to stop the vampires in my realm from preying on unwilling humans.

Granny Mariotti's tiny bungalow was overflowing with humans and witches and vampires alike. They were all talking at once, and it was giving me a headache.

"I don't know how to be a queen," I wailed to Skyler. Rose remained impassive, but I caught Thorn snickering. She saw me staring and gave me a blindingly bright smile.

"Make it up as you go along," Skyler said. "You can't be any worse at it than Jure was."

I made a face at her. "That's comforting. There's still his son to worry about."

"Travis won't give you any more trouble," she said.

"That's an interesting theory," I said. "Maybe I need to find him to test it out."

I peeked over at her to see if she was disturbed by my suggestion.

"That's not the only thing you'd be testing," she said. "Tansy, I'm over him. I'm over that compulsion to be with him no matter what."

"Are you sure?" I asked. "Nothing seemed to shake it before."

"Your magic worked," she said. "The other girls are getting better, too."

Her eyes were clear and bright—no sign of compulsion. I was so relieved she was back home, I didn't even argue with her about what the future might bring. The teeth marks all over her body were fading, but I knew there were other scars we couldn't see. And I hadn't helped her to heal them. Not when it mattered.

"I'm sorry," I said, looking her in the eye. "I shouldn't have lashed out at you like that. I was hurting over Opal Ann. And so scared about Granny."

"We all were," Skyler said back. "I understand."

We still had a long way to go toward healing, and I wasn't sure if our friendship would ever go back to the way it was before. But something told me Skyler and I would be all right.

Her dad was still out of the country, but Gertie came by to visit her. First, Gertie and Granny had a hushed conversation in the garden, and then Gertie and Skyler talked in private in Granny's office.

When they came out, I could tell they'd both been crying, but Skyler looked less unhappy somehow.

It was dark now, and I needed a break from all the drama, so I took out the trash. I was dragging the bins to the curb when I spotted her, watching me from across the street.

She was the last person I expected to see. I walked over to her. "Vanessa."

My mother had the nerve to show her face? She was either trying to goad me into fighting her or she had a death wish.

"You tried to kill my grandmother," I said.

"If I wanted to kill her, she'd be dead," she replied.

I absorbed that information. Because it was possible she'd spared my grandmother, I wouldn't kill her right now. Unless she made it impossible not to.

"Aren't you going to bow to your queen?" I asked.

"You are not fit to be queen. A queen does not take out her own trash," she said.

"This queen does," I said. "This queen also doesn't treat her subjects like her personal blood bank."

"Do you even know what it takes to be queen?" she asked. "Have you even chosen your Executioner?"

"I won't need one," I said.

"Every ruler in the PAC has one," she said.

"Not me. I'll be a different kind of queen."

She sucked in a breath. "You think you have what it takes to be queen?"

I studied her a moment and then bared my golden fangs. "I know I do."

"We'll see," she said. I thought she would challenge me, but instead, she walked away into the darkness.

It wasn't a surprise to see my mother walk away from me. It was what she did. But that didn't mean it didn't hurt.

And the hurts kept coming.

When I looked over at the house, Vaughn was standing on the front porch, watching me with a frown on his face.

I joined him. "Everything okay?" I asked. I'd taken a lot of his blood, and he still looked pale. He had dark circles under his eyes, and his summer tan had faded.

Still, he was beautiful.

"You let her go?" That's why he was all frowny-face?

"She's my mother," I said. Then I changed the subject. "I have a lot to do before school starts. Rose and Thorn said they can stay a little while longer to help with the transition. And maybe we'll have time to go out on a real date."

He looked at his feet. "I've been meaning to talk to you about that."

I sucked in a breath. "Are you going to break up with me?" I asked.

He shook his head. "Jesus, no. Tansy, you're my favorite person. I…I really care about you. It's something else. Thorn thinks that with some training, I can be useful to the PAC," he said.

"You want to help the PAC?"

"I want to help *you*," he replied. "And now you're part of the PAC."

"What would you be doing?" I asked.

"I'd meet up with some vampire hunters in Texas," he replied. "Correction. *We*'d meet up with some of the observation team in Texas. She asked me to train with them."

"Are you sure you want to do this?" I asked.

"I am. Jure almost killed you, Tansy," he said.

"I'm aware," I said. "But this isn't about me."

"It's always about you," he said. "I want to protect you."

"And you think joining the PAC will help me?"

"I do," he said.

I wasn't sure about that. I didn't know anyone else in the PAC. I liked Rose and Thorn, but they weren't in charge. What would happen if Vaughn had to choose between me and some random group of vampires-in-charge?

"You're going to be gone the rest of the summer," I said, my voice coming out whinier than I meant it to.

"It's only a month," he replied.

"That's not an answer. Are we breaking up?"

"You're not getting rid of me that easily," he said, and I relaxed.

"I could use a little extra muscle," I told him. "Bobbie Jean just basically threatened my life before she took off."

"She's still mourning Opal Ann," he said.

"I don't trust her," I said.

"She'll calm down," he assured me. "Just give her some time. But if she doesn't…"

I wrapped my arm around his biceps. "I know I can count on you."

"You can," he said. "Count on me, I mean." He shot me a warm smile. "Thorn said I'm a natural," he added.

A natural aptitude for killing vampires? That could be convenient…or very, very inconvenient.

He ran a hand through his hair and looked away. A muscle ticked in his jaw. "I'll miss you," he finally said.

"I'll miss you, too," I said. I cleared my throat. "What if I go full-on vamp while you're gone?"

"You won't," he said.

"But what if I do?"

He kissed me gently, just a peck. "We'll figure it out."

"It makes me so angry," I said. "I didn't choose this. My life has been turned upside down. If I could just press rewind and change the past, I would. I would have never gone to that party, never met Travis. But I can't, and now I'm stuck with my decision for the rest of my undead life."

"It wasn't your fault."

"What if I become like them? What if I become a monster?" I knew the truth. Even if Vaughn didn't think I was a monster, that didn't mean I wasn't going to become one.

"Not you, Tansy," he said. "You're not—"

"Not a vampire? But I am. At least part of me is."

He moved closer and brushed a stray strand of hair away from my face. I opened my mouth, but nothing came out. I wanted to tell him not to go, that I'd miss him too much, but I couldn't. Vaughn had made up his mind.

"I'll call you every night," I promised.

"Your skin is so soft," he said. He touched my cheek. "I've wanted you for so long. I don't want anything to come between us, Tansy." He kissed me again, more thoroughly this time.

When we drew apart, he took my hand. I looked into his eyes and smiled ruefully. "A vampire queen and a vampire hunter are dating. What could possibly go wrong?"

He smiled back. "We'll make it work."

"Tansy," came Skyler's voice. "We have a problem."

Of course we did.

I sighed and dropped Vaughn's hand, then walked away, tossing over my shoulder, "Duty calls."

Don't miss Tansy's second adventure in
I'm With the Banned

Coming soon!

Turn the page for a sneak peek...

Chapter 1

My heartbeat accelerated when I saw who was leaning against my locker the first day of school. Vaughn Sheridan, long-time best friend, first-time boyfriend, and avowed vampire hunter. Too bad that this summer I became the queen of the vampires.

It wasn't all bad news, Skyler was back home, Vaughn still wanted to date me, and I was learning to manage my allergy to the sun. Since I was a striga vie, a vampire-witch hybrid, I didn't turn to ash in the sun, like other vampires, but without my tonic, I did get violently ill, which is why I'd guzzled a big ol' glass of the stuff right before school.

I was getting better at taming the monster inside me, but I still had to deal with my fangs descending when I was angry or upset. I was learning to control it, at least in public.

"Tansy," Vaughn said. "I missed you." His skin was golden brown from his month in the Texas sun, which made his gray eyes shine. His dark hair was longer than he normally wore it and it made me want to run my fingers through the strands.

I melted when he linked his hand in mine and pulled me into a supply closet. He cupped my face in his hands, his thumb brushing over the scar on my cheek before he leaned down to kiss me. His lips felt so good that I could barely stand it. He broke the kiss, but I leaned in for more and he chuckled. "You missed me, too."

He was smiling. I always felt like I had won a prize when Vaughn smiled at me, even back when we'd simply been friends. He hoarded smiles like librarians hoarded books.

There was a small patch of wall not occupied by shelving and he walked me backwards until my back was against it. I didn't mind. I had missed him since he'd been off training with Rose and Thorn to hunt vampires.

"I wasn't sure I'd see you at school today," he said, slightly emphasizing day.

"Granny bought me a parasol," I said. "And Edna is a dermatologist, so she wrote me a note excusing me from outside activities due to a rare skin condition." It wasn't a lie. If I stayed in the sun too long, I'd roast like a marshmallow by the campfire.

He touched my shoulder lightly. "I like this shirt."

I like you, I thought, but kept my mouth shut and instead, I stared at him. I was glad Skyler had convinced me to make an effort. I wore a green top and a long skirt and sandals. I was wearing make-up because my eyes looked squinty without mascara and eye liner.

I put out a hand, looking for an excuse to touch him like he was touching me. "When did you get back from Texas?" I breathed him in. He always smelled like sunshine and sand, like summer. Like home.

"Late last night," he replied, leaning in a fraction. "I would have called you, but I figured you were already asleep."

We were so close in the tiny room that I could smell the shampoo he used. "What did you want to talk to me about?" I asked, hoping he hadn't changed his mind about us. Dating me was complicated.

"You look really pretty today," he said, his hand brushing mine. I stepped closer.

"You look good, too," I said. He seemed to realize how our bodies were pressed together and took a step back. I had to admit that stung.

He could see the hurt in my eyes. "Tansy, I'm sorry. As much as I'm enjoying this, I need to talk to you."

I turned away from him and studied the shelf of cleaning products like they held the secret to life itself.

I cleared my throat. I hadn't been happy about his decision to go to Texas, but Vaughn had made up his mind. The important thing was that he'd made it back home in one piece.

"What did you want to talk to me about?" I asked. "Because I have class in like five minutes."

"Do you want to hear the bad news or the worse news?" he asked.

"Neither sounds great, Vaughn," I said. It wasn't like Vaughn to be dramatic. I tensed, expecting him to tell me something heartbreaking.

"Okay, bad first. Remember how my dad is dating someone new?" he replied.

"Vaguely," I said. "He started dating her right before we…"

"Went on the road with a vampire band?" Vaughn replied. "Yep, that's her. He's going to ask her to move in."

"When did you meet her?" I asked, surprised because he hadn't mentioned anything.

"I haven't," he admitted. "Dad's setting up a meet and greet on Saturday."

"Why don't I come over Saturday, too?" I asked.

His face softened. "I'd love that."

"I'm assuming you haven't told your dad about what happened?" I asked.

He shook his head. "Not sure he'd believe me about what we did last summer anyway."

"I worked mostly night shifts while you were gone," I told him, "So I didn't see him very much." I hesitated and then asked, "He doesn't know about your new career?"

"No," he said. "I told him I was at conditioning camp." He paused and then added, "He's been distracted, but maybe it's because I've never seen my dad act so infatuated before."

"I'm glad he found someone," I said.

"Me, too," Vaughn said. "But tell me what I missed while I was gone. Besides you, I mean."

"It was quiet," I said. "Honestly, it was kind of nice."

"No phone calls?" Vaughn asked.

"What do you mean?" I gave him a puzzled frown.

"Connor texted me that he wanted to talk to Skyler," he said.

I flinched at my best friend Skyler's ex-boyfriend's name.

Vaughn added hastily, "I didn't tell him anything, I swear, but somehow, he knew something was wrong."

"Skyler didn't say anything," I said. "And I'm sure she would have told me if she'd gotten a call."

He nodded and I changed the subject.

"Okay, back to the subject at hand," I said. "Saturday

night? I'll come over."

He'd been gone half the summer. Okay, maybe that was an exaggeration. He'd been gone a month, but it had felt like half the summer.

"No, I mean, I'll pick you up," he clarified. "I'm blowing this." He ran his hand through his hair, then stepped closer until we were nearly touching. "Tansy, I'm sorry. I want you to come over and not just because I need your help. I want to spend time with you."

Before I could answer, the bell rang. We snuck out of the supply closet as soon as the coast was clear. I headed to my first class but then Skyler fell into step next to me. "A little supply closet action. Nice," she said, then sighed. "Connor and I used to love that closet."

"No action," I said.

She gave me a skeptical look.

"Okay, a little action and a lot of problems," I admitted.

"What's wrong, Tansy?" Skyler asked.

"Vaughn wants us to have dinner together on Saturday," I said. "To meet his dad's new girlfriend."

"Aw, a double-date," she said. "With his dad."

I ignored Skyler's giggles as we slid into our seat barely missing the tardy bell. "Classic," she finally said between giggles. "That is so frickin twisted."

It was my turn to sigh. "Tell me about it."

"What are you going to wear?" Skyler asked.

"That's what you're worried about?"

"You know, this is an opportunity to remind Vaughn what he missed," she replied, wiggling her eyebrows meaningfully.

"What's with the eyebrows?"

She giggled. "Maybe you can remind him what he left behind when he went to Texas."

I flinched at the reminder that he had left me behind. I knew she wasn't trying to hurt me, but it did. "How exactly am I supposed to do that?"

Again, with the eyebrows.

"Skyler," I said. So much had happened between Vaughn and me this summer. We'd gone from friends to a couple, but that was the least weird thing about it.

He was back home, and he'd missed me. The thought brought a smile to my face.

"Senior year is looking up," I said. "I was beginning to wonder if Vaughn was ever coming back."

Class started before she could answer, but then Ms. Townsend was interrupted mid-lecture about nineteenth-century poets when the principal walked in.

Principal Ferrell cleared her throat. "Sorry to disturb you, but we have two new students joining us today, Rose and Thorn Assassin." She paused. "Unusual last name."

Someone in the back row choked back a laugh.

"What the hell?" Skyler mouthed to me. My sentiments exactly.

What were the two vampire hunters doing at my high school? They'd tried to blend in, which meant that Thorn's dagger was nowhere in sight, but I had no doubt it was concealed on her somewhere.

"You are not enrolled here," I hissed at Thorn, who took the desk in front of me, after shoving the guy in it out of it when the teacher turned her back.

"My queen, I hate to contradict you, but yes, we are," Rose said. She was sitting right behind me, studying a perfume bottle that probably didn't contain perfume.

Thorn was polishing her dagger. "Queen Tansy doesn't like to be called queen."

Whenever someone used that word about me, my

body felt as though I'd guzzled about a thousand cups of coffee.

"Not for long," I hissed. "And, Thorn, put that away." I wasn't a hundred percent certain that the sisters were friend or foe, but at least they'd shared some information about the shadowy organization they worked for.

Rose and Thorn were identical twins who at first glance, looked nothing alike. Rose's hair was pink, and Thorn's was black. Rose dressed in floral dresses and looked like woodland creatures would do her laundry while Thorn looked like she'd hunt and kill those woodland creatures and preferred leggings and leather jackets. Rose's weapon of choice was poison and Thorn's was her pointy dagger.

"Why are you here?" I asked them.

"In English Literature?" Rose asked, sounding confused.

"Why are you at my school?" I said. "Aren't you too old for high school?" I wasn't actually sure how old they were, but I thought they were around twenty or so.

"We go where you go," Thorn said. "Until further notice." Given Rose's love of deadly nightshade and Thorn's fondness for her dagger, they were probably more than bodyguards.

"You can't kill anybody," I said, then amended it. "Unless you have to."

They didn't work for me, they worked for the Paranormal Activities Committee, aka PAC, which from what I'd learned had oversight in supernatural busines in every realm, including mine. I hadn't wanted to be queen, but I didn't get a vote. I'd killed the king of the California vampires and now I had to suck it up and learn to be a good ruler.

They'd also cleaned up after me when I'd killed The

Drainers' drummer with his own drumstick, but none of that explained what they'd been doing in my class.

"We were bored," Thorn said. She gave me a long look. "We'll start your training this weekend."

"My training?"

Thorn nodded as if it were decided and turned her attention to the teacher at the front of the room.

"Don't you have PAC business to attend to?" I asked. I was pretty sure the twins were a couple of years older than me and had already graduated from high school. Or assassin school. Whichever.

"We're…on vacation."

I exchanged a look with my best friend. Doubtful.

Skyler and I met Vaughn for lunch. We were seniors so we could go off campus. I held my parasol over my head, feeling kind of foolish, but most of the student body was eager to leave so nobody seemed to be paying me any attention.

Vaughn drove, but I noticed something different about his car.

"You got your windows tinted," I said.

He glanced at me and smiled. "I thought it might help with the whole sun issue."

I wondered how much it cost and if I could do the same for the Deathtrap.

"That reminds me," I said. "Time for my tonic." I dug the thermos out of my bag and took a sip before recapping it.

"Did you know that Rose and Thorn have enrolled here?"

"What?" he replied. "They never said a word."

"You were hanging out with them for a whole month," Skyler replied.

"We weren't exactly hanging out," he said. "We spent twelve-hour days training. Most nights, I was so tired I laid on the bed and groaned. I thought I was in shape until I trained with those two."

"Where'd you stay?" Skyler asked curiously. I knew because Vaughn, tired or not, had video called or texted almost every night.

"This big house in Austin," Vaughn said. "Rose said one of the P.A.C. members owned it. I can't believe they're attending school here. How many classes do you have with them?"

"They're in our Lit class," I replied. "But who knows? They'll probably just show up whenever they feel like it."

"We never decided where we're eating," Vaughn said.

"Anywhere but Chicken Clucks," Skyler replied.

"Understood," Vaughn said. "How about Diamonds? They have a drive-through."

After a quick lunch, we headed back to school. Vaughn had a meeting with his adviser that he couldn't miss.

When the final bell rang, Rose and Thorn trailed Skyler and me from our lockers to the big double doors at the entrance of the school. We were prepared to make our escape, but Ashley stepped in front of us, her toned frame vibrating with curiosity. Her brown hair had perfect highlights from the sun or perhaps an excellent stylist and she was dressed in an expensive but understated cream dress.

I lived in band tees, faded jeans and sunscreen and during our sixth-grade beach trip, I'd stayed in the sun too

long and fried my skin. My classmates had called me Rock
Lobster for six months. Christian C. even did the song's
choreography from Just Dance every time he saw me.

"Who're your friends?"

"None of your business," Skyler drawled.

I felt Ashley's eyes on me as we swept past her. Rose
and Thorn stayed on our heels as we walked to Skyler's
car.

In the parking lot, there were a bunch of guys crowded
around a souped-up Challenger. I caught the scent of Axe
body spray and underneath that, something like wet dog.

Rose and Thorn stopped and sniffed the air, but before
they said anything, the boys piled into the Challenger and
took off.

My best friend and I had carpooled to school. She
lived a few houses down from me and Vaughn lived two
streets over.

"Want to come over and raid Gertie's going to Goodwill
bag?"

"Who am I to turn down free clothes?" I replied.

Gertie, Sky's stepmother, had a credit card with no
limit and a serious shopping addiction, which was a bad
combination. But since Gertie was a former Vegas showgirl
with showgirl curves, her hand-me-downs didn't fit Skyler's
slimmer build.

I had what Granny Mariotti described as bounty. Or
maybe she meant booty. Either way, I had it. I plopped
said booty on Skyler's king-sized bed while she rummaged
through a bag of discarded clothing.

"This would look great on you," Skyler said, throwing
me a jade colored top. I held it against me and looked in
the mirror. That shade of green did something wonderful
for my eyes.

I also snagged a pair of expensive, downy soft jean shorts with the tag still on them. I narrowed my eyes at Skyler. "It almost seems as if someone went out and bought these especially for me."

She held her hands up. "Gertie bought them, I swear."

I was still suspicious. The one good thing that had happened after the whole Drainers' fiasco was that we found out that Gertie was nicer than we'd given her credit for. She and Sky were getting along much better now that Sky didn't see her as merely a gold digger looking for a sugar daddy and no prenup.

"Thanks, Skyler," I said. Then silence. She hated when I asked, but I had to. "How are you doing?"

"Not craving human blood, if that's what you're asking," she said. "Also not hooking up with vampire musicians."

"All good, then," I replied, but there was a look on her face I didn't like. "What?"

"You never talk about it," she said.

"It?" I repeated, but I knew what she was talking about.

"It happened to you, too," she said.

"I know," I replied. "I was there. I'm just not ready to talk about it."

Skyler wrapped an arm around me. "Okay." She paused and then added, "I thought I saw Connor the other day."

"Fuck Connor," I said, fury boiling out of me suddenly. If her ex hadn't bailed on her, she'd never have hooked up with Travis, the vampire d-bag musician.

"Tansy," she said. "I just worry about him, you know."

"Vaughn told me Connor's been back for months," I spit out. "And no one's seen him, not even Vaughn. They text sometimes and that's it."

"That's not like Connor," she said.

"Neither was dumping you without a word and taking

off to another country for a year," I said.

"True," she said. "I honestly thought he loved me." Connor's callousness toward Skyler had set off a chain reaction, one that had left me with fang marks on my neck.

"I know," I replied, trying not to sound bitter, but I was. Bitter was the new black.

Acknowledgments

The seed of this book was planted when Melissa Wyatt, Mary Pearson, and I had a discussion about vampires and consent. Thank you, my friends! Also, whatever you do, don't google your favorite band's name and groupies. Reality is worse than fiction.

Many thanks to my agent Stephen Barbara, who never even blinks when I tell him story ideas, even the outlandish ones.

I'm so grateful for the amazing welcome I've received from everyone at Entangled. Heather, Meredith, and Riki let me join in on *The Masked Singer* chats, even though I always got it wrong. I still say Morris Day was a solid guess. And big thanks to Lydia, Stacy, and Liz, who managed to make it all come together.

My husband and kids make me smile even when I'm deadlining. (It's a word. I'm gonna make deadlining happen.)

Sink your teeth into the smash-hit
series from *New York Times* bestselling
author Tracy Wolff

c r a v e

My whole world changed when I stepped inside the academy.
Nothing is right about this place or the other students in it. Here
I am, a mere mortal among gods…or monsters. I still can't decide
which of these warring factions I belong to, if I belong at all. I
only know the one thing that unites them is their hatred of me.

Then there's Jaxon Vega. A vampire with deadly secrets who
hasn't felt anything for a hundred years. But there's something
about him that calls to me, something broken in him that
somehow fits with what's broken in me.

Which could spell death for us all.

Because Jaxon walled himself off for a reason. And now someone
wants to wake a sleeping monster, and I'm wondering if I was
brought here intentionally—as the bait.

Let's be friends!

🐦 @EntangledTeen

📷 @EntangledTeen

📘 @EntangledTeen

📰 bit.ly/TeenNewsletter

entangled teen

an imprint of Entangled Publishing LLC